THE CAVALIER OF MÁLAGA

David Raphael [M]

Carmi House Press

Carmi House Press
P.O. Box 4796
North Hollywood, California 91607

Library of Congress Catalog Card Number 89-091080

ISBN 0-9620772-1-6

**To my beloved children
Abraham, Nehama, Miriam, and Rina**

'Del bien lo más, y del mal lo menos'

Chapter 1

The camp outside the fortress of Málaga was brimming with excitement. The finest swordsmen in all Spain, dressed in fine silk and lavish plumes, their swords gleaming in the sunlight, readied themselves for a visit from the Queen. Alberto Galante, captain of the forces under the Marquis of Cádiz, also sensed the excitement. The visit from Queen Isabella would be a welcome lift in morale to his war-weary troops.

The war against the Moors had been continuing for close to ten years now. Always the courageous troops of the Marquis of Cádiz had led the way, proving themselves time and again the bravest soldiers during attacks on the infidel fortresses. Skilled in the martial arts, they always sought the most dangerous positions. In the course of the years, the Moors had been forced to give up garrison after garrison to the Spanish cavaliers. The troops of the Marquis had distinguished themselves at Alhama, the first of the Moorish fortresses to fall, at Loja, Zahara, Alora, Moclín, and Vélez-Málaga. Each of these fortresses had fallen into Christian hands.

The campaign against the infidel Moors was progressing favorably; its ultimate goal was the conquest of the city of Granada. Every cavalier dreamt of the downfall of this fabled Moorish center. Its fall would mark the end of the war; more important, it would terminate the seven-century occupation by the Moors, invaders from the African continent. Alberto yearned for the victory, but he knew it would not come without the shedding of much blood. While everything in this campaign was going well up to now, Málaga would prove a different challenge from other Moorish fortresses. It was no minor garrison on

1

the outskirts of the Moorish kingdom, but a well-fortified rock, against which the Spanish cannons and other artillery pieces were helpless. The Moors were ready to fight to the end, and the prospect of a long, drawn-out battle was not a pleasant thought. Alberto cast it from his consciousness, straightened his shoulders, and headed for the tent of the Marquis of Cádiz.

The striped, multi-colored tent was lined with costly tapestries. While fingering the workmanship, Alberto marveled at these tapestries with their mythical scenes. As he did so, the Marquis of Cádiz entered and put his hand on Alberto's shoulder.

"Aha! Alberto, my good man, what you are feeling are only the trappings of nobility. Tonight you will dine with the King and Queen of Castile and Aragon and feel with your mind and heart the presence and personalities of our rulers. It is to them we owe allegiance, and it is to them that we give our highest respect and honors."

"Marquis, I am most honored," replied Alberto, "that you have dignified me with this honor and privilege. I hope I will continue to be worthy of your good graces."

"My dear Alberto, I esteem you most highly because I have seen you in combat. I have seen the look in my men's eyes when they hear you will be leading them into battle. They believe in you, and you believe in yourself. You have proven yourself time and again. But it is not for this reason alone that I have chosen you to sit at the table with us tonight."

"Marquis, your kind words warm my heart, but truly I wonder if I am deserving of such praise."

The Marquis, his gaunt face becoming serious, continued, "Flattery is not one of my traits, nor do I give credit to others when it is not due. While it becomes a cavalier to show humility, it is not fitting to be too humble; an excess of humility is as bad as too much pride."

Alberto felt uneasy at these remarks, but he nevertheless nodded his assent. "Why yes, Marquis, it is no doubt true that things done to excess are never good."

What was the Marquis trying to say? Alberto seemed puzzled by the invitation to join the Catholic monarchs for supper in the company of the great nobles and prelates of Spain. Alberto was from a well-to-do family in Sevilla; his father was a successful spice merchant. But the Galante family, well off as it was, was not nobility. Alberto knew it, and so did the Marquis. What was the reason for this grand gesture? The Marquis semed to be opening doors for him, but he could not fathom why.

"Alberto, I have carefully considered your performance on the battlefield and outside it. True, you are a man of action, but you are more than that. You are a tactician. On the occasions that I have consulted with you about assault measures during the sieges of Alhama and Moclín, I sensed you had an insight, an intuitive military sense beyond that commonly seen in our ranks. It is for this reason that you were selected initially as one of the captains in the camp. Your experience, your leadership is of great value to us."

"Yes, sir," Alberto replied.

"Alberto, you are like a son to me. Consider what I am about to offer you and do not disappoint me. I want you to be my second in command."

Alberto gasped slightly, his eyes open wide with astonishment. "But Marquis, if I may be so bold to ask, is not such a position more fitting for one of noble birth? There are in our very camp many distinguished cavaliers who would doubtless be offended that I, a mere commoner, am chosen to be the right hand man of the Marquis of Cádiz.

"Bah! Aristocratic puffery is all they know. To dress up in their latest outfit, to hunt for hares, and revel in the late hours with ladies of high station — this is all they know. They dabble in games rather than the art of war. Their tactical knowledge is almost nil, and although many show bravery on occasion, they cannot be relied on day in and day out. I want someone I can rely on and whom the men under my command respect. I want someone who can think and plan as well as he can fight. I want you, Alberto Galante, at my side to be my second in command. Well . . . what do you say?"

Alberto considered this, trying to relate it to the Marquis' comments about humility and pride. The Marquis wanted a clear answer, not some meek affirmation or a polite refusal. He wanted the answer of a man, of a cavalier.

"I am most honored, Marquis sir, and I accept your proposal."

The Marquis hugged Alberto and told him warmly, "I knew I could count on you . . . *caballero*."

Alberto, his hand resting on the Marquis' arm, vowed, "I shall do everything in my power, sir, to fulfill my duties as your second in command. I accept the responsibility you have entrusted to me and will fulfill my duties to the best of my abilities. I thank you, sir, for this opportunity."

"I shall announce your selection at the dinner table tonight." With that remark, the Marquis spun around and left the tent, leaving Alberto to contemplate his change of fortune.

The King and Queen walked slowly up the path leading to the camp of the Marquis of Cádiz, accompanied by their royal guard of five soldiers. Isabella was wearing a dress of purple brocade lined with gold; her gold crown and reddish-brown hair shone radiantly in the Málaga sun, its rays brilliantly reflecting the jewels in her crown. Her face was pale, her eyebrows thin and highly arched, and her mouth had a hint of a pucker. Glancing with approving eyes first at one soldier and then the next, she was able to inspire devotion with a mere kindly nod of the head or with one of her measured facial expressions. She was the Queen, the prime regent of Castile, whose every movement and step was weighted with regal power."

At her side was Ferdinand. Elegantly dressed, sword at his side, he looked like a man engrossed in the physical element of war rather than in the administration of a kingdom. His carriage was erect, his handsome face tanned, and his eyes piercing. But this was not the day to upstage his royal partner, so he adjusted his crown with sufficient deliberation to avoid distracting the crowd from the Queen. This was a day for Isabella, he thought to himself, not for the supreme commander of the Spanish forces. So be it.

As the royal retinue arrived at the summit of the mountain, the surrounding troops cheered their sovereigns while a quartet of musicians received the royal duo with festive music. The Marquis of Cádiz strode gallantly toward the King and Queen, doffed his orange-plumed hat, and bowed graciously: "Your Majesties, it is with great honor that we welcome our revered King and Queen. Nothing gives us greater pleasure than to serve as your hosts, and we hope that we will prove to be worthy of your visit."

Isabella nodded graciously, accepting his bow, "Health and grace unto you, Don Rodrigo Ponce de Leon, Marquis of Cádiz. Know that we are thankful to you for your many years of devoted service to the crown. Were it not for men like yourself and those who surround you, men of valor, men of sacrifice, we could not have aspired to this victory, a victory that has not been seen in Christendom for centuries. It is our dream and your dream that we rid our soil of this Arab menace once and for all. And we shall do it . . . together."

The sumptuous meal prepared for the sovereigns was served on glistening silverware and jeweled glass goblets. Wines flowed liberally amidst an atmosphere of gaiety; ample portions of roast mutton and pork were heaped on the plates along with a staggering variety of vegetables and fresh bread. The prelates, the chancellors, the royal ladies — all were in a playful spirit. At the head of the table were the King and Queen; seated at their side was the radiant Marquis, savoring every moment of their presence. It was difficult to believe that here, in the shadow of the massive Gibralfaro castle of Málaga, in the very midst of a siege that sapped the strength of friend and foe alike, such levity and good humor could prevail. It was a dizzying experience for Alberto who was now thrust amid a company that only a short while before would have found his presence below their dignity.

Suddenly, Ruy López of Jaén, a well-known but obnoxious cavalier, addressed him with a scowl, "Pardon me, Captain Galante, but since when do sons of spice merchants invite themselves to dine with the grandees of Spain? I should think that for someone of your birth and your station, it would be more fitting for you to eat our droppings and scraps, and maybe . . . not even that."

Alberto countered ferociously, "Better to be one of the pearls of the lowly than be the disreputable lot of a vaunted class."

Ruy López's drunken breath was repugnant to all about him. The young lady across from Alberto, captivated by his tales of battle, now squirmed nervously in her seat, embarrassed by the reference to a social inequality. Frightened by the drunk cavalier, she cast about for a polite way to extricate herself. She stood up excitedly and murmured, "Pardon me, sir, I see someone by that bench I must speak with."

Alberto looked at Ruy López de Jáen with disdain. Ruy López was a loudmouth son of a grandee, prone to bouts of drunkenness. Alberto hated him, not because of his privileged birth, but because Ruy López had endangered his men, provided them with wine before combat, weakened their concentration, encouraged them to lead lives of dissipation, made them lose their fighting edge. Alberto hated him passionately. But this was not the right moment to vent his anger, not now, when he was to be introduced as a cavalier.

Ruy López cast a malicious grin at his adversary, and angrily challenged, "You dare trade words with a nobleman, you . . . you peasant?"

Alberto answered, "I trade words only with those whose speech is a disgrace to the accident of their noble birth."

Ruy López reached to slap Alberto, but Alberto countered the blow with his forearm, grabbing Ruy López's hand and twisting it behind his back. With this movement, Alberto pulled Ruy López away from the table and thrust him into a crowd of soldiers. He stripped Ruy López of his sword, threw it to one of his men, and instructed them, "Watch this drunken fool until he wakes up, and don't allow him to return to the dinner party until you check with me."

Ruy López screamed at Alberto, "You bastard, you'll pay dearly for this insult. You'll pay, you hear me? Damn you, damn you to hell."

As Alberto began to leave the crowd of soldiers, Ruy López screamed one last time, "Damn you, you think you're going to get away with this? I know who you are and where you come from . . . I know you are a *Marrano* . . . you and all your family. Your mother is a *Marrano* whore and your father is a *Marrano* spice merchant pig."

Alberto, stung by these insults, was frozen where he stood. He could not let this insult to his honor pass and still maintain the soldiers' respect. He turned around slowly, deliberately, and faced Ruy López. He signaled to his men to surround them so they would be out of sight of the royal dinner party. Ruy López stood there grinning, "Well, is that not the truth, bastard Jew?" Ruy López lunged at him.

Seething with rage, Alberto smashed a powerful right hand into López's face. The force of the blow sent López crashing to the ground in an instant, rendering him unconscious. Alberto wiped his hands, spat at the floored drunk, and signaled to his men to take Lopez away. "Scum of the rich," Alberto remarked. Amid the approving glances of his comrades-in-arms, he walked back to the dinner table.

At the dinner table, Alberto engaged in the usual pleasantries, resuming his small talk with the aristocratic young woman who now returned to her seat next to his. She listened attentively to his accounts of his soldiers' exploits. But it was not the same. Alberto had been disturbed, indeed unnerved by the insults Ruy López had flung at him. True, Ruy López was drunk and angry, but the question remained: did López suspect anything or was it just a reaching for straws, an outpouring of whatever epithet happened to flicker through his intoxicated mind? Alberto was concerned, even when the Marquis of Cádiz formally announced his designation as second in command. While everyone applauded, Alberto managed to force a smile and gracefully bow in acknowledgment of the honor, allowing his internal fears to be disguised as cavalier humility.

The dinner party ended. The Marquis of Cádiz proudly led the way around the campsite, little more than an arrow's trajectory from the Moorish castle. Precautions were taken to ensure that the King and Queen were not endangered, and while the Queen toured the periphery of the campsite, she was able to view the entire Gibralfaro castle with its several towers and ramparts. Because it was a huge castle, as the Marquis pointed out, the cannon balls from the siege guns were not able to breach the defenses of the outer walls; furthermore, the Moors were able to speedily repair whatever breaches did appear. Hence, there was little opportunity for heroics on the part of the *escaladores*, troops who specialized in scaling walls and needed only a small crack to take their advantage. The fighting men allowed the artillery to provide the major part of the assault, engaging in only a series of minor hand-to-hand skirmishes. Since the Moors were superior to the Christians in hand-to-hand combat, the soldiers allowed the Lombards, the German-made cannons, to pound away at the walls even if their effect was insignificant. To demonstrate the artillery, the Marquis ordered a series of bombardments for the pleasure of his guests. The cannon balls shattered the air with ear-deafening noise; blow after blow pounded at the massive castle; fragments of fortification crashed down from the walls to the ground, where they were buried in clouds of dust. The guests were much impressed. Alberto could see the Marquis' pleasure in the spectacle provided for his guests, and Alberto noticed how his men strutted about the campsite with pride.

Suddenly, the face of the Marquis paled and his body stiffened; he lowered his eyes. Alberto found this behavior unusual for the Marquis . . . until he looked at the closest tower atop Gibralfaro castle. Flying in the distance was the blue and red banner of the Marquis, the banner that had been taken during the single defeat he had suffered at the hands of the Moors. It was his banner of shame, the symbol of his ignominy and loss. And now, the Moors, seeing the moment ripe for embarrassing the Marquis, brazenly unfurled the pennant. Ladies gasped. Cavaliers whispered. Others, tight-lipped, resisted all queries about the banner. The King and Queen showed no signs of emotion, accepting the display as of no special importance.

The Marquis, his face coloring with shame, guided the royal couple and their following back to the campsite amid the Moors' howls and jeers. The relentless mocking and jeering intensified as the party departed, and the cannonades stopped abruptly. This round was won by the Moors.

Walking back with the Marquis, the King was acutely aware of his nobleman's inner torment and knew the deed would not remain unanswered. While the dignity and pride of the Marquis was wounded, it was not a mortal wound; it would only serve to arouse him to action. The royal party departed slowly. Just before taking her leave, Isabella's parting words were, "My Marquis, please allow me to thank you for your hospitality. Your friendship, your company, your support are most valuable to myself and the King. Know that we confide in you as in no other, and that you are for us more than any other compatriot. You are like a brother to us. Your victories are our victories, and your losses are our losses. Your happiness is ours, and when sadness strikes your heart, we feel it too."

The words of the Queen had a comforting effect on the Marquis. The tension in his face relaxed.

The Marquis replied, "You are most gracious, your Majesty, to allow me to continue to serve you even when my failings, which are so great, have been brought to your attention. I ask you to forgive the shortcomings of this cavalier, your most humble servant."

The Queen placed her hand gently on the Marquis' hand, "Chivalry and courage have seen no finer example in our day than in your person, Don Rodrigo. We love you and your men love you. Do not be troubled by the past — it cannot be altered. Struggle instead with the problems of the present — and conquer them, and with it, you shall find the contentment that will cleanse the lingering blemishes of the past."

As the King and Queen walked away, the Marquis stood contemplating Isabella's parting words. Then he turned around to face his men arranged in a semi-circle. Their faces were inflamed, their swords drawn, their spirits ready for action — ready to avenge the public humiliation. Many of the cavaliers had been with him when the banner had been lost, and they too personally felt the Moorish insult. They thirsted for revenge.

One cavalier asked, "Marquis, sir, our honor has been defiled by the Moors in the eyes of our King and Queen. How can we hold our heads high in front of them anymore? How can we? We have vowed to avenge you and ourselves. The Moors will pay for their insult with their lives, so help us God. Marquis, tell us what you want us to do, and we will do it now, this very moment."

The voices of the cavaliers followed rapidly one after another in a chorus of discontent.

"Now, Marquis, sir, now! Let us attack them!"

"And chop their heads off . . . sir!"

"Let's teach those treacherous Moors a lesson they'll never forget, let's kill them all — now!"

The cavaliers shouted their approval of these exhortations to battle, flinging their hats, brandishing their swords.

But the Marquis, listening calmly, raised his arm to signal for silence and answered his men. "My good cavaliers, our good name, my good name, has been sullied in a vile and shameless manner. The insult must be avenged quickly and honorably. But I must inform you that to attack our foe at this moment would be a mistake."

The silence turned into a soft rumble of whispered curses voiced by individuals who shook their lowered heads in disagreement. The Marquis sensed the frustration of his fighting men who, while they were ready to go to battle, were restrained by his words.

The Marquis continued, "I repeat, cavaliers, and heed my words: To attack now would be a mistake. We have not planned sufficiently the details and tactics of any such attack. Nor are we ready for battle. Our stomachs are heavy with food, and our minds are dulled by drink. It is late in the day, and night will be soon upon us. And even if we were to scale the walls of the castle, we would then have to fight on the foe's terrain, a terrain with which we are unfamiliar. Besides, it would be dark, and they will have the advantage. Our losses would be great, and the risk of defeat high. I will not allow my honor and your honor to be jeopardized by failure or by exposing ourselves to needless danger. We must plan our attack with forethought, so that we will have the advantage. No, we do not attack tonight."

The group of soldiers disbanded slowly. While a few stayed behind to try to convince the Marquis to attack now, his mind was made up. The Marquis strode to his tent and closed the entrance to prevent any further argument. He went straight to bed.

So did Alberto. It had been enough for one day, and he would need his sleep for the days to come. The smell of battle was in the air.

In the morning, the full fury of the cannons at the Marquis' disposal was unleashed upon the castle. All of the projectiles were directed at the tower from which the banner had been raised. Foul smoke and thundering roars poured forth from the engines operated by rotating crews. They ferried gunpowder by cart from a series of underground storage pits, where it was guarded day and night by three hundred men. Stonecutters chiseled the cannon balls into shape from raw stone extracted from a local quarry by hundreds of workers. Wagon after wagon brought scores of the balls to be hurled at the enemy's bastion. It was a well-organized operation, involving many secondary services: charcoal burners who made charcoal for the forges, blacksmiths who forged the spare parts of the cannon carriages, carpenters who repaired the wagons, munitions experts who made the gunpowder, as well other backup services. This was the backbone of the royal army: without cannons, without the artillery force and its army of artisans, the Christians could never have advanced so far. This was the first time that cannons had been used against the Moors; indeed, all were in agreement that this German invention made a critical difference. Without the cannons, the Moors would have been able to hold their own against the onslaught of the Christians, and Alberto would be caught up in a war without end. It was for this reason that Alberto was grateful for the cannons. He wanted to go home soon.

Shower after shower of cannon balls rained upon the infamous tower, gouging out holes, shattering the air with the whistle of flying rock and the pounding of the balls. But the Moors were nowhere to be seen. Some of the incendiary balls had set part of the interior woodwork on fire, and a shroud of black smoke enveloped the tower.

The effect was cumulative, and after two days and nights of relentless cannonades, the result had been achieved; the tower was no more. It had been gradually demolished to a smoking heap of rock and ashes. But it was only a minor victory: the bulk of the Gibralfaro castle remained. For this reason, the two-day hammering of the tower into a pile of dust was not enough to alleviate the wrath of the cavaliers. Furious and obstinate, the men of the Marquis demanded vengeance; a few of his advisers counseled caution, but they were in the minority.

"Marquis, are we to sit around like women waiting for the Moors to decide when we should engage them in battle? I say we take the battle to them. Let us make a full scale assault by way of the very tower that we have just destroyed and which they cannot adequately defend. We need to attack now before the Moors have an opportunity to repair the damage and erect a new tower in its place."

"But the cannons could stop any repair work," answered a cavalier at his side.

"Yes, true, and for how long should we wait? Weeks? Months? Until when? Wait for what? Until we break their defense, as we have now? What, I ask you, are we waiting for? Marquis, forgive me for saying so, but I don't understand this at all. Now, Marquis, now, cavaliers, now — this very moment is the time to attack."

The Marquis considered this argument and turned to Alberto, who had been quiet. Alberto wanted his words to reflect good judgment, to be respected by his peers and, of course, by the Marquis.

"Marquis, sir," Alberto said carefully, "Great is the dishonor that has been done, but great also is the damage that has been inflicted on the Moorish tower. It is a good beginning, but it is not enough to justify a full-scale assault. The two towers that remain intact may easily serve to defend the castle, such that the Moorish archers could pick off our men at will as they attempt to scale the wall on ladders. We must wait until the two other towers have been destroyed by our cannons. After that we can advance against the Moors."

"Those are the words of a woman, not of a cavalier," Alberto turned to face his critic, Ruy López de Jaén, his lips still swollen from the blow Alberto had dealt him, his eyes flashing malice.

Alberto countered quickly, "The only women in our ranks I am aware of are the ones who wait for the last wave of each attack, leaving the real combat to others. I am not one who has sought protection in the skirts of the rear . . . as some who sit at this table have done."

Ruy López's face turned red, his hateful eyes still bulging. López reached for his sword, as did Alberto. Both positioned themselves to strike, when suddenly the sword of the Marquis smashed down on the table, startling the two antagonists.

"Stop it, both of you. I'll have none of this foolishness in my tents. Now put your swords away. You heard me. I said put your swords away and sit down."

Alberto and Ruy López did as they were told, reluctantly guiding their swords back into their scabbards. Alberto cursed himself for his loss of self-control, for allowing Ruy López to make him look like an easily angered fool. Did the Marquis think less of him for this outburst? He saw his dreams of becoming a captain, a counselor, and a palace courtier fade. He must not appear hot-headed; he must be ruled by his head, not his heart. He silenced himself.

"Cavaliers," the Marquis spoke crisply, "we will act today in preparation for a full assault tomorrow. Today all our camp will be moved next to the wall beside the destroyed tower. We will keep a steady fire on the remaining towers to prevent the Moors from firing their arrows at us while we are setting up. Alberto Galante and Ruy López de Jaén, you will each lead separate companies of wall-scalers adja-

cent to the wall, and you will report directly to me. Garcilaso de la
Vega, you will lead the second wave of wall-scalers along with me. My
brother, Diego Ponce de León, will participate in the third wave with
my son-in-law, Luis Ponce. Artillery cover will be handled by Francisco
Ramirez de Madrid. Archers and crossbowmen, Manuel Gómez.
Shield bearers, Armando de Córdoba. Four-fifths of all booty will be
divided among the captains, the rest to the crown. Now prepare for
the attack."

It was a bold move: brilliant, fearless — those were the words used
by the chief cavaliers as they emerged from the Marquis' tent. It
would show the Moors what unflinching courage the cavaliers of
Spain possessed, how they were willing to expose themselves to
assaults from above, how they would dare the Moors to shoot at them
as they approached within crossbow's range, nay, within the range of
a lance. It was bold, it was daring — Alberto muttered to himself — it
was also dangerous, very dangerous, and he knew he would soon be
placed in a position of great physical peril. Tonight he would write his
parents and sister a letter: it might even be his last.

Ruy López de Jaén brushed by him, pushing Alberto aside.

"Oh, pardon me, have I offended you again?"

Alberto did not answer and kept on walking, López tailing behind
him.

"No matter," Ruy López added, "By nightfall, your true character
will be known to all. Tomorrow, maybe, I shall die as we scale the
walls, but if the Moors do not get you, Galante, I will. And I will die
with the satisfaction that you and all of your rotten kind will burn
to a crisp."

Alberto continued on his way, paying no attention to the pathetic
noises López directed his way. He continued walking, advancing
further into the campsite, snorting in contempt at the carryings-on of
this so-called noble cavalier. After a short distance, Alberto scrambled
behind a tree to watch Ruy López from afar. In the distance, López
sauntered down the hillside into the gully below in the direction of
army headquarters. Alberto abandoned the protection of the tree and
carefully edged up to the hillside beyond which Ruy López had disappeared from view. He looked about and spotted López again, now
a tiny figure meandering its way through the colored tents of the siege
grounds. Alberto followed him as best he could until López disappeared once again from sight.

Where was López going? Did he really know something about

Alberto and his family? And even if some damaging report were to be submitted, what action would be taken and when? And if action were to be taken against him, what should he do? Alberto had no idea. He had no plan of action, nothing in mind, except to fight like a caged animal, to slash his way to freedom. But he knew instinctively, everyone knew, that was the wrong answer. That strategy would only be effective against a concrete enemy like the Moors. You could see the Moor, you could touch him, and ultimately you could defeat him. But this was a different foe, far more formidable than any he had met so far. Its web stretched throughout all of Spain; it waited patiently for its victims who strayed into its clutch or who were denounced by informers. It waited for the right moment, pounced upon the prey, and ruthlessly wracked the bodies and consumed the souls of its victims.

Alberto was not of a mind to be devoured by this predator, or by his own imaginings. Perhaps López's threats were unfounded. He decided to bide his time, to delay further thought or action on this matter until the more immediate one of the the forthcoming assault on the Moorish fortress had been solved. If he was still alive after tomorrow, then he would rethink the matter. He wrenched his concentration back to reality, back to the war and to the responsibilities of guiding his men and preparing them for battle, back to checking their armaments and provisions, back to the only reality he knew.

The camp was transplanted within a matter of hours and the cannons began to blast away at the flanking towers. Although the Moorish towers were still largely intact, despite the incessant battering, this time the artillery was intended to hold the Moors off until the combatants met face-to-face. But many of Alberto's men were unable to sleep from the continuous din of the thundering machines. Alberto would have preferred to attack after a good night's sleep, but he reasoned that what was true for his men was also true for the Moors. They would be tired and sleepless too. He sensed the fatigue within himself of two near-sleepless nights in succession, of the ominous threats of Ruy López, of his intemperate outburst in the tent of the Marquis. Then his mind and body relaxed into slumber, oblivious to the cacophony of gunfire that punctuated the stillness of the cool Málaga air. He slept poorly that night.

"Yaaa!"

Alberto heard the muted cry in his sleep, slowly turning in bed, barely able to open his eyes.

"Yaaa! Yaaa!"

It was a Moorish battle cry. Alberto bolted from his bed, drew his sword, and bellowed at the top of his lungs.

"Attack! Moorish attack! On your feet!"

His soldiers, still half-asleep, dragged themselves out of bed, rubbing their eyes to respond.

Alberto could not believe his eyes. The Moors were spilling through the gate in a full-scale sortie against the contingent of Christian soldiers led by Ruy López. There were hundreds and hundreds of Moors, no, more than that, maybe two thousand of them, all in full coats of mail, fighting furiously. Cavalier after cavalier fell before their onslaught. Leading the Moors was the ferocious Abrahen Zenete, the peerless Moorish captain who, sword in hand, urged them on as he fatally struck down his opponents with the full power and skillful grace of his weapon.

Ruy Lopez's men started to flee before the Moorish advance, destroying what was left of the Christian line of defense. Breaking formation, the cavaliers ran for their lives over the rocks. Ruy López, seeing himself abandoned by his men, shouted, "Retreat! Retreat!," but his order was unnecessary in view of the already chaotic retreat. Abandoning his heroics, López joined his men in withdrawal. But a Moorish foot soldier caught up with him and speared López in the back with his lance. The wild retreat continued, and the screams of the fleeing cavaliers awoke the entire camp of the Marquis of Cádiz. Some ran through the camps, alarming their comrades to battle; some continued to run even further, beyond the point of perceivable danger. Terror had gripped them and sent them flying in pursuit of safety.

Alberto regrouped his men to launch an attack upon the main body of the Moorish force, by now totally in control.

"Yaaa! Yaaa!"

The savage battlecries of the Moors pierced the air; nothing could stop them. Finally Alberto and his soldiers met them head on. Alberto, parrying their swords and lances with his shield, swung at one after another. He stabbed one in the chest, while two others came after him simultaneously. He blocked one blow, then the other, and countered with a slashing blow to one Moor's neck, whipping the blade through his spine. Jets of blood spurted from him. The other Moor, baring his teeth with rage, unleashed a series of thrusts, and Alberto downed him, too.

"Yaaa! Yaaa!"

The Moors were gaining ground, pushing the cavaliers backwards. Alberto's men stood their ground courageously, but some of his first-rate soldiers, such as Ortega de Prado, had fallen. Indeed, some of his men were deserting him, a thing he had never witnessed before. Facing an overwhelming Moorish force, the cavaliers were being beaten, but there was still hope. The wiry Garcilaso de la Vega, in fierce hand-to-hand combat with a huge Moor, was struggling to overpower him. Garcilaso ducked to avoid the wide swish of the Moor's knife, tripped him with his foot, and stabbed the Moor in the stomach.

The losses continued. Cavaliers fell, one by one, to the Moorish blades and lances. The lustrous steel of the Arab infidels shined no brighter than in the hands of Abrahen Zenete, the valiant Moorish warrior who slew all in his path. Zenete was the perfect fighting machine: tall, bearded, handsomely muscled, with unbelievably quick reflexes and superior sword training. He was a born leader, the champion of the Moors, and was held in awe by Moor and Christian alike.

The Marquis of Cádiz emerged from his tent, saw his troops fleeing in disarray, and shouted for all to hear:

"Cavaliers! Cavaliers! Do not fear. I am here, the Marquis of Cádiz. Follow me. Unto them! Unto them!"

Many of the soldiers, hearing the heartening words of the Marquis, doubled back and regrouped. Diego Ponce de Leon grabbed the banner of the Marquis and held it high in the air. The sight of the banner, the sight of the Marquis leading his men into battle stirred the cavaliers, and they took courage and began a massive counterattack, aided by fresh troops from the Holy Brotherhood. The huge bodyguards of the Marquis paved the way, carving out the Moorish flesh as they tried to wrest the momentum from the infidels.

Alberto saw that the lead force of Abrahen Zenete was headed directly for the Marquis' group. The Moorish captain and his guard accelerated their pace, slaying all who stood in their way. Then the two forces — that of Zenete, and that of the Marquis — collided with awesome force.

While the bodyguards of the Marquis were able to hold their own against Zenete's warriors, they could not cope with Zenete himself, who took to the front line of battle. Zenete's blows weakened the defense about the Marquis, carrying off one bodyguard after another. When the Marquis' son-in-law stepped in to fill the breach, he was sent reeling to the ground with a side blow from a Moorish sword that slashed his left arm. The banner of the Marquis began to waver as the Marquis' brother Diego lost his footing.

Alberto sensed an impending defeat and, crossing the field and ravine, plunged through the thick Andalusian brush onto the field below. The wounded Diego, having dropped the banner, retrieved it and took it away from the center of action. Zenete was in deadly one-to-one combat with the Marquis, with Zenete landing the better of the blows, forcing the Marquis to retreat. The Marquis rallied briefly, but the Moor recovered and was pounding the cavalier with hammer blows delivered with incredible speed. And then the Moor, with one crashing blow, knocked the sword out of the Marquis' hand, leaving him defenseless. As the Moor raised his weapon to deliver the final thrust, he let out a terrifying yell: "Yaaa!"

His sword plummeted toward the Marquis, but before it reached its target it met with the cold, hardened steel of Alberto's extended sword. Alberto — furious, inspired — flung back Zenete's sword, and followed with a brilliant series of rapid thrusts. For the first time in the battle, Zenete was forced to take the defense.

Lunging at his aggressor, Alberto pushed Zenete backward with a vicious shove to his chest, sending the Moor backward and causing him to almost fall. Alberto lunged again, attempting to exploit the situation by thrusting his sword for the kill, but Zenete recovered his balance and parried Alberto's near-fatal stab. Furious, the Moor retaliated with blazing ferocity, driving Alberto backwards. But Zenete's blows were unable to penetrate Alberto's darting protective shield. Then Alberto stopped the Moor's advance and struck back with crashing blows of his own.

Both were of equal skill, so the duel continued, with neither party able to gain the upper hand. The Marquis and the other cavaliers watched closely this contest between the champion of the Moors and the courageous cavalier who was his match. It was evident to all it was a draw.

Finally, Zenete perceived he had met his equal. While he knew he would not lose, he feared he would not win against this cavalier. Besides, the Christian reinforcements were pouring in and wiping out whatever small advantage the surprise attack had provided. His men were now greatly outnumbered, and his losses would escalate the longer he prolonged the contest. Zenete had wanted one prize: the head of the Marquis. And but for a split second and the hand of another, it would have been his.

"Yaaa! Retreat!"

Zenete and his men retreated back to the first campsite, and then further through the gates of the castle. The cessation of the Moorish battlecries caused the Marquis and his forces to be strangely uneasy.

But it was not over. Now the Moorish archers from atop the two towers and the breach in the wall unleashed a new attack. Their rain of arrows caught the thousands of cavaliers below unawares. The cavaliers were easy targets, and many were struck by the arrows. When the archers spotted the Marquis, who was still with his men, they singled him out and directed a fresh barrage of arrows at him. One of the arrows struck his cuirass near his belt, but caused no harm. He plucked the arrow out of his belt and flung it away angrily.

"Retreat, cavaliers! Back to the first camp," he shouted, realizing the foolhardiness of his decision to move his campsite within range of the Moorish archers. The Marquis realized he had compromised his judgment in the name of chivalry; he should have listened to the words of caution. His brother and son-in-law were seriously wounded; fifty good fighting men were dead, and the wounded numbered in the hundreds. The Moorish losses were equal to his own, but this was no consolation. His rashness was inexcusable, but that was not the worst of it. The worst was that he had lost honor. He had been humbled by Zenete and lost face in the eyes of his men. Had he not turned his flee-ing soldiers around in time, it would have been a disastrous rout, a catastrophe from which his good name would never recover. He vowed he would never make the same mistake, and returned to his tent without speaking to anyone.

Alberto was surrounded by his soldiers.

"*Bravo, matamoros!* Praises to the Moor-slayer!" they shouted in unison, and Alberto thanked them and praised them in turn. Men shook his hand in admiration; others signaled their approval of his performance by doffing their helmets, raising their shields, or smiling and nodding their heads. Garcilaso de la Vega pushed his way through the group of well-wishers to embrace Alberto, squeezing his shoulders with affection, as a comrade in arms, as a fellow cavalier.

"You were marvelous," said Garcilaso, one arm around Alberto's shoulder. "Simply and truly marvelous. I don't know how you did it, but I, for one, can say that no cavalier ever fought more brilliantly than you fought here today. Believe me when I tell you that tonight you have preserved our honor. By your battle with Zenete, by saving the life of the Marquis, we are all indebted to you, Alberto. You are truly a *caballero*.

Congratulations continued to be accorded to Alberto. He took this all in a spirit of humility, as a cavalier should. It was all a dream, he thought to himself, surely it was all a dream. His sense of the unreality of it all persisted through the night. The euphoric giddiness was still with him in the morn as he walked through the camp and the men whispered to each other and pointed in his direction.

"There goes the Moor-slayer," they would say in awe, "That is the one Zenete could not beat." Accounts of his daring rescue of the Marquis spread quickly to the other camps.

Chroniclers of the war recorded his exploits to preserve them for posterity. First the deeds were enhanced and then came elaborations and exaggerations, many of them created by the men under his command: Zenete, they said, was in extreme peril throughout the contest; and the Moor was lucky to have escaped with his life. Some discovered Alberto had a pedigree of unimpeachable lineage, while others maintained he came from an illustrious family of Castilian knights.

While Alberto ignored the embellishments, his face beamed with pride and his speech became more authoritative. Before the incident, he had been a captain of note — courageous, responsible, but he had been only one among hundreds equally brave. But there was only one Zenete, and there was only one man who had faced him in hand-to-hand combat and lived. Alberto was that man.

He was a new legend. Many of the ladies of the court began to take interest in this dashing cavalier from Sevilla, the right hand man of the Marquis of Cádiz, a knight destined for a great and glorious future. The curious ladies of the court began to take longer walks, often strolling past the camp of the Marquis, hoping to be noticed by the captain. But Alberto, embarrassed by all the attention, kept to his tent. He had pledged to protect women, to respect them, to uphold their honor, and it was not becoming for a cavalier to pursue his advantage with the fair sex. He would be pure, righteous, and chaste just as the Marquis was. He would curb his temptations, conquer his carnal appetite by ignoring the impulses of his flesh that urged him to violate his code of honor.

What Alberto denied himself in body, he achieved in spirit. The bond between himself and the Marquis became stronger than ever. The Marquis drew closer to Alberto, gave him greater say in the strategy decisions, and showered him with praises in front of his peers.

Inspired by the Marquis, Alberto performed his duties with increased zeal. As the camp returned to normal, the cannons again punctuated the coastal air. Two weeks had passed without combat, and Zenete had failed to emerge from the castle. Rumors circulated that Alberto had dealt the Moor a fatal blow, but Alberto knew it was not so, and he denied the rumors that the Moor was dead. Zenete would return, Alberto assured them. Zenete was still very much alive and would seek him out one day to make Alberto pay with his life for his audacity.

Alberto would fall asleep thinking about the fateful day when he would be tested again, when he would pit his courage against the vengeance of the Moorish champion.

A hand shook Alberto's shoulder.

"Wake up, Alberto, wake up," whispered the voice.

Alberto's eyes opened and adjusted themselves quickly to the darkness inside the tent. It was Garcilaso.

"'Get dressed and come with me. Hurry and don't ask any questions," Garcilaso whispered.

This was very strange, Alberto thought to himself, but then again everything had been strange lately. Alberto dressed quickly, slipped on his boots, and adjusted his sword. Together, the two men walked outside the beaten paths of the campsite, trying to avoid being spotted by the guards.

They walked until they arrived at the horse corral, where two horses were saddled and ready. Garcilaso climbed quietly on his horse, and signaled to Alberto to climb onto his. He did so. At first the horses moved slowly around the perimeter of the camp, away from the campsite, until they came to the ravine. The pair proceeded slowly down the ravine and ultimately climbed out of it onto a side road.

"What's this all about, Garcilaso? What's going on?" Alberto asked. He spoke in a whisper, although they were well out of hearing range.

Garcilaso answered, "Alberto Galante, you are banished from the camp of cavaliers and you are forbidden to return."

"Banished? What do you mean 'banished'? That's ... that's ... I ... I ... don't believe it. My God, what have I done that I should be treated so? And who has ordered all this? I *demand* an answer,

Garcilaso."

Garcilaso looked at Alberto without emotion, weighing his words carefully. Putting his finger to his mouth, he said, "*Con el rey y la Inquisición, chitón.*"

The words struck like a dagger at Alberto's heart.

Having said these words, Garcilaso did not need to say more. He spun his horse around and galloped down the road.

Alberto stood in the middle of the road, silent, stunned by Garcilaso's words: "Concerning the King and the Inquisition, one remains silent."

He had been found out. There was no hiding it any more. By the morning, everyone in the camp would know the truth about him. Garcilaso was right; there was no returning to the camp or to the cavalier's way of life that he held so dear. From that day he would be an outcast, a fugitive from the Crown and the Holy Office of the Inquisition, an exile in his own country. Ruy López de Jaén, that lowly scoundrel of a cavalier, had reported him to the Holy Office and with one stroke had accomplished what he promised to do. Alberto was dishonored.

A spiritless Alberto asked himself: What was left for him to do? How could he, a cavalier, live without honor? Why not end it all now, this moment? He pondered this option but quickly rejected it. The silence of the night matched the emptiness of his soul, the gloomy blackness penetrating into his being. Slowly, the dejected cavalier of Málaga turned his horse around and headed down the nightmare road of his new existence.

Chapter 2

Alberto avoided the main trails, taking backroads and cutting across the Andalusian landscape. He guided his horse through the moonlit night, watching to avoid the check points and toll bridges. As dawn approached, he headed for the cover of the mountains. At nightfall, his lonely trek would start again until he arrived at his destination, the city where his parents and sister lived — Sevilla, the marvel of Andalusia. He tied his horse to a jutting rock and took off the horse's saddle. He spread out a wool blanket on the ground in a shaded area and slowly eased down on the blanket, allowing his sore muscles to relax. He removed his boots, propped up his knees, covered his face with his wide-brimmed hat, and sighed with relief.

He tried to sleep, but the event of the day had shaken him. His thoughts returned to his parents in Sevilla, his sister, his relatives and friends — were they safe? And if so, for how long? How long before the Inquisition caught up with them, too? If Alberto was the first to be reported, then his family was in great danger, and it was only a matter of time, perhaps days, before the Inquisition pounced upon his family, dragged them into its net, and confiscated their possessions. He must hurry to Sevilla and warn them to escape. But escape to where? The Inquisition was setting up in other cities of Spain, and Alberto felt that it would be wise to keep away from its centers of activity.

The Andalusian sun beat down upon the mountain outside Alberto's shelter. Its brilliant light bleached the landscape, creating an undulating haze in the air above the heated rocks. It reminded Alberto of the hearth in his home, of his grandfather Jacobo, and of the tales he used to tell. From long ago, Alberto recalled the hearth with its warmth, its flickering blades of flame licking at the air, causing shimmering undulations above the blazing logs. It seemed only a short while ago that Alberto listened to his grandfather Jacobo warming himself by the fire, his voice unsteady with age, but his mind and memory still sharp. Grandfather worked for the municipal council in Sevilla, helping local representatives called away by the king to participate in the national assembly of the Cortés. Because of his position, Grandfather was well informed about current affairs, but usually he talked about things past. After the evening meal, Grandfather would sit Alberto down next to the fire and recount tales of grandeur, of kings and knights, of Jews and Christians and Moors, of the Biblical prophets and of the great sages of Israel. It was from his grandfather Jacobo that Alberto learned who he was and where he came from. Alberto was a secret Jew, as were all the members of his family. Grandfather Jacobo used to love to tell of how the Galante family came to be Jews in hiding, of how they had adopted their double life: Christians on the outside, Jews on the inside. Grandfather told the story a certain way, as if he had learned it by heart. And Alberto could hear him even now, many years later, speaking to him as he once did.

"It all began with the Black Death, young Alberto, it all began with the Black Death. Throughout Spain, and in the rest of Europe, the plague attacked men, women, and children. It consumed millions of victims, leaving death and sorrow. It spared no one, Jew and Christian alike, priests and rabbis. No matter who you were or what you believed, the Black Death could strike you dead. The corpses would be taken on carts, one body piled on top of the other, and thrown outside the city gates. There were sores on them, awful looking sores that covered their bodies. And as the disease spread, people tried to understand why such a terrible thing had happened. Some saw it as a punishment from heaven. But there were those Christians who tried to blame the black Death on Jews."

"On Jews? How could anyone believe that?" Alberto remembered asking.

"But they did. The Christians blamed the Jews for the Black Death. They claimed that the Jews poisoned their wells, and that this was all part of a plot by the Jews to destroy the Christians. The rumors of well poisoning spread throughout the lands of Europe. In southern France, a certain Jew was reported as saying that he had made a potion of spiders, frogs, lizards, and the flesh of Christians whose hearts were mixed with the flour of the sacred host — and that he had poured the potion into the wells and the rivers of the Christians."

"Ugh! Ugh! Why did he do it?" shuddered the youthful Alberto, as he spat out the imagined potion from his mouth.

"He never did any such thing. It was all a lie, an awful, malicious lie made up by the Christians. They could not understand why they had been visited by such a calamity. Nor were they willing to believe that their sins were so great as to merit the wrath of their God. No, they had to blame it on someone or something. So they picked on the Jews because the Jews were the known servants of Satan, the Devil. Only the Devil, they believed, could have caused something this awful, this dreadful. Therefore, the Jews, loyal aides of the Devil in this world, must be responsible for the Black Death. So we, the Jews, were blamed and tormented as we always are for every misfortune and disaster that occurs in this world. It was said the Jewish plot to spread the Black Death started in Toledo and, from there, the deadly potion was secretly transported to other parts of Europe. And wherever people spread the story of the Jewish plot, they believed it because they wanted to believe it. So what happened? Entire Jewish communities were destroyed in France and Germany by Christians, our Jewish brothers and sisters dying by the thousands for acts which they never committed.

"Here in Spain, the only trouble we had was in the north. The lower classes, when they heard the rumor, took to the streets to kill the Jews. They had murdered some Jews in Barcelona and destroyed a few communities in Aragon, but the royal authorities intervened to stop the madness. Steps were taken to protect the Jews of the area by banning sermons that fanned the fury. Thus it was that the Jews in the south of Spain were spared the fate of their brethren in northern Spain and other parts of Europe. But the hatred continued despite what the authorities did.

"The hatred grew and grew. It spread from mother to child, from father to son, in the streets and in the fields, in the churches, everywhere in Spain. Everywhere you could feel the hatred in the way the Christians looked at you, in the way they spoke to you."

Then Grandfather shook his head slowly, his eyes became tearful and glassy-eyed, a look of sorrow spread over his face. He continued slowly, "I will tell you what I saw with my own eyes when I was a boy of nine here in Sevilla. I remember it today like the day it happened.

Who could forget such a day?"

"It was Ash Wednesday in the year 1391. All our family was in the *judería*, the Jewish quarter, when the mob arrived at the gates. My five-year-old brother clung to our mother's dress as we heard the shouts and screams of the Christian mob pounding on the entrance gates. My father stood next to the window trembling with fear, unable to move or speak, not knowing what to say or do. We were all scared, so very scared. I, too, clung to my mother as she stood by the window looking towards the gates. Through a break in the window, we could see what was going on, we could see the gate being set on fire and giving way to the mob. My mother tried to shoo us away, but I refused. I wanted to see what was going on, but she insisted and forced me to the back of the house. But even there I could see from the window in our bedroom. I saw everything . . . everything.

"As the gates opened, the mob rushed in with torches in their hands, setting fire to one Jewish home after another. Smoke and fire filled the air. Those who lived closest to the gates were the first to be attacked. The mob pulled the Benozillo family out of their home and forced them to their knees. The father and mother and their two beautiful daughters begged for mercy, raising their hands to heaven, pleading with the mob not to hurt them.

"It was then that I saw Ferrant Martínez, the archdeacon of Sevilla, raise the cross over their head, shouting at them, 'Convert or die! Convert or die!' The Benozillos kissed the rim of his robe, kissed his feet, kissed his hands, kissed the cross, urging him to spare their lives. The pleas, the sobs went on, but Ferrant Martínez would not listen. He wanted them to convert, but they would not. He pushed the Benozillos back and gave them to the mob. The father was run through quickly with a sword; the mother fell back screaming and put her arms around her two young daughters. She cried, 'In the name of heaven, in the name of God . . . ' before they, too, were struck down by the sword and set on fire.

"On and on it went. Home after home, family after family was destroyed by these animals who swore by the cross and murdered in the name of Jesus. Our saintly rabbi, Rabbi Todros Almosnino, walked out to meet them. He covered himself with his prayer shawl and put on his phylacteries, preparing himself for the mob. They grabbed him and flung him viciously to the ground. They cut him up into little pieces and threw them into a bonfire. His wife Sarica fainted in the middle of the square when she saw what was being done to her husband.

A ruffian, a youth of no more than twenty, ran up to her unconscious body and pierced her heart with a lance. She died in holiness like her husband; they sanctified the name of the Holy One, blessed be He, through their deaths.

"Our synagogue was set ablaze, its flames reaching high into the air. I saw one person running off with the silver ornaments of the Torah scrolls tucked under his shirt. Another Christian ran out of the smoke-filled building carrying the scroll itself and unraveled it on the street, stamping on it and ripping it to shreds, and then setting fire to the pieces of parchment.

"Twenty-three synagogues were consumed by fire that terrible day. The flames, the smoke, the smell of burning flesh — I smell it, I see it today as I have seen it every day since that blackest of days. I cannot forget it. No, I cannot forget, and I cannot forgive.

"Four thousand men, women, and children died that Ash Wednesday. But the ashes that day were for the people of Israel, not for Christ. They made ashes of our holy places and of our holy books. They made ashes of our community and of our souls. They slaughtered babes and sucklings till their bodies were drenched with the blood of the Jews. In the name of their savior, whose death they sought to avenge, they killed and killed a thousand times over and more. And always it was that monster Ferrant Martínez, that ignorant Catholic priest, who roused the Christians, inflaming them with his speeches to force us to convert to Christianity. And if we refused to submit to baptism, he gave us to the mob to be killed. That was the kind of man Martínez was. I blame him for all that happened, for the death of all my relatives, God rest their soul.

'One of my uncles died the death of a true martyr. His name was Hasdai . . . Hasdai Yehiel. Rather than submit to baptism, Hasdai took his family in a back room, while the mob was beating on his door. He took a sharp knife and, with his own hand, he slit the throats of his in-laws, his wife, and his three innocent children. Then he killed himself. There were others, many others, who did the same. The mob looted their homes and took everything they had.

"When the mob reached our home, they flung the door open, and swords and torches in hand, they found us — my father and my mother, my little brother and me — all of us on our knees, saying 'We accept Jesus as our Lord. Baptize us into the Church.'"

With that, Grandfather Jacobo spat to the side of his chair, a look of disgust distorting his face. He continued, "Martínez came towards us and looked us right in the eye, and he sprinkled the holy water on our heads. The angry mob then dragged us out of our home to the nearby church where we were instructed in our new faith. There were other Jews like ourselves who preferred baptism to death, maybe four or five thousand of us. From then on we were regarded as 'New Christians'. That's what they called us, not 'Christians', but 'New Christians', by which they meant converted Jews. They still despised us after we converted, and we despised them, too, because of their brutal fanaticism. Because we were still Jews at heart, we wanted nothing to do with their religion, although we had to pretend otherwise. So that is what I am, Alberto, and that is what you are. We are Jews, secret Jews, but Jews nonetheless. Say it for your grandfather, Alberto. I want to hear it from you."

A puzzled Alberto asked, "Say what, Grandfather?"

"Say that you are Jewish, and that you are proud to be one of us."

Alberto's eyes shone with affection. "I am a Jew, of the House of Israel — always have been and always will be . . . and I am proud to be one . . . like you are, Grandfather."

Alberto went up and put his arm around his Grandfather Jacobo and kissed him. He dearly loved his grandfather. Jacobo with one hand ran his fingers playfully through Alberto's straight light brown hair, and with the other pulled his grandchild towards him, hugging him tightly. Alberto reciprocated the hug, clinging to his grandfather's swaying frame.

Grandfather Jacobo continued, "Let me tell you what happened in the months that followed. The riots spread from Sevilla to the other towns. In nearby Carmona and Écija, all the Jews were killed. Not one person was spared. In Córdoba, two thousand Jews perished, but many survived by allowing themselves to be baptized. Throughout Spain, Martínez and his blood-thirsty men spread hatred for the Jews. They spread it to Toledo, to Valencia, to Barcelona, Burgos, and other places — the madness spread like wildfire. The people, spurred to religious hatred by Martínez, within a matter of three months attacked 70 Jewish communities and plundered them all. When it was over, 50 thousand Jews were killed; over 100 thousand were forced to submit to baptism. My guess is that maybe the same number of Jews managed to remain alive and unconverted. That was all that was left of the once proud House of Israel. They broke us in two as if we were a stick; they murdered our brothers and sisters and disgraced the survivors. But listen to me, Alberto, there is still one way to live with pride and honor, and that is to be what we are. Promise me this one thing."

"What, Grandfather?"

"Promise me."

"I promise."

"Promise me that one day you will leave Spain and that you will return to the Jewish people, to the House of Israel. Promise me that you will leave this double life as a New Christian. Promise me that you will do what I was unable to do in my own life. Promise me that and I shall die a happy man."

"I promise you, Grandfather. I swear to you, I promise you."

Alberto recalled his promise. And now it came back to him in a rush of memory, prompting a feeling of guilt that he had made no effort to satisfy it. Alberto thought about his grandfather and how he had been able to see the future, the way of things to come for the New Christians, and how it would never be good. He remembered this youthful commitment to a faith, a people, his people, and he used its newfound power to strengthen him against the troubles ahead. A resolute Alberto swore anew the vow that he had made as a child.

The day had come to leave Spain. Sleep finally overtook his body and put his mind at ease.

The massacres in Spain in 1391 had produced close to a hundred thousand new converts to Christianity. The Jewish communities of Spain were shattered by the ferocity of the popular uprising against them. In Sevilla proper, as in other cities of Spain, the few remaining Jews struggled to retain their dignity. One main synagogue was converted into a church, Santa María La Blanca, and the Jewish quarter was to be known as the Santa Cruz quarter. While the Jewish community — or what remained of it — was slowly reestablished in Sevilla, it could barely afford to pay the annual community tax of two or three thousand maravedis.

At the head of the Jewish community was Rabbi Judah Ibn Verga, a renowned Talmudic scholar, who did what he could to help the converts. The rabbi regarded the Conversos, or 'New Christians', as lost sheep from the House of Israel, as Jews who must one way or another be brought back into the fold. Patiently, and with the utmost discretion, the rabbi maintained secret connections with his brethren, encouraging them to maintain their ancestral rites, to observe the Jewish customs of old, to preserve their identities as Jews.

Even without the rabbi's prompting, there were many such Conversos who practiced their Jewish ways in secret, not only in Sevilla but in other cities of Spain. Crypto-Judaism was a flourishing underground movement in Spain: many of the converted Jews detested their new religion and despised the hypocritical Catholic priests who had inflamed the rabble in their frenzy. The Conversos hated their new status and attempted to revert to their former Jewish ways whenever opportunity arose. But to practice Judaism was not without risk: once baptized, you were forever regarded as a Christian by the Church, and any relapse was severely punished.

But the fear of punishment did not deter the Conversos, nor did it deter the rabbis. In Sevilla, Rabbi Ibn Verga ministered to the Galante family. He urged them to leave Sevilla, to start life anew as Jews elsewhere — perhaps in North Africa or in the empire of the Ottoman Turk. But Alberto's father, Vicente Galante, always postponed the decision. His business as a spice merchant was improving, and the thought of giving up what he had accomplished, of going to a strange new land and having to speak a foreign tongue did not appeal to him. It was better to wait and see what the future would bring in Spain. After all, as a New Christian, Vicente was no longer subject to the harsh regulations against the Jews that limited where they lived and what they did. Now he was a Christian, in name if not in spirit, and many obstacles towards his advancement in Spanish society were removed by Grandfather Jacobo's conversion. The social comforts and the business opportunities, now available to him as a Christian, weakened his resolve to leave despite Rabbi Ibn Verga's pleas to leave before it was too late.

But then troubles began. Resentment of the New Christians grew as they entered Spanish society, the newcomers competing aggressively in all spheres of Castilian economic life. In Castilian society where reading and writing skills were rare, the literate Conversos advanced quickly. Some amassed fortunes in commerce and married into aristocratic families; others distinguished themselves in medicine, diplomacy, and the sciences. The rapid ascent of certain Conversos to social prominence contrasted sharply with the inhibited status of their unconverted Jewish brethren. And with each conspicuous success of a New Christian, the Old Christians grew angry and jealous of this thriving minority in their midst. The Old Christians had granted social entry to these neophytes only to end up being pushed aside by the latter's greater vigor and superior education. Not only were they being advanced over 'true' Christians, many of the converts were continuing to adhere to their Jewish ways. The act of baptism had been little more than a farce.

Outbreaks against the Conversos began, first in Córdoba, then in Sevilla. The New Christians suddenly became aware that they were not free from danger. In the eyes of the populace, they were viewed as insincere Christians, as backsliding heretics. The Old Christians called them *Marranos* or "swine". The signs of the times were evident to many, and the Conversos began to flee Sevilla, often at the urging of Rabbi Verga.

The rabbi made use of a story to prove his point. One evening, Rabbi Ibn Verga brought several Conversos together to impress upon them the need to emigrate. He was short and ruddy-faced, and his manner soft and engaging, but he could be forceful when the occasion demanded. As the ten or so Conversos gathered around him, Vicente Galante included, he asked an assistant to bring in three covered trays.

"What is this, rabbi?" asked one Converso.

"Observe and you will understand, my son," answered the rabbi calmly.

The rabbi uncovered the first tray. The Conversos gasped as they saw a pair of dead pigeons whose feathers had been plucked. Around their neck was a paper: "These are the *anusim*, the forced converts, who will be the last to flee."

Then the rabbi uncovered the second pair of pigeons, alive, but also with feathers plucked. "These are the ones in the middle group who will escape — they will escape alive, but with all their wealth plucked away."

Finally, the rabbi removed the cover from the third tray and revealed the last pair of pigeons, alive and unplucked. The rabbi concluded, "And these are the wise ones — they are the first to flee, and so they will escape untouched."

But Vicente Galante was not one of those who left. He remained unmoved by the rabbi's arguments and did not share the Converso community's fears of worse things to come.

And so the Galante family stayed behind.

In 1477 Alonso de Hojeda, head of the San Pablo Dominican monastery in Sevilla apprised Ferdinand and Isabella of the serious laxity of religious observance among the New Christians. Startled by this information, the King and Queen requested a Papal Bull from Pope Sixtus IV to establish an Inquisition in Spain, charging it with the task of investigating heretical activities. The Papal authorization was granted and, by 1481, the Inquisition was fully operational in Sevilla. Many Conversos fled to neighboring regions. Eight thousand fled to the lands of the nobleman, the Marquis of Cádiz, Rodrigo Ponce De León, who took them under his protective shelter. But the Marquis, despite his protests, was threatened with charges of contempt for the activities of the Holy Tribunal, and was forced by the crown to surrender the fugitives who had sought refuge in his marquisate. The renegade Conversos were brought back to Sevilla in chains, imprisoned, tortured, and many were ultimately burned at the stake. The rabbi's words were prophetic.

When in December, 1481, the Moors stormed the fortress of Zahara, the Marquis of Cádiz retaliated by assaulting and capturing the Moorish town of Alhama. He did this without Ferdinand's authorization, but the attack suited the interests of the king. Once the gauntlet was thrown down by the Moors, it was readily picked up by Ferdinand and Isabella, and the war was on. By 1483, Ferdinand himself was directing campaign strategy. Ardor for the religious crusade against the infidel Moors ran high in Andalusia. Conscription began with each town or municipality required to provide troops to fulfill the royal summons. Members of the municipal communal assembly were expected to volunteer their services. To pay the conscripts, communities had to contribute funds from their treasuries or impose new levies.

Alberto, then twenty years of age and eager for the thrill of combat, had volunteered to become part of the Sevillan military contingent. Alberto wanted to be a cavalier, to be a man of honor and valor, to fight alongside the nobles of Spain.

Vicente's rage upon hearing of his son's decision was fierce.

"Alberto, this is a very foolish thing you have done. Your mother will worry about you night and day. Is that what you want? To bring sorrow and heartbreak to your dear mother?"

"No, Father, I want to be with my friends. They're all going to join in the battle. Alonso de Murillo is going and so is Pedro Ibarra. Everyone of importance is going. I can't, I won't stay behind here in Sevilla to mind your store . . . to worry about when the next shipment of ginger and pepper is going to arrive at the port. I want to be a cavalier, to take part in the greatest war of our day."

Vicente Galante shook his head incredulously, "What's so great about it? The Moors have been our friends, the friends of the Jews, much more than the Christians have. If you have an enemy, it is not the Moor, it is the Christian. Fight the Christian . . . not by doing his bloody battles for God's sake, but by staying a Jew at heart . . . by staying alive at all costs. That is what you should be doing."

"I'm leaving, Papa. And nothing you say is going to convince me otherwise."

Vicente Galante raised his arms skywards, "Rabbi Ibn Verga, where are you? Forgive me for not listening to you."

Alberto's mother cut in. "Son, do not go. Alberto, please, I beg of you, do not go."

"I am sorry, Mama. My mind is made up. I am going, but I want to go with your blessing."

"Can I do otherwise? . . . I will bless you, my son, I will bless you. May the God of Israel protect you wherever you go. Think of us and write to us when you can. And when you have done all that you feel you must do, come back to us and let our family be united once again. Take care, my son, be well, and God be with you."

Alberto embraced his mother tightly and then kissed his sister, their soft cries making him feel uneasy. Finally his father and he embraced each other with a long and firm hug. As he stepped out the door, his father's last words rang out: "Come back to us, Alberto. In the name of God, come back to us. Come back to us, my son."

Alberto was returning home. He had driven his horse hard all night long after a poor daytime sleep. As he approached the city of Sevilla, his mind evoked past memories of his growing up in this city: the merriment of a teenager at the regional fair, the courting of the ladies, the playing of the lute with his friends. He remembered the time when his father had punished him when he went wading in the Guadalquivir River, and how relieved his mother was when his father finally found him and brought him back home. He remembered pulling his little sister's hair and then running out the door before his father could catch him. He remembered the secret coming of age ceremony that Rabbi Ibn Verga had performed for him — a Bar Mitzvah. But most of all, he remembered the feeling of belonging to this place called Sevilla; he was one of its sons, and Sevilla was as much a part of him as he was a part of Sevilla. It was Sevilla where everything from his past had taken place, a city that he could and did call his own. The city was a witness to his birth and growth, an accomplice to his escapades, a silent partner to all the commotion of his existence. Sevilla was his home.

As he approached the city, familiar sites came into view. He saw the Giralda, the minaret of the former mosque now converted into a cathedral. Close by stood the Mudéjar palace called the Alcázar, its massive Moorish architecture captivating the vista from afar. Alberto could almost smell the fruity fragrance of the gardens of the Alcázar: the orange groves, roses, and palm trees in a network of cascading waterways and leafy hedges. The morning dew glistened on the shrubbery and the brush in the coolness of the Andalusian dawn, bringing renewed energy to Alberto's fatigued body. As he drew near, he saw sailors loading ships on one of the quays. Alberto was surprised that there were only two ships that lay in the harbor.

As he entered the city gates, he saw the Sevilla he remembered, and yet there was something different. He could not specify what the difference was, but *something* was changed. The city, awakening from the silence of night, was still, except for the clatter of his horse's hooves on the cobblestones of the main street. Alberto realized what the difference was: Sevilla was too silent, even for this hour. With dawn, Sevilla always bustled with activity: merchants carrying their wares to the main plaza, farmers bringing in cartfuls of olives and oranges, cavaliers riding on horses, people running to and fro. Today there was an eerie tomblike silence in the city.

A door slammed as Alberto went by. Then another. Alberto continued on his way, perplexed. He guided his horse to the *Calle de las Sierpes*, the Street of the Serpents, where many New Christian families resided, his own included. At the far end of the street he saw someone dressed in black driving a shaky horse-driven two-wheeled cart. A black scarf completely covered the driver's head, except for two holes cut out for the eyes. His robe was black, as were his leather mittens. Alberto slowed his horse's pace to look at the cart and its mysterious hooded driver as they rattled by. At least here, Alberto mumbled to himself, there were still signs of life.

"Out of my way!"

Alberto, puzzled, moved away slightly, but was still within arm's reach of the cart.

"Plague victims, you fool! Can't you see? Now get out of my way, you damn fool!"

Alberto, suddenly realizing the danger, jerked his horse away from the cart bearing the Black Death.

The curses of the enraged driver continued as the cart clattered down the street. On the back of the cart, a black wool blanket barely covered the corpses festering with purulent sores, their discolored arms and legs protruding underneath. The stench of rotting flesh penetrated his nostrils, and he felt a sudden urge to vomit. Alberto was petrified and, for an instant, he shared the silence of the city, its muteness now understood.

But his fears went beyond concern for his own survival. What of the Galante family? Were they victims of the pestilence? And then another fear came to mind, one which Grandfather Jacobo would have not hesitated to articulate. The Jews, what of them? Everyone blamed them for the Black Death. But all the Jews had been driven out of Sevilla three years ago; there were no more Jews in Sevilla. So who was to blame for the plague now? The answer came to Alberto like a thunderbolt: the New Christians!

Alberto spurred his horse and sped it down the Street of the Serpents. House after house became one dizzying blur as the steed galloped down the street; suddenly, Alberto pulled on the reins and stopped the charging animal in front of the Galante household.

Alberto dismounted and looked about. Everything looked the same. The garden looked well-kept and the plaster walls were still shining white, an indication to Alberto that the house had been recently lived in. He walked over to the wrought iron gate and found it open. He walked to the door and banged on it, but there was no response. He banged again. Still no response.

A white sheet of paper on the wall next to the door caught his attention. He read the notice:

"By order of the Holy Office of the Bishopric of Sevilla, this property is sequestered and assigned to the custody of the Inquisitional office until the accused — Vicente Galante, his wife Rosa, daughter Ana, and son Alberto — do hereby present themselves to the Holy Office at the castle of Triana for interrogation relating to their alleged Judaizing activities and to their sudden departure from the city of Sevilla. Any person having information regarding the whereabouts of members of the Galante family are to report immediately to the Holy Tribunal. If any persons, knowing the whereabouts of the aforementioned, fail to do so forthwith, they are to be hereby excommunicated and may not be absolved by their confessors."

Signed,

Juan de San Martin
Inquisitor, Bishopric of Sevilla.

Alberto ripped the sheet off the wall and tore it to shreds, grinding the shreds into the ground with his boots. Quickly, he ran around the house, gazing in one window after another. Everything looked the same as the day he had left Sevilla. The rooms, the furniture, the cooking wares in the kitchen — all had been untouched, unmoved. In his bedroom, Alberto could even see the books on chivalry and knighthood that he had read as a youth. The hearth where Grandfather Jacobo had recounted his tales was stacked with fresh firewood. He saw soiled clothes strewn about, and outside on a thin rope, there were still clothes hanging to dry in the sun.

Painful as it was to see his home and not be able to go inside it, Alberto realized his parents left it thus to create the impression they would soon return. It would have given them just a little more time to escape before the neighbors began to wonder why the Galante household was so silent. Perhaps the neighbors would drop by for a visit. Upon seeing the house this way, the neighbor would return home, unsuspecting. As day after day passed, suspicion would grow, and the neighbor would feel duty-bound to report it to the Holy Tribunal. Thus informed of their flight, the Inquisition posted the order taking over the property and outlawing the Galantes.

Alberto did not give voice to his despair; he was a cavalier now, and he could not cry and scream as women do at the empty loneliness of his fate. Rabbi Ibn Verga, where are you now?, he remembered his father saying. Papa, Mama, Ana, where are you? He had no idea where they had gone. Now he was alone, cut off from the closed circle of cavaliers, cut off from his home and family.

And worse, now he was a fugitive.

As Alberto rode back toward Sevilla's city gates, a strange site caught his attention. A young man, barefoot, head bent in shame, wearing a tall mitre and a yellow robe, and carrying a lit taper, walked by. When he passed, people crossed to the other side of the street to avoid the dejected figure. Alberto had never seen such a sight before.

Was he somehow infected with the plague that people wished to avoid him? Alberto slowed his horse. As he drew closer, he could see the young man more clearly. His long yellow robe covered his knees. Painted on it were flames pointing downwards and devils with whips and hooks punishing sinners. One more detail became clearer to Alberto: the face of the young man. It was Manuel de Castro, an old school friend. Their gaze crossed, and de Castro lowered his eyes to avoid Alberto's look of astonishment. Alberto dismounted and tried to speak with him, but de Castro walked quickly away

"Manuel de Castro, wait! It is I, Alberto Galante. Wait!"

But de Castro kept on walking hurriedly, paying no heed to Alberto's call or to the fearful people who scurried out of his way. Alberto ran after him.

"Manuel de Castro, don't you recognize me? It is I, Alberto Galante. I am your friend."

Alberto caught up with him, placed an arm on the man's shoulder, and turned him around. Alberto could not believe what he saw. De Castro's left cheek was riddled with maggots, his eyes bloodshot and draining a yellowish discharge, his lips blistered black and blue, his face gaunt and heavily lined. The taper's flame cast stark shadows on his horrid face.

"My God, Manuel, what's happened to you?" Alberto uttered softly.

De Castro looked at him, "I am afraid I do not know who you are, sir. I have never met you before. Leave me alone . . . please."

De Castro turned again and began to walk away. Alberto again followed, seizing his arm.

"Listen, you cannot say you never met me, Manuel de Castro. You cannot deny knowing me. You know very well who I am, just as I know who you are. I will not let you go until I have some idea where my parents are. Do you hear that? The Inquisition is after us, and I must find out about them before I leave Sevilla. Now, tell me, do you know anything of them . . . or not?"

De Castro looked at Alberto again and said loudly for all to hear, "I am afraid I do not know who you are, sir. I have never met you before. Leave me alone!"

And then, very very softly, De Castro added, "Quickly now, meet me in the alley there to the left."

Alberto did as he was told and waited for de Castro to join him. Perhaps de Castro would have some information about his family's whereabouts. He saw de Castro stand by the entrance of the alley, his yellow robe billowing in the wind. After a short while, de Castro dragged his ailing body toward Alberto.

De Castro put the taper aside and sat down on the floor. He bowed his head and spoke without urging, although his voice broke with occasional sobs.

"I am a fool and you are a fool, Alberto Galante. I am a fool for allowing myself to speak with you. And you are more of a fool for endangering your life by speaking with me. I have no more of a life to live, but at least you are still young, you are still full of life, and . . . and I do not wish anyone to suffer as I am suffering — especially not someone who was once my friend."

"I am still your friend, Manuel," Alberto answered.

De Castro did not look up. He continued speaking, "Do not interrupt me. Your friendship means nothing to me. Feelings, love, hate, truth, falsehood — they all mean nothing. Everything I was or had has been taken away. They have taken away my spirit, they have racked and tortured my body, and they have left me diseased, an object of scorn for all to see and laugh at. My time is short, I know that. Very short. But I do not wish anyone to share my cursed fate."

"You have obviously been away and do not know what is happening here in Sevilla. The Inquisition has been busy in this city. Those of us who escaped the flames have done so by confessing to what they regard as our sins. I was one of the lucky ones, if you want to call it that. Under torture, I confessed to everything they wanted, swore to everything they demanded, admitted to believing whatever they wanted me to believe. Yes, I escaped the stake, but as my penance they made me wear this *san benito* robe in public so that all who see me will know I am a confessed sinner. After I have paid my penance, they will hang up my *san benito* robe in the local church with my family name sewn on it so our descendants will also have to bear my shame. But enough of me. My pain will soon come to an end when this wretched body of mine breathes its last wretched breath.

"Now you ask me where your parents are. I answer you, I do not know. If I knew, I would tell you. All I know is that many have fled to the north where Jewish communities are still permitted to exist. Some have fled to the Moorish kingdom of Granada. That is all I know. The only advice I can give you is simple: get out of Sevilla. Go as far away as you can. The city is full of evil. It is evil. The pestilence has killed over ten thousand here, including the Inquisitor de Hojeda, cursed be his soul! He was one of the first to fall prey to its deathly grip. Perhaps God has seen fit to punish this city and its evil Inquisition with this pestilence.

"But why me? Why has God selected me to suffer in this way? I tell you I do not understand. If I had been a cruel person, if I had done people harm, perhaps I could accept this fate as my due punishment. But I search my past and I search my soul, and I know that, imperfect as I am, I am not deserving of such unjust treatment. I do not understand God at all.

"Go, Alberto. Do not ask me any more questions, for I have no answers to offer you — only tales of misery and woe."

De Castro rose from the ground, his head still bowed. He picked up the taper and began walking out slowly. After a few steps, de Castro turned around, not quite looking at Alberto, and said, "In the city of Carmona, there is a woman called La Susanna. Go to her. Maybe she can help you."

With this, de Castro walked out of the alley, holding the lighted taper in front of him. Suddenly he was gone from view.

Alberto did not try to go after him. He had heard enough. He emerged from the alley and climbed on his horse. Without looking back at the city he had once called his own, he left Sevilla forever.

As his penitent friend had suggested, Alberto went to Carmona to meet La Susanna. He wanted to hear news of his family as well as to meet the infamous La Susanna. She was the daughter of Diego de Susan, a rich Converso merchant who was one of the first victims of the Inquisition, and she was shunned and despised by all.

It was Diego de Susan who, with seven other Conversos, had plotted the local resistance in Sevilla against the newly established Holy Office. Conspiring to strike quickly before the Inquisition made its first move, the Converso leader had gathered enough weapons and money to arm a hundred men. But all was in vain, for La Susanna betrayed her father's secret to her lover. The Converso conspirators were apprehended, tried, and sentenced to be burned at the stake. When the Inquisition confiscated her father's estate, La Susanna was left penniless. Although her confession of her family's Judaizing activities saved her life, she lost everything else: family, friends, wealth. All that was left was her phenomenal beauty, for which she was called "*la hermosa hembre*," or "the beautiful woman." She it was whom Alberto searched for through the narrow streets of Carmona. He asked every passer-by for her house. As he asked one elderly woman about her, she spat on the ground and walked away. A toothless muleteer smiled knowingly at Alberto in response to his question. Alberto would not let him go until he had wrested some information from him. The muleteer spoke, "La Susanna, you say, it is you want? She'll charge you plenty for what you want, my boy. Beautiful she is, they say, I've never seen her, you know, but she's expensive, and if you have the maravedis, she will give you what you want, you know what I mean, eh, boy?"

Alberto all of a sudden understood, "You mean she's a . . . a . . . lady of ill repute?"

The muleteer guffawed, "A lady . . . of ill repute?!" The muleteer guffawed again, then became somber in his manner.

"Yes, a lady of ill repute . . . a *Marrano* slut, that's what she is . . . A stinking, no-good, Jewess of a whore that should be burned with the rest of her filthy rotten kind." Then the muleteer, too, spat on the ground.

"Just give me the directions to her house," Alberto persisted.

"You want her that bad, eh, boy? . . . If you're that bad off, better you should sleep with one of them than a Christian girl. This La Susanna . . . she's a lovely bitch, you know what I mean, real beautiful, but she's bad, real bad, or so they say. Won't do anything except for lots of money, you know, like the rest of them Jews. Anybody who has a little bit of money in town has had her, even the town grocer wasted a small fortune on her. She'll take you for all you've got."

Alberto insisted, and the muleteer showed him the way to La Susanna's house. Alberto handed the muleteer a maravedi, but the muleteer refused, shaking his head, "No, boy, I want no part of Satan's work. Besides, you're going to need every maravedi you've got for this one."

Once the muleteer left, Alberto drew close to the wooden door and knocked. The door opened, and there she was: more beautiful than anyone he had ever seen. Her hair was reddish-brown, and she had fiery hazel eyes; her lips were perfect, her body full and beckoning. Alberto fought the forces within him that made him want to reach out and consume her.

"Well, don't just stand there and gawk. You want it or not?", La Susanna asked.

"Pardon me, señorita, but if I may, I would like to speak to you concerning the whereabouts of my family . . . the family of Vicente Galante."

"How the devil should I know where they are? Is that all you want from me?"

Alberto nodded, continuing, "A friend of mine thought you might know. I ask for your help."

"Why should I? Who are you, anyway?" La Susanna answered.

"Alberto Galante, they call me. I'm one of your kind, I mean, the kind the Inquisition is after, you know . . . "

"Oh, oh, I see," La Susanna said, peering slowly and sharply at his face. "Still, why should I? You haven't done anything for me. You say you don't want me, but that's how I support myself. You have me first, and then you can have your precious information. Five hundred maravedis it'll cost you, sweetheart."

La Susanna approached Alberto, placing her hand caressingly on his shoulder. Alberto pulled her hand away, his heart pounding, his face flushed and perspiring from the rising passion of his feelings.

"Señorita, please, all I want is information about my family."

La Susanna studied him, her eyes darting about nervously, "I don't believe you, Alberto whatever your name is. Your eyes betray you. You want me . . . you want me very much . . . I can tell," La Susanna said as she nudged against Alberto.

Alberto backed away, "Señorita, I mean you no dishonor. I am a cavalier . . . I did not come here today to take advantage of you or to add to your shame."

La Susanna stopped suddenly, her eyes blazing with anger.

"Don't you talk to me about dishonor! What do you know such things? That's right, what do you know, all of you honorable people? Spanish honor, cavalier honor, I spit on your honor! I've seen your kind. I know all about you and your disgusting kind, you hear? I know all about you! I've had them all . . . dukes, knight commanders, judges, the whole lot of them. I even had a bishop or two, how else do you think I got out of that nunnery they tried to put me in?

"No, my dear cavalier, you can stop your act. It doesn't fool me, and you might as well stop fooling yourself."

Recovering his composure, Alberto cooly replied, "It is very important, and I will repeat my question: do you know where the family of Vicente Galante has fled?"

La Susanna was inflamed by his reply. Her eyes blazed angrily, her eyebrows pressed into a menacing frown, "Bad as you think I am, I am not stupid. For all I know, you're an agent of the Inquisition, and

I'm not about to help you slaughter any more innocent people. That's right, that's who I think you are. So get out of my house!"

Alberto started back towards the door; about to leave, he suddenly turned to her, "As you wish, señorita. One last question though: what if I'm not?"

"Not what?!" La Susanna blared.

"Not from the Inquisition. What if I am a runaway Converso fleeing from the Inquisition?"

"Get out! Out! Out of here! Out of my house before I report you," yelled Susanna as she slammed the door on his face.

Alberto stood on the street, unsettled by the encounter, his head whirling, his mind still troubled about where to go and what to do next. Slowly he climbed on his horse, grabbed at the reins, and checked to make sure his sword was secure. As he drove his heels into the animal's side, the door to La Susanna's home suddenly opened wide. She stepped out, speaking to the air about her, taking no notice of his presence, "The mountain air of Segovia is the purest there is in all Castile." With this pronouncement, La Susanna retreated inside and slammed the door behind her. The "beautiful woman" had come and gone. Alberto now knew the direction in which he must travel.

Chapter 3

Segovia. It was a logical choice. Alberto remembered his father mentioning a Converso cousin in Segovia, a wealthy physician who ministered to royalty and nobility. He remembered the name: Pinto. Such a cousin could easily bear the financial burden of fugitive Converso relatives fleeing from the Inquisition, hide them in his household, and provide them with the means to escape to safety. Segovia was such an obvious choice that he wondered why he had not thought of it before. The only problem was getting there.

Alberto arrived on the outskirts of Segovia after using backroads through deserted Castilian terrain, routes that would have presented substantial difficulty to the common traveler. For weeks, he lived off the land; he ate wild figs, honey, and berries. On rare occasions, he would enter a small town to replenish his supplies, talk with the local townspeople, and then continue on his way. He passed through tiny hamlets, such as Andújar and Ocaña, and within sight of the fortified castles of Maqueda and Escalona, named after the ancient Israelite cities of Makeda and Ashkelon.

Castile was studded with pockets of villages nestling in isolation with limited communication between the neighboring towns. Because of their isolation, Alberto felt that he had little to fear from being seen in an out-of-the-way town. No one would know who he was; nonetheless, he took all precautions to avoid attracting attention. Whenever he stayed in a tavern, he would pay nine or ten maravedis for a day's worth of food or lodging. The plain, unvarying food he ate there — cabbages seasoned with garlic and oil, served on simple clay dishes along with hard bread and flat-tasting wine — made him wonder if this was any improvement over the food he picked in the fields. The accommodations were equally spare: a bed made of two pieces of thick cloth on a vermin-infested floor. Despite the lack of comfort, Alberto enjoyed being around the simple villagers accustomed to little, but willing to share the tavern fire and their tales of the road, thus making the journey a more pleasant one.

It was to such a tavern in Segovia that Alberto came in search of his father's cousin. If this Doctor Pinto was as famous as his father claimed, it should be no problem to locate him. Indeed, even the burly tavern owner had heard of him. While polishing the cauldrons, the innkeeper explained to Alberto how to reach the distinguished physician, but only after he added a word of severe caution.

According to the tavern owner, Doctor Pinto was a sorcerer of the healing arts. The infamous doctor had magical powers of healing conferred by no less than Satan himself, and he was now selling his dark powers and demonic incantations to the highest bidders. Moreover, he read medical books written in the Arabic language of the infidels, which made him even more suspect. The man was a Jew doctor, although a Christian in name only, but he was neither Christian nor Jew; he was an *alborayco*, like the steed of Mohammed, al-Burak, that was neither horse nor mule, neither male nor female, neither this nor that, like the rest of those *Marrano* Conversos.

"The man heals through the devil, and not through God's will," said the innkeeper angrily. "It is terrible that some Christians, ay, especially the rich ones, put their trust in the hands of this money-grabbing Jewish doctor."

Alberto answered him forthrightly, "But the man is a learned and brilliant physician. Everyone says so. That is why the rich and the powerful go to him. He produces results. He heals people and he makes them well again."

The innkeeper slammed the pot he was polishing down, and said, "I would rather be sick from God's will than be healed through the magic of the devil and his Jewish serpent doctors. Go on, you want him? You can have him. But leave my tavern first, for I'll have no Jew lovers under this roof, you hear?"

Alberto countered, "You are mistaken, sir. It is well known that the Jewish doctors have much knowledge and skill. That is why rich and poor alike go to them. And that is the reason why I, too, will go to Doctor Pinto for my illness."

"Yes, is that so? Well then, get out of my inn before I beat the devil out of the likes of you. Better to die with Christ than be healed by a Jew doctor!"

The innkeeper raised his pot menacingly, and signaled with his free hand toward the door. Alberto cooly tipped his hat in the innkeeper's direction and walked leisurely out the door. The action provoked a series of curses and name-calling from the tavern within.

Alberto was angry at himself for allowing the conversation to take such a direction. He had drawn unnecessary attention to himself, and he resolved in the future to refrain from being drawn into a similar situation. Nonetheless, he felt good that he had in some way protected his relative's honor. He was proud that one of his relatives, even though he had never met him, was a physician of the Spanish grandees and was reputed to have extraordinary skill and much knowledge. Alberto concluded Doctor Pinto must be a very special person, and he looked forward to meeting him.

The Jewish physicians were known throughout Europe, as were the Moorish practitioners. Christian physicians usually dispensed amulets and benedictions to ward off demons and evil spirits, while the Jewish physicians adopted a rational, scientific approach to guide them in treating diseases and wounds. Versed in the Arabic and Greek medical treatises, the Jews became preeminent in this field. As a result, they were in great demand. Kings and nobles sought them when in need, despite the exhortations of churchmen. The common people believed the Jewish medical practices were really sorcery, a belief that the Church fostered. Each important cure effected by a Jewish or Converso physician brought with it popular scorn and superstitious fear of the Jew's diabolic pharmacopoeia. But when all was said and done, when disease racked the body with pain or threatened a close family member with death, people ignored the official prohibitions and sought out the best medical care available, regardless of the practitioner's religion.

Doctor Pinto's office was close to the Alcázar, the turreted castle on the western ridge of Segovia. The location was well chosen because it was within walking distance to his common patients as well as close to the castle.

At midday, Doctor Pinto's office was packed with people — some groaning with abdominal pain, others with a purulent discharge from their eyes, still others suffering from shortness of breath. Most sat on benches waiting patiently for Dr. Pinto to call the next patient inside.

Alberto was asked to wait his turn. He was struck by the patients; they came from all classes: nobleman and commoner, Jew and Christian, young and old. Disease was no respecter of religion and high station. Alberto waited his turn as instructed. From time to time, he would catch a glimpse of Dr. Pinto as he went from one ailing person to another. Some left with herbal medications; others with a more pressing illness were referred to one of the local infirmaries for further care.

Alberto looked closely at Dr. Pinto, hoping to discern what kind of person he was. Dr. Pinto wore a long white robe that extended from neck to ankles. Pinto was tall, lean, and held himself very erect; he had a broad forehead and an aquiline nose. His dignified bearing was tempered with kindness, but he did not often smile.

When it was Alberto's turn, he went in the examining room and closed the door behind him.

Doctor Pinto was sitting behind his desk, hands in his lap. "Yes, young man, good day. Please, come in and sit down. I am Dr. Pinto . . . and you are . . . ?"

"Alberto Galante, sir."

Alberto sat down.

"Galante? That's a good name. Now, Señor Galante, how can I be of service to you?"

"Dr. Pinto, I am not sick. I am here for a different reason. Do you know someone by the name of Vicente Galante in Sevilla?"

"Why do you ask? " the physician asked.

"I am his son," Alberto said.

The physician's face became deathly pale as he peered at Alberto, rapidly scrutinizing the facial features. However, he did not speak, but remained strangely silent. Finally he spoke in a whisper.

"And what is it you want? " the doctor asked cautiously.

Alberto said, "Shelter. A place to hide. My family has fled Sevilla. My father often spoke of you, very highly as a matter of fact, and I thought perhaps that he might have come here to get away from the Inquisition."

Doctor Pinto's face became taut with fear, "Señor Galante, I do not know what you are talking about. None of my relatives are fugitives from the Holy Office. I think there must be a mistake."

"But my father and you are cousins," Alberto retorted, "he told me so."

"Surely you are confusing me with someone else," said Doctor

Pinto, increasingly agitated. "My family and I are Old Christians of the purest stock. I have documents to prove it."

"What?" asked Alberto incredulously.

"You heard me. I am of Old Christian stock, but I am not going to repeat myself. Nor am I going to waste my time with any further explanations, young man. Now please leave."

Alberto got up slowly, uncomprehendingly, and said, "My father loved you. He admired you. He said you were a great physician and a great man. You are correct, sir, perhaps I am confusing you with another person."

An expression of pain crossed Doctor Pinto's face. He stared at Alberto once again, looked down at the table with a resigned expression, and looked carefully once again at Alberto. He scratched his nose, tapped his fingers, pouted his lips. And then, as Alberto was about to open the door to leave, he said, "Wait. I have a question for you, Señor Galante. Before you leave, tell me, what does one stand on?"

Alberto sensed immediately that the entire conversation hinged on this cryptic question. It was a question within a question, and only those taught the right answer would pass the test. Every Converso child was taught the answer, and Pinto was obviously testing him. While Alberto was familiar with the question and the answer, he had heard it so long ago that the words were no longer readily brought to mind. He was frustrated beyond measure, as he searched furiously within himself for the solution.

"Is it 'two legs'?" said the doctor in a nervous half-laugh.

Suddenly, Alberto remembered, and his face lit up. He had the answer.

"One stands on one's thirteen," Alberto said jubilantly.

"Yes, one stands on one's thirteen," the physician repeated softly, nodding his head affirmatively. "Allow me to prescribe something for your bad bile, Señor Galante."

Doctor Pinto scribbled something on a piece of parchment and handed it to Alberto. "I hope to see you again sometime soon. In the meantime, take these medications as prescribed. There is no charge for this . . . ah . . . service."

The physician showed Alberto to the door. In the anteroom, in the hearing range of all the patients, he instructed Alberto aloud further, "Remember, follow the prescription directions exactly as I have written here."

"Yes, Doctor Pinto," said Alberto, "thank you very much, sir."

The physician called the next patient into his examining room. Alberto walked outside, and opened up the parchment with the prescription. On it was a message:

"Meet me at the Plaza del Azoguejo underneath the aqueduct at sunset."

He put the message into his saddle bag and rode off happily on his horse.

Yes, Dr. Pinto was his father's cousin. And yes, Alberto had been saved by remembering his thirteen. "*Se para uno en sus trece*," the saying went, "One stands on one's Thirteen." It was a saying that was used to describe those Conversos tortured by the Holy Office but who, to their last breath, had stood on Maimonides' Thirteen Principles of Jewish faith.

Alberto waited for Dr. Pinto at the aqueduct till shortly after sunset. The physician arrived on foot and signaled to Alberto to follow him. They walked to the large open plaza next to the aqueduct. In the middle, where no one could hear what they were saying, they began to speak.

"Doctor Pinto, are my parents with you? " he asked.

"I will ask the questions," snapped the physician. "First I must be satisfied that you are truly who you say you are."

"Very well, sir . . .," Alberto said.

Doctor Pinto proceeded to interrogate Alberto about his parents and his grandparents, where they were born and what they were like. He asked about their tastes and their habits; he asked about the family business and where the various spices were imported from. He asked question after question in rapid succession, and Alberto answered them completely. He asked for information about Grandfather Jacobo, about the origins of the Galante family, and of any secret rites that they practiced. Alberto satisfied him on all counts.

Dr. Pinto finally said, "I am satisfied that you are indeed Alberto Galante, the son of my cousin Vicente. Now, as to your question, your parents are not here in Segovia. I have no idea where they may be."

Alberto was crushed; he had expected that his family would be here. Now, he was alone again. He had not a friend anywhere.

"Come with me, Alberto," said the doctor, "and leave your horse behind."

Alberto followed the physician through the labyrinth of streets around the aqueduct. They walked down the major street under the aqueduct and turned left into a small alley that wound its way uphill. With the approach of night, it was becoming difficult to distinguish figures in the distance. As they walked from one alley to another, Dr. Pinto would glance behind his shoulder to make sure no one was following them. Having arrived at an obscure alley, and satisfied that they were not being trailed, the physician unlatched the bolt of a courtyard gate. He allowed Alberto to pass through, and then closed the gate behind them. Dr. Pinto led the way through a very neglected courtyard filled with weeds, knee-high shrubbery, and stacked bricks.

A dilapidated building stood at the far side of the courtyard. The window and front door of the building were closed. It was dark inside, except for a few narrow shafts of light penetrating through the crevices of the makeshift wooden roof. The floor was covered with dust that the two of them kicked up with their boots. At one corner of the adjacent room was a slab of rock.

Dr. Pinto pushed on the rock until it moved to one side, revealing a trap door underneath. The physician lifted the trap door and descended through it. "Close the trap door after you," he said as he disappeared from sight.

Alberto did as he was told and followed the physician, closing the trap door after him.

An oily, stale air assaulted Alberto's nostrils. It was the smell of burning torches. When Alberto arrived at the bottom of the ladder, he looked about and saw he was at the end of a long subterranean tunnel. The tunnel was lit only with burning torches placed on the tunnel walls at carefully spaced distances.

Alberto followed the physician down the tunnel. Once or twice he lost his footing in the uneven dirt floor beneath him, unable to see its irregularities in this submerged world of flickering shadows and indistinct light. In this surrounding, Alberto imagined the figure in front of him to be some strange apparition, its velvet cloak shimmering like some ghastly shroud on a walking corpse raised from the dead to show Alberto the way to the nether world. It was an eerie feeling. Alberto had the disturbing sensation that he was sinking slowly into the mouth of a dark abyss from which there was no return.

Dr. Pinto continued to walk down the tunnel, lighting the torches on the walls. He walked down one corridor and then down another, with Alberto immediately behind him. Finally, at the end of an especially long, dark tunnel, they came upon a large, well-lit central cavern. In the center was an oblong wooden table at which two men were seated. Dr. Marco Pinto interrupted their conversation as he arrived, torch in hand, "Good evening, gentlemen."

One of the men jumped up from his chair. It was the Converso merchant Armando Fonseca. He shouted at the physician: "Marco! What is the meaning of this? Who . . . who is this man with you?"

The physician replied, "He is a relative of mine . . . from Sevilla . . . he is fleeing the Inquisition."

The Converso merchant was furious and drew his sword. "You idiot! How dare you bring him here to our secret meeting place?"

Angry, Fonseca advanced with his sword toward the doctor and Alberto. Dr. Pinto became equally angry, "Put your sword away, Fonseca. He is one of us. You heard me, put your sword away!"

Fonseca, somewhat miffed at being shouted down by the physician, lowered his sword slowly but did not put it back into its scabbard. He held on to it, saying: "I presume that you took all the usual precautions. Did you look to see if anyone was following you?"

The physician replied, "No one followed me."

Now it was the other person seated at the table, the tailor Mario de Aguilar, who spoke, "Marco, we are in this together, we and our families. We have stood together for years, and we have never brought any outsiders into our group. In the name of Heaven, I cannot understand why you have done such a thing. You have made my . . . our situation more dangerous."

Doctor Pinto continued his plea, "I swear to both of you that no one followed me . . . or him. For the love of God, don't abandon this young man. The Inquisition has a warrant for his arrest and for all his family. I tell you, Mario, this man is of our own flesh and blood. We cannot abandon him."

The tailor was unmoved. "Yes, and it may cost us our own flesh and blood if we are not careful. I do not know this man you bring and, therefore, I do not trust him. The burden is on you, Marco, to prove that he merits our trust. You tell us now, who is this person?"

Dr. Pinto told Armando and Mario Alberto's story, providing the details he had corroborated through questioning. He added, "I tell you, I knew his parents in Sevilla. They were Conversos, as we are. I believe that this man can be trusted. He knew about standing on one's Thirteen. He knew about certain facts and incidents known only to members of my cousin's family. He is who he says he is, señores, and I beg of you to accept him into our secret organization."

A long silence followed as the two sullen Conversos considered the plea. Finally, the merchant Fonseca gave a long sigh, sheathed his sword, and said, "On the word of Dr. Marco Pinto, we welcome you into our fold, young man, but only until we can verify your tale."

"We have no choice," added the tailor Mario, "he already knows too much. What is your name?"

Alberto, who had been deliberately silent thus far, replied, "Ah ... Alberto Galante ... at your service, sir."

The merchant asked, "Is it true what Marco said ... about your being a warrior?"

"Yes, it is true ... I have fought in many battles against the Moors."

"And under whose banner did you fight?"

'I fought with the Marquis of Cádiz."

"The Marquis of Cádiz! Everyone has heard of him."

The tailor joined in, "He is the greatest cavalier there is."

"A very great cavalier," the physician affirmed.

The Converso merchant warmed to Alberto and, in a congratulatory tone, remarked, "You have an instinctive ability for finding yourself in good company, young man. Allow me, Señor Galante, to offer a toast in the hope that your battle has not been in vain."

The merchant poured wine for all those present. He raised his wine cup into the air, "A toast to the new member of our group, Alberto Galante. May he fight our battle for freedom as he has fought in the past against the Moors. May he become one of us in name, in spirit, and in fact. A toast to you, Señor Galante. *L'Hayim!* To life!"

"*L'Hayim!*," shouted the others present.

The four of them raised and clinked their wine cups, hurriedly downing their drinks.

"Where's Hernando?" asked Marco Pinto.

"I hear footsteps," said the tailor, "that may be him coming."

It was Hernando, the blacksmith, who was arriving. The blacksmith was always late, but his great physical strength made up for his shortcomings. He was a massive hulk of a man with bulging, muscular arms. Only his temper matched his strength, and it was the blacksmith whom Dr. Pinto feared might be most unwilling to accept newcomers into the group.

Strong as the blacksmith was, he was torpid as an ox, and his solution to all the problems was physical violence. The blacksmith arrived, stared at the foursome — and especially at Alberto, and wondered what was happening.

Dr. Pinto approached the blacksmith and placed his hand gently on the man's shoulder, "Hernando, we have a new member in our group . . . He has been cleared by all of us. He is safe. He is a Converso as we are. Hernando, I would like to present to you Señor Alberto Galante."

Alberto came forward with stretched hand, "It gives me great pleasure to meet you, sir."

"Hrrumph!" growled the blacksmith as he stared at Alberto. He shook Alberto's hand grudgingly and sat down at the table, arms crossed in disgust.

Alberto shrugged his shoulders at the blacksmith's uncouth manners, but took the slight without response. Dr. Pinto was relieved there was no major confrontation between them and he, too, took his chair.

The Converso merchant began the meeting. "Good. Everyone is here now. The meeting can begin. We have a serious matter to attend to. Gentlemen, I regret to inform you that the Inquisition . . . "

The tailor interrupted, "May its name be blotted out!"

The merchant persisted, "Kindly allow me to speak without interruption. As you well know, there is a permanent Inquisition tribunal in Valladolid. I regret to inform you that a temporary Inquisition tribunal is to be set up here in Segovia."

"Oh, no!," exclaimed the startled Pinto.

The tailor shook his head, and let out a long sigh. Only the blacksmith and Alberto remained silent.

The merchant continued, "Furthermore, the Inquisition . . . has decided to pronounce an Edict of Grace in Segovia. What it means is this: any person, Christian or Jew, who has knowledge about the Judaizing activities of any citizen of the city must report it within 30 days to the Hermandad or face its punishment."

The tailor shouted, "By the devil of Alicante! They are at our doorstep. What will we do?"

Suddenly the blacksmith slammed his hammer on the table, startling everyone, and said, "I say fight back. Attack! Attack before they attack us!" The blacksmith then raised his hammer menacingly in the air.

The merchant responded, "Fight? Fight what? Fight the army of soldiers that protects the Inquisitors? Only a fool would attack." The blacksmith leered angrily, but the merchant continued, "Do you not know what happened in Zaragoza? The Converso leaders in that city arranged for the assassination of the Inquisitor Pedro Arbúes, hoping that this would prevent the establishment of the tribunal in that city. But the plot backfired. All the city turned against them when it was found out that Judaizing Conversos were behind the murder. Fifteen members of the powerful Santángel family were burned at the stake, others had their hands and heads chopped off, and you want to fight?"

Marco Pinto buttressed the merchant's reply, "No, no, not attack. We must not arouse their suspicions under any circumstances. We must continue to behave as if we were good Christians until we can find a way of escape."

Now it was the tailor's turn. "Our grandfathers were Jews, believing Jews, converted by force against their will during the riots of the last century. And though they were Christians on the outside, in their hearts they remained Jews. It was the secret of our grandfathers, and of our fathers, and it is our secret today . . . a secret we *must* pass on to our children."

The blacksmith roared, "No one hates this double life more than I do. I hate it, you hear, I hate it."

The blacksmith banged his hammer on the table again, shattering the air in the cavern.

"Silence!" screamed the merchant. "We have no choice. Either we deceive or we die."

"I agree. We must lay low until the storm has passed," said Pinto.

"Hrrumph! It may never pass," countered the blacksmith, pouting with his lips as he once again reverted to his position of silent anger and crossed arms.

The merchant went to other matters, "I think that you should know that some Conversos have already left town and fled to God knows where. We are in a similar position, and we must make a decision about what to do now that the Inquisition is in our midst. I have been able to make the arrangements we discussed earlier. I mean, I have found a captain with a ship of his own who is willing to take us and our families to Morocco, or if need be, even to the land of the Turk. The Inquisition has inspectors at every port, and it will be risky. Nonetheless, this captain I speak of is willing to take the chance . . . if the price is right. And the price is steep . . . five hundred ducats a head."

"What! That is robbery!" said Dr. Pinto angrily.

"But it is our only hope. Take it or leave it, the captain told me," said the merchant.

"Leave it we will," the tailor replied. "We do not have this much money ... except perhaps for the good doctor here."

Dr. Pinto did not acknowledge the tailor's remark. The tailor was always trying to embarrass him, but he tried not to pay attention.

"This captain is a robber, that's for sure," Dr. Pinto commented, "and no one knows if he will stop here. I think we do better to stay away from such so-called friends. For now, the best strategy is, I feel, to stay where we are and to continue exactly as we are doing."

The merchant turned to the blacksmith, who was still sulking. The blacksmith turned his head slowly, looked up at the merchant, and then turned his head back. He continued staring straight ahead, seemingly indifferent to the question under discussion.

"Leave it," said the blacksmith curtly.

It was unanimous.

"Very well," said the merchant, "it is decided. We continue as we are doing. Marco, it is your duty to find the forged documents for this relative of yours. If he is to stay with us any length of time, he must be given a new identity, a new baptismal certificate ... you know, the usual. I presume you will obtain it through the usual secret channels."

Marco nodded his head affirmatively.

The merchant, however, was not finished. "I, on the other hand, will continue to search for a sympathetic captain willing to take us and our families to some place where we can openly be Jews."

"Amen," intoned the tailor ... "and for a better price, I should hope."

"Such a captain will not be easy to find," continued the merchant, "everyone lives in fear of the Holy Office, and there will be a high price to pay, but not anything as absurd as the price that I mentioned earlier. We must have courage, my friends, and we must have patience. Difficult times are coming, and we must be ready to face them. Our task is simpler for the moment. We have to prepare ourselves for the Jewish New Year, *Rosh Hashana*, which is but two weeks away. I have found someone to lead the prayers and to teach us about the holiday."

"A Jew or a Converso?" asked the tailor.

Pinto noted, "I do not like the way you put the question. For your information, we are all Jews!"

"Is that so?" answered the tailor sardonically, "Pardon me, good doctor, for my indelicate choice of words."

The meeting was becoming charged with hostility. Conversos had enough problems of their own without creating petty squabbles. The merchant decided to end the fighting.

"The teacher is, how can I put it, an unconverted Jew," stated the merchant.

'Ah, now I know," said the tailor, "an unconverted Jew . . . ahh."

"Hrrumph!" snorted the blacksmith. But it was not clear what he meant by the snort.

The merchant decided to put a quick end to the meeting, requesting them to reconvene the following week at the same time to prepare for the New Year.

Each went his own way. Dr. Pinto led Alberto through the tunnel, back to the trapdoor area, out into the neglected courtyard, and back to the now abandoned streets of Segovia. The blacksmith had his own special tunnel that led to his shop; the tailor and the merchant also left via a separate connecting tunnel.

The underground web of shafts and tunnels fulfilled the Converso need for absolute secrecy. Here in the subterranean passageways the Conversos shared their darkest secrets, poured out their longings, and spoke of their dreams to flee to freedom. Here it was that their other selves, their Jewish selves, emerged, showing that the light within themselves had not been extinguished. Here, in the depths, their spirits reached for the heavens above. Here, in the depths, they drew from the wellsprings of their own tradition, and prepared for the day when they could walk without shame and be what they really were.

It was Segovia's social event of the year. Beatriz de Bobadilla, the Marchioness of Moya, had returned to the Alcázar from the battlefront, and her husband Andrés de Cabrera, governor of the castle, was organizing festivities in her honor. Everyone heard how she had miraculously escaped being killed by a crazed Moor during her visit to the queen in Málaga, and everyone was eager to see her again. La Bobadilla, as she was fondly called, was a close friend and confidante of the queen; she and Isabella had known each other since childhood, and their friendship had grown over the years. She knew the queen's darkest secrets, and the queen knew hers. It was for good reason then that people would say, "*Después de la reina, La Bobadilla . . .* " "After the queen comes the Bobadilla," for she was acknowledged as the second lady of Spain.

It was through his wife that Andrés de Cabrera found a way to influence the queen. As the queen's loyal supporter since her marriage to Ferdinand, Andrés served her as he had served the late King Henry IV — as administrator for the city of Segovia. It was he who mediated the terms of transition between the two reigns. As a result, Cabrera received the new queen's respect and gratitude. In due time, he was introduced into the nobility and was officially known as the Marquis of Moya. Despite royal patronage, Cabrera was disliked by the townspeople over whom he ruled, partly because he was a strict disciplinarian, partly because he was known to be of Converso origin. The whisperings of his Jewish ancestry added to his lack of popularity. Nonetheless, his unwavering loyalty to the queen, his excellent skills as an administrator and as an able implementor of royal policy, secured his position as ruler of the Alcázar. He was also designated protector of the royal treasure and its crown jewels.

Andrés de Cabrera had the Alcázar castle ready for the occasion. He wanted to please his wife, to make her forget the unsettling episode at Málaga. In addition to various types of fowl and beef and lamb dishes, he ordered diverse confections to be readied: quince dishes cooked in sugar, citron fruits steeped in honey, lemon preserves, candied pumpkin, along with cartloads of peaches, pears, and nuts. He wanted it to be an affair everyone would remember. The estate rooms of the castle, decorated with Moorish friezes and caissoned ceilings, were scrubbed and polished and outfitted with new tapestries. The turrets, the staircases, the stained glass windows, the damask walls of the chapel, and its altar pieces — all shone with a brilliance not seen since the day of Isabella's coronation in Segovia back in 1474. The castle glistened as never before. The main courtyard, where the reception was to take place, was lined with flowers encircling the base of each arch as well as the central fountain.

For the occasion, Cabrera secured the services of local musicians who played many different instruments, including a lute, recorder, tambourines, sackbut, oboe, flutes, guitars, drums, the Moorish pipe called the añafil, and others. He was looking forward to hearing them play.

Everyone of local and regional importance was invited — the city magnates, the nobles, the renowned Bishop Dávila, the heads of the local monasteries, and of course, the new local Inquisitor. Other Segovian men and women of distinction were invited as well, including Marco Pinto, the city's eminent physician, and Don Abraham Senior, the Chief Judge of the Jews of the kingdom. It would be a splendid affair, and Andrés de Cabrera knew it would also be an unqualified success.

Dr. Pinto, his wife Regina, and his daughter Hermosa were all invited to the festive affair at the Alcázar castle. The physician had been requested to examine Señora Bobadilla upon her return to the castle and found her to be in excellent physical condition, except for a touch of melancholy. The problem, as he saw it, was not with the governor's wife, but with his own wife.

Regina Pinto was furious. She had been angry from the moment Marco had brought Alberto into the household via the secret passageway. Although she did not vent her anger in front of Alberto, she made it clear to her husband that she was extremely unhappy and wanted to be rid of the uninvited intruder. Regina tolerated no nonsense, and she believed in strong, swift action on matters affecting family survival and fortune. Even as they walked towards the entrance gate of the castle, she made her husband feel the pressure of her will.

Regina asked, "Why did you endanger our lives like that, Marco? There was no need to do so."

Pinto replied, "I've told you. He is of the Jewish nation, as we are. One cannot hand over one's flesh and blood to the hounds of the Inquisition."

Regina continued, "But one cannot be so careless either. They are fanatics — out for blood and money. Give them a chance, and they will kill us all."

Hermosa, their daughter, interjected, "Mama, we are careful. Everyone in our secret group can be trusted. You know that."

Regina was unmoved, "All it takes is one mistake, one mistake, and I am afraid we may have already made it."

Marco walked on, not responding to the statement.

Regina said further, "Remember the nurse at the office who was spying on you? Or the clerk who would look into your papers till you caught her? Or the other people who you thought were following you as you walked home? No, my sweet, we are under suspicion without question. Everyone knows about our Converso background, despite our forged documents. And now that the Inquisition is establishing a local tribunal here, there will be those who will seek every opportunity to turn us over to the Inquisition."

Hermosa said, "Oh, Mama, surely it couldn't be that bad."

Regina looked sternly at her daughter, "Couldn't it? Allow me to correct myself. We have not made one mistake. No, we have made *two* of them . . . the first was allowing this Alberto into our house. The second was not taking that ship and getting as far away from Spain as possible."

The physician suddenly spoke, "And pay that outrageous price?"

Regina countered, "And pay with our lives instead? I want it to be perfectly understood that this Alberto Galante is not going to take one step into my house until I say so. Is that clear? Not one step! He stays in the underground tunnel until his papers are ready, and even then I may not let him out. It is my decision. Is that clear?"

The physician answered in a resigned voice, "Yes, Regina . . . as you wish."

The three arrived at the castle. Hermosa placed her hand on her mother's, "Please, Mama, no more of this kind of talk. Let's have a good time at this fiesta . . . please, Mama."

Regina squeezed her daughter's hand and gave her an understanding smile. She would grant her daughter's wish.

Upon arriving at the Alcázar, the Pinto family was escorted into the main courtyard by a uniformed guard. They presented themselves to the governor Don Andrés de Cabrera and to Beatriz de Bobadilla, exchanging the customary courtesies and salutations. Don Andrés drew Dr. Pinto aside and thanked him once again for his medical services and assurances that all was well with his wife.

The celebrations were already in progress. To the courtly music of the orchestra, splendidly dressed young men and women promenaded their way across the courtyard: ladies in rich silk skirts with arabesque motifs and gold-lined tabards, their laced headdresses *a la Morisco* bobbing in the air; the men in short, loose velvet coats and silk breeches held up by leather belts at the waist. Pendulous gold chains hung about the ruffled necks of the nobles; at their sides were jeweled gilded swords, and at their feet were shoes tapered to a fine point.

Dukes, ecclesiastics, jurists, and heads of military orders mingled in the central courtyard and entered the magnificent estate rooms within, eating and talking on the castle patio with its panoramic view of the Eresma Valley and the River Clamores far below.

As Doctor Pinto helped himself to a goblet of red wine, Hermosa was approached by an attractive blond Christian youth, Juan de Gonzalo. Infatuated with her, he bowed respectfully and asked, "May I have the pleasure of this dance, my lady?"

Hermosa curtsied in return, "Why, thank you . . . with your permission, Father." Hermosa accompanied Juan to the center courtyard, and they joined in the stately court dance. Juan held Hermosa's hand tightly, "Ah, my lady, your cheeks are like the roses of Toledo . . . with soft petals that need a gardener's caressing."

Hermosa answered, "But watch for its thorn, Juan. It may not be worth plucking."

The debonair Juan replied, "Ah, my lady, would that my fingers could bleed for such a chance."

The two continued dancing.

Marco Pinto and his wife watched as their lovely daughter danced with the handsome Juan. To many it would have have been thought a perfect match.

But Regina remarked, "I don't like the way they're looking at each other. I don't like it at all."

Marco replied, "Regina, I've told you before . . . we will not discuss this matter here."

Regina gave her husband an icy stare and kept quiet.

One nobleman, noting the physician's watchful eye on his daughter, came over to Marco's side and whispered something.

Marco did not hear him well, so he asked the gentleman to repeat what he had said.

The nobleman bent over and slowly repeated, "A very fine young man, this Juan de Gonzalo. Good family."

"So I hear," Marco noted politely.

Winking at Pinto, the noble nudged him and said knowingly, "Good *Old* Christian stock, if you know what I mean."

Marco studied the aristocrat's eyes to search for an ulterior motive, but it seemed to be a simple comment.

He acknowledged it as such. "Yes, I can see that . . . very fine stock, indeed . . . I'm delighted. Thank you for your information, sir."

The aristocrat smiled knowingly and walked on. Marco continued to sip indifferently on his glass of red wine, as he watched the gentlemen move on to another sector of the courtyard. It was nothing, he assured himself; the man, whoever he was, knew nothing at all. He took in a deep breath and sighed with relief.

A hand reached out slowly and grabbed Marco Pinto by the shoulder. The tense physician jerked violently upon being startled so, and spilled the contents of the wine glass on the floor. He spun around to face the person to whom the hand belonged. The man was heavy-set, with thick jowls, bug black eyes, and a full beard. Pinto had never seen him before.

"Pardon me, sir," said the man cooly, "I did not mean to frighten you . . . but have we met before?"

"Why . . . uh . . . ah . . .," said Marco, sizing up the stranger while regaining his composure, "I do not believe that we have."

"Then allow me to introduce myself. I am Don Enrique Domínguez de Córdoba, head of the local Hermandad . . ."

"Oh," said Regina upon joining the pair.

The man continued, ". . . Protector of Segovia and authorized representative of the Holy Office of the Inquisition."

"And I am Marco Pinto, a humble physician at your services, Don Enrique . . . My wife, Regina."

Regina curtsied upon being introduced and Domínguez bowed in return. Marco continued, "We are most honored to meet someone as distinguished as yourself."

Domínguez said, "The pleasure is mine, Dr. Pinto. It is not every day that one has the opportunity to meet a famous physician such as yourself. You see, I have a problem . . ."

Marco smiled. The man had a problem. Of course, a medical problem. And understandably the man wanted to discuss it with the best physician in the city. It all made sense.

"Yes, go on," said Dr. Pinto.

"Well, to be quite frank, I am looking for the leader of a band of brigands. We caught up with his outfit in the mountains. He was badly wounded during our attack, and we think he may have gone in search of a physician. I wanted to talk with you if perhaps he might have secretly come to you."

"Well, that is perhaps understandable. I am quite well known as a physician," said Marco.

"Yes, I am aware of that, Doctor Pinto," said Domínguez. "I merely wish to ask you whether you have seen the man. He was wounded in the thigh by one of our archers."

"I don't recall seeing anyone with such a problem. I'd have to check my records. I see so many patients I can't remember them all. You understand that, I hope."

"Is he dangerous?" asked Regina.

"All I know about him is that he is an excellent swordsman," said Domínguez. "That makes him dangerous enough . . . for those of us who have to catch him."

"And you haven't caught him? Pity," said Marco sympathetically. "He sounds like a dangerous man."

Domínguez answered slowly, "The man has eluded us. Other Hermandad officers in the area have been instructed to keep a look-out for him. In any case, I would appreciate your reporting to our office if you see him. We need to know."

"I will certainly do so immediately," said Dr. Pinto emphatically, "I will check my records first thing tomorrow. I will do my utmost to help you bring this fugitive to justice."

"Very well, thank you," Domínguez said, his attention apparently distracted by someone signaling to him from the other side of the courtyard, "Excuse me, Señor and Señora Pinto . . . I must take leave. I hope to be seeing more of you."

Marco said, "By all means, do come and visit us."

"Oh yes," added Regina, "please let us know when we can expect you."

Dominguez bowed one last time and said, "Thank you most kindly for your generous invitation." He kissed Regina's hand and left the two of them standing, and full of fear.

In the meantime Juan and Hermosa disappeared from view on the patio. They climbed to the top of the John II tower and were breathless and exhausted from the climb. As they stood there, high in the castle turret overlooking the valley below, they felt increasingly drawn to each other. Not knowing exactly what to say or do, Hermosa pulled out a hand fan and began to cool herself.

"That was a climb . . . don't you think so, Juan?" asked Hermosa.

Juan nodded his head in agreement, gazing into Hermosa's blue eyes. He was entranced by her beauty: every movement she made was graceful, everything about her was magical. Juan was exhilarated by Hermosa, and most of all by the feelings he felt growing within himself.

Church bells began to ring loudly and continuously. From their vantage point, Juan and Hermosa could see a group of worshippers in the distance heading in the direction of the cathedral. They looked at each other, puzzled by these continuous peals from afar.

Hermosa asked, "The church bells . . . why are they ringing?"

Juan put his hand softly on hers, "Could it be that one day we will hear them ring for us . . . together in matrimony."

"Ay, Juan, what daydreams," Hermosa said coquettishly, pulling her hand away and fanning herself as before. She walked away from Juan, trying to cool his ardor.

A few curious stragglers from the courtyard had now come out onto the turret roof in response to the bells, interrupting their privacy.

"It is best we return to the courtyard," advised Hermosa.

"As you wish," said Juan, and they wound their way down the turret to the courtyard.

"Look. It's the *juglar*," shouted Hermosa happily when she realized what was about to happen.

Suddenly, an ebullient tanned elf of a man, his grey hair curled into locks, his red cloak tightened about his waist with a wide leather belt, skipped into the courtyard, somersaulting and cavorting as he went, standing on his hands, twisting and turning his body to the vagabond tune he was singing. He moved around the ladies, making comical expressions of pain and wide-eyed joy, and then jumped onto the fountain rim. It was the *juglar*, the folk minstrel, with his ballads and tales and witty sayings, who now joined the festivities.

> Gather around me, all you ladies so dear,
> To hear my stories of far and near
> Great ballads have I — beyond compare,
> And were I you, I would listen — if you dare!

> I've been to Granada, where the Moors are still bold,
> Where wine is missing, and the women are sold,
> Their horses are steeds, of a kind never seen,
> But their armies are falling, to the likes of our Queen!

> Alhambra's their castle, it's a beauty I miss,
> I've sold my sweet songs there, a poem for a kiss,
> Their wine barrels are empty, much to my dismay,
> But my heart's lute I've strummed there on many a day.

The women gathered about the *juglar* or troubadour who had seen faraway places and sang about them. He told of the wiles and ways of strange peoples and of his own adventures, tales of love and courage, jumping and cavorting to the tunes to the delight of his audience. There were many roving troubadours wandering through the countryside: some sang their ribald ditties in the village streets, while some went from castle to castle for royal patronage. While the *juglar* at the

Alcázar fiesta sang less coarse verses, he, too, would insert on occasion more common touches.

When Bishop Dávila heard some of the *juglar's* baser verses, he was pained to have them sung at such dignified festivities. The stout, grey-haired churchman would have to speak to Don Andrés de Cabrera about this matter at a more opportune time. Dávila, the blood rushing to his square-jawed face, got up from the bench and walked away; the local Inquisitor Lucero and other ecclesiastics followed him.

"What's the matter, Bishop? Upset about the *juglar*?," asked Don Andrés, his face taut with worry, as he pursued the Bishop in the hallway.

The Bishop spun around, his face in an angry scowl. "Yes, I am very upset. Are you trying to make us descend to the tastelessness of the court of Castile, bringing its tomfoolery and clowns here to Segovia? I'm not about to condone this spectacle, and I tell you to your face: it is not fitting. But you think it is right for you to do it, because you consider yourself beyond reproach. Don't you agree, Inquisitor Lucero?"

"Absolutely," parroted the Inquisitor, "Absolutely."

"Please, Bishop Dávila," said Don Andrés, "surely it is not so bad. I admit, some of his songs are in questionable taste, but I beg of you not to put an end to the minstrel's show, if that is what you are thinking. The *juglar* makes her forget her sufferings at Málaga. It is proper for you and the Inquisitor to walk away, but Bishop, surely that is enough."

"It is *not* enough," said the Bishop forcefully, "and I will not accept being taught morality by the likes of you. Nor will I allow God-fearing people to be exposed any more to the corrupting mouthings of this uncouth minstrel."

"Do what you must," said Don Andrés, realizing that it was pointless to argue with the Bishop. Cabrera and Dávila had been long-standing antagonists on several issues. Not able to count the disputatious Bishop as one of his supporters, Don Andrés felt it would be wise not to alienate the new Inquisitor, Diego Lucero. With Andres' Converso background and Dávila's known detestation of Converso backsliders, it would only cause him trouble.

A stern Bishop Dávila moved to the center of the courtyard, his cross raised high. Upon seeing Dávila, the merry spirit created by the minstrel disappeared. In its place was an uneasy silence. The frightened minstrel took a final subservient bow and melted into the shadows.

Dávila planted himself in front of the orchestra. He raised his cross and said, "The infidel Moors have been been beaten at Málaga and they have surrendered the fortress of Gibralfaro. Let us give thanks unto the Lord, our savior Jesus Christ, who has made this great thing to pass.

"Let us give thanks for entrusting our Catholic kings with this divine mission in which they have succeeded for the glory of God and for the glory of all Castile and León.

"Let us pray."

Everyone made the sign of the cross and knelt on the courtyard floor. Now it was the Inquisitor's turn to add a few words:

"And just as the infidel foe is being beaten outside of Castile, so shall we eliminate those infidels who are hiding in our very midst."

All in attendance knelt in prayer in the presence of the Bishop and the Inquisitor. The would-be lovers Juan and Hermosa exchanged understanding glances, while Marco and Regina Pinto shook their heads. It was in the midst of observing his daughter's playful antics that Marco realized that Domínguez was closely watching them. Out of the corner of his eye, the physician sensed the intense stare of Domínguez. Marco wondered how much the Hermandad officer knew and what he only suspected. Could it be that the Pinto family was now the object of suspicion? To Marco it was evident that life in Segovia was becoming difficult. Perhaps, just perhaps, his wife was right after all; perhaps they should have paid the price, left Segovia, left their friends, left his medical practice, left everything behind. Then he would be free of all this needless worry. But then maybe he was worrying over nothing. He really did not know what to think any longer, and it troubled him that he could not reason his way out of this predicament. Perhaps he had made a mistake after all.

Chapter 4

Alberto wanted to leave. He hated living like a rat in the subterranean tunnel, napping on its oily walls and inhaling its oppressive thick air. He detested the dark and dreary surroundings, the lifeless shadows substituting for the light of day. He hated it all, and he hated himself.

He hated himself because he thought he was a burden. The coldness of Regina from the moment he arrived made him feel unwanted. Although Regina never actually insulted him outright, nor voiced her animosity, he could feel the hostility in her eyes. He was a burden, a threat, and he knew it.

Alberto would have left had it not been for the insistence of Doctor Pinto that he stay at least until his documents arrived. Hermosa Pinto had also been gracious and understanding. Father and daughter tried to soften the unpleasantness of Alberto's position, for which they felt themselves in part to blame. At least once a day, each would descend through the kitchen trap door to pay Alberto a brief social call. It was a fleeting respite from the boredom of the day, but Alberto admitted it was better than no respite at all. The first two days Alberto spent walking up and down the underground tunnels until he knew them by heart. The scheme was simple: there were four different tunnels, all converging upon the central cavern — one to the Pinto home, the others to the homes of the merchant, the blacksmith, and the tailor. The tunneling required had been difficult, and Alberto admired the diligence that had resulted in the creation of such a perfect subterfuge. It was well worth the effort, he admitted to himself and to Doctor Pinto.

The physician's conversation with Alberto usually dealt with the events of the day. Most of all, Dr.Pinto talked apprehensively about the local Inquisitorial tribunal and its activities. Thus far, the physician said, only a handful of Conversos had been denounced to the Holy Office for suspected Judaizing activities. All precautions, he added, had to be taken; it was imperative that Alberto not set foot above ground until he had adequate legal documentation concerning his Old Christian character. Proper persons had been contacted, and it would be only a matter of days before the costly documents would be ready. Dr. Pinto urged Alberto to be patient, difficult as it was under such trying physical conditions. Possessing such papers, while not a guarantee, was important, especially for anyone wanting to advance within the higher echelons of Spanish society. Alberto told Dr. Pinto to save his money; he did not need the papers. The physician, however, was insistent and would have it no other way. He made it clear to Alberto that a movement was afoot to exclude Conversos from holding either municipal office or membership in the guilds. This had already happened in Toledo after the riots there 30 or 40 years earlier. You could never be sure when such documents would prove to be invaluable. Alberto conceded Dr. Pinto was right and allowed the physician to proceed with his plan. It was, Alberto sensed, the physician's way of making amends for his wife's coldness and, indeed, for the frigid reception that the healer himself had given Alberto in his office.

It was with Hermosa that Alberto came up for fresh air. He loved her company. When her mother was gone, she would find some excuse to send the servants away on some petty errand and allow Alberto to enter the house above. Upon surfacing, Alberto would stretch his arms and take several deep breaths. Hermosa took special pleasure in watching. After Alberto basked in the warm sunlight of the courtyard and moved about to limber up his stiff joints, she would bring him a basin of hot water to wash himself, and a cloth to dry himself. On other occasions, she prepared some warm broth for him to eat. She did everything she could to make him feel like a welcome guest of the family. She saw Alberto not as a threat, but as a companion, a friend, a young Converso who was in hiding, someone who had the same things to hide as she did. And, besides, he was most interesting.

Everyone agreed that Hermosa lived up to her name: goodness of soul, sweetness of character — all of this came as natural to her as her gentle smile and good humor. She was the personification of beauty, with a creamy, olive-colored skin and curly brown hair, large, soft blue eyes with naturally curled eyelashes, and a perfectly shaped straight nose — all added to her look of womanly softness. She had learned to be tender hearted from her secret Jewish tutors who taught her the importance of virtuous and benevolent behavior. She tried to be a good person, to be a 'woman of valor' as the Sabbath song had it, to be someone valued for her excellence of character rather than for her physical beauty. But she knew she was pleasant to look at. Everyone told her so, and she had already several potential suitors, among them the aristocratic Juan de Gonzalo. Yet she found most men her age vapid and arrogant, seeking to press their physical advantage. She despised men without principle, men who sought nothing but selfish physical gratification at the expense of others.

Hermosa had never met a Converso cavalier, nor any *genuine* cavalier for that matter. She found the chivalrous tales of errant knights pure fantasy. The real-life knights and cavaliers she knew were pompous, empty-headed peacocks, reeking of vanity and self-glorification. She wanted nothing to do with them. Alberto, she sensed, was different, far different, from any cavalier or knight she had ever met. Alberto had character, almost storybook character, and she began to develop a growing interest in him. Alberto was chaste, respectful, kind, intelligent, and from all accounts, brave. And, best of all, he was a Converso as she was.

Whenever Alberto talked about his childhood in Sevilla or his exploits at Málaga, Hermosa listened attentively. She learned about Converso life in Sevilla, about the Moors, about the Marquis of Cádiz, and many other things. And she in turn talked about her own experiences while growing up in Segovia. As the only child of a prominent physician, she had never been lacking in the social comforts. Indeed, until she was thirteen years of age, she had not even known that she was of Converso origin. Her parents never spoke of their Jewish activities until they felt she was old enough to keep the family secret. It was only then she understood why her parents spoke so little about the Church. At 13 she was given a tutor to provide her with initial instruction in Jewish religious beliefs and practices, and only then was she allowed into the activities of the clan.

Hermosa learned Hebrew prayers as well as how to perform the ritual benedictions; she learned the *Shema* and the *Shmoneh Esreh* (the Eighteen Benedictions) almost by heart. Periodicaly, she would attend the clandestine gatherings to listen to explanations of the Bible and the Midrash. In her discussions with Alberto, she related how the tailor, who was the most learned of the clan in religious matters, would lead the discussions. When major holidays such as *Yom Kippur* or Passover came, the tailor made secret contacts with the local Jewish community to arrange for a special teacher for the group. Through such instruction, her knowledge of Judaism, and her sense of identification with the Jewish people, increased each year. The religion of her fathers, denied to her in childhood, had finally come to be her own as an adult.

When she was 13, it became Hermosa's duty on Friday evening to change the linen and to light the Sabbath candles. She would then place the lit candles in a pitcher or in the underground tunnel until the candle had burned itself out. On the Sabbath, and on most other days, the family would abstain from pork. When a Christian guest arrived for dinner, pork dishes of necessity would have to be served to lessen suspicions. But to avoid contaminating the kosher utensils, a special set of plates and utensils was kept on hand for such occasions. The Pintos tried to keep the Jewish dietary laws as much as possible — washing the meat to remove all traces of blood, cooking with oil instead of animal fat, and of course, separating milk from meat dishes. Only servants who were also Converso could prepare the food. It was too dangerous to employ an Old Christian within the household.

Jewish law forbade work on the Sabbath. Yet not to work on the Sabbath created immediate suspicion of being a Judaizer. Because the Inquisition was known on Sabbath days to be on the lookout for homes from which no chimney smoke emerged, Hermosa was told to add logs to the fire at meal times, but not to use it for cooking purposes. Hermosa related to Alberto how her mother would set up her spinning wheel in the front room on the Sabbath so that, whenever a guest arrived, she would appear to be busy. They had to take continual precautions and maintain a pretense of being practicing Catholics, or else it could mean total ruin for the family.

Even when they went to the cathedral, the Pinto family made it a point to be conspicuous. They always took their place in the first few pews to be visible to everyone. Their faithful attendance, their generous contributions to the church coffers, their annual partaking of the sacramental host of the Holy Eucharist — all this helped to allay suspicions they were anything less than truly observant Catholics.

But in her heart, Hermosa denied the validity of the Christian faith.

She denied the divinity of Christ, she denied the virginity of Mary, she denied the Christian concept of salvation.

As she denied everything that was crucial to the Catholic faith, she yearned to know more about her Jewish ancestral religion. All that she was made to avow in public, she disavowed in private. All that she avowed in private, she admitted to none except to the trusted few. It was evident that, as she matured, so did the dichotomy within herself, a chasm bridged only by the lie that she was forced to live. This, she admitted to Alberto, was the greatest tragedy of every Converso.

The Converso community announced a special underground meeting to meet the new teacher sent by the local Jewish community to provide religious instruction for the high holy days. Hermosa heard rumors about the new teacher, one of the Jewish Morisco worthies rescued from the recently captured fortress of Málaga. Hermosa heard that the teacher, or 'Hacham' as he was called, from the Andalusian south still wore the exotic, alien dress of the Moors. Luckily, he knew enough Castilian to make himself understood. Her curiosity to meet the Hacham was no less intense than that of the Hacham who wanted to meet the crypto-Jews of the Segovia Converso underworld.

There was little time for the Hacham to think about the underground labyrinth into which he had been brought. The tailor whisked him along without a word as they advanced from one corridor to the other. Finally they arrived at the central cavern.

Seated about the main table were the Conversos and their older children. Alberto and Hermosa sat next to each other, sharing a bench with the merchant and his three children.

The tailor introduced the swarthy, gaunt-faced Hacham, his thin frame draped with a loosely hanging tunic.

"Fellow Jews, I have the honor today of introducing the Reverend Hacham Isaac Alhadeff, former head of the Jewish community of Málaga and present instructor at the Talmudic college of Segovia. He has agreed to talk to us about how to prepare ourselves for the upcoming holy days of *Rosh Hashana* and *Yom Kippur* ... Señores y señoras, Hacham Isaac Alhadeff."

The Hacham looked about at this new group of pupils. He knew that their formal Jewish education was limited, but he sensed their thirst for knowledge. From his past experiences as a teacher of Conversos in Córdoba, he knew it was not only knowledge they wanted: they wanted recognition as Jews by someone who was a *real* Jew, by someone untainted by ancestral conversion. They wanted recognition by a *sefardí tahor*, a pure Sephardic Jew, unsoiled by baptism and by Christian upbringing. And it was he, the Hacham, who had been chosen to make them feel worthy again, to make them feel and believe that they were as good as any other Jew.

"The period of *Rosh Hashana* and *Yom Kippur* is a very important time in the year. It is a time of preparation for repentance, it is a time to examine one's deeds over the past year and to ask forgiveness from those we have injured. If you have committed a sin against your fellow man, you must go directly to him and ask for forgiveness. If you have sinned against God, you must ask forgiveness from the Holy One, blessed be He, through prayer and through a genuine feeling of repentance for your misdeeds. This is the Jewish way of atonement.

"There are no intermediaries in our religion. You do not confess your sin to a priest to obtain forgiveness. You must go directly to the injured party if you wish to achieve the state of *teshuva*, of a returning to a state of holiness in the eyes of God and man . . ."

The Conversos listened closely to the words of the Hacham. Occasionally, Alberto and Hermosa would glance at each other, exchange a smile, and then they would again listen to the spiritual emissary from southern Spain.

The Hacham continued to talk about the introspective spirit required during the holiday. He spoke of daily penitential prayers, called *selihot*, recited in the week before *Rosh Hashana*. He spoke of blowing the ram's horn, or *shofar*, on this sacred day and described the festive meal eaten on the eve of the New Year and the traditional ceremony. The final day was *Yom Kippur*, the Day of Atonement, marked by fasting to reach a state of spiritual purity. *Yom Kippur* was the day of judgment. It was the day the Almighty decided who would live and who would die, who would be raised up and who would be brought low, who would rejoice and who would be saddened in the next year. It was the day that sealed one's fate.

Many asked questions of the Hacham. Hermosa asked about *Kol Nidrei*, one of the opening prayers of *Yom Kippur*.

The Hacham replied, "*Kol Nidrei* is a formula for annulling oaths made to God. It does not apply to oaths made to other people."

Hermosa asked further, "But what about the vows of faith in Christianity that we were forced to make over the last year? Does *Kol Nidrei* apply to that?"

"Yes, it does," said the Hacham, "the formula of the prayer indicates that all such vows are null and void; and that those of you of the children of Israel who have made this error will be forgiven."

A feeling of relief emanated from the group. The Hacham had said the most soothing words possible — that all would be forgiven, that Conversos were still part of the people of Israel, that there was still hope for them all. These were the words the Conversos wanted to hear. It was not that they had not heard them before, but that they did not hear them often enough.

The session ended. Each of the Conversos thanked the Hacham and departed through the tunnels leading back to their homes. The tailor led the Hacham by the way they had come. Alberto and Hermosa walked slowly down the tunnel that led to the Pinto home.

As they walked, Alberto spoke, "You know, the Hacham's talk was very good. I learned a lot today. Yet one thing bothered me. And it was this: that he was inside the fortress of Málaga when we, the cavaliers, were attacking it. It disturbs me to think we could have killed people like the Hacham, people who are wise and so learned, and yet not know what we were doing. How many Hachams have I killed? How can I undo the damage that I may have done as a cavalier? How can I bring back to life all those dead Hachams, all those dead Moors, back to life?"

Hermosa saw the troubled look on Alberto's face. She put her hand comfortingly on Alberto's arm and said, "What you did, Alberto, you did because you could not do otherwise. It was your duty then, and you did your duty as a soldier should. You do not usually find people such as the Hacham in battle. You fought only warriors such as yourself, people trained to kill, and who would have killed you if they'd had the opportunity."

"That is true," conceded Alberto.

Hermosa continued, "Besides, you are experiencing a change of heart. You know and feel in your heart that there is only one situation where the taking of another person's life is permitted."

"And what is that?" asked Alberto.

"In self-defense. In such a situation, it is permitted to take the life of the person who wants to kill you."

"That is also reasonable," said Alberto, his guilt beginning to dissipate. But Hermosa was not finished. She added, "You must also not forget that you saved the life of another. Did you not tell me that you saved the Marquis of Cádiz from sure death?"

"Yes . . . yes, I did," noted Alberto. "I loved the Marquis like I loved my father. I would have given my life to protect him from harm. Everyone loves him. He is a cavalier's cavalier . . . all the ladies of the court love him too."

Hermosa took this opportunity to give the conversation a more pleasant turn. Hermosa remarked, "A ladies man . . . well! I suppose you also had some pretty ladies running after you."

Alberto said, "None as pretty as you."

Hermosa was flattered, and said, "Oh . . . come now, truly you jest."

Alberto looked directly into Hermosa's soft blue eyes, and with a tender voice said, "How can I jest about things so dear to my heart? Hermosa, to make a declaration of one's affection is a most difficult thing to do. Yet night after night, as I gaze upon your womanly sweetness, I fear that my eyes will look too intently, and that I will lose the presence of the one lady by whom I wish to be esteemed."

"Alberto, your eyes have not revealed your intentions. What do you mean by these words?"

"Hermosa, I hope that you will allow me to gain your favor by pleasing you and serving you. Allow me to express my gentle affection in ways that will win your heart, never once hoping to obtain something dishonorable from you."

Hermosa experienced a flush of confusion. She did not expect such a statement of affection. She glanced at Alberto as they stood at the bottom of the trap door ladder, her parted lips and blinking eyes revealing her loss of inner composure. She stuttered, "I . . . I must set the table now . . . and light the Sabbath candles . . . uh . . . Perhaps one of these nights you can join us. Father would enjoy speaking with you."

Alberto smiled, "But I doubt your mother would allow it. If it were up to me, the choice of being next to you each night would be no choice at all."

Hermosa did not respond. She smiled softly, climbed up the ladder, opened the trap door, and walked into the adjoining kitchen. She looked about and noted that her mother was busy preparing dinner. She peeked into her father's study and found him pouring over a massive medical treatise.

Hermosa pulled a small candle from the wall. The candlelight flickered gently on and off her face, casting soft, muted shadows. She covered her head with a scarf as custom dictated. Hermosa then propped up two small candles on a two-pronged silver candelabrum, lit the two candles, and said the traditional blessing. Having done so, she went to the bedrooms, tidied them and changed the linens. Finally, she came back to the living room and set out the spinning wheel along with various rolls of yarn. Everything was as it should be. Now the only thing remaining was to hide the Sabbath candles.

Hermosa went into the kitchen and poured a bowl of stew. Her mother slapped her playfully on the wrist, "Hermosa, no! . . . Wait your turn. It's not suppertime yet."

Hermosa answered, "It's for the young man downstairs. He hasn't eaten yet . . . unless you want him to eat with us."

Regina said angrily, "I'll have nothing of the sort. He stays down below until I say so. Take him his bowl and hide the candles while you're at it."

"Yes, Mama," said Hermosa.

Returning to the trapdoor area, Hermosa lowered herself down the trap door while carrying the candelabrum and the bowl of stew. As she came down, Alberto came up to meet her, "Here, let me help you."

"This is not a duty for a cavalier," Hermosa remarked.

"Please . . . I assure you, it is my pleasure."

Hermosa was not moved by Alberto's plea. She held tightly on the ladder until she reached the lowest step. She placed the candelabrum and the bowl on the table, and handed a pair of clean eating utensils to Alberto.

"*Shabbat Shalom!* Sabbath peace!" Hermosa announced energetically.

Alberto acknowledged the greeting, "*Shabbat Shalom!* Sabbath peace to you, my princess. For none in the court of Spain is as lovely as you."

"Oh, Alberto," Hermosa said, the blush returning to her face.

"Tonight, on this holy day of the Sabbath, I swear unto you my affection and my deepest devotion."

"Alberto, we know each other but just two weeks. How can you say such a thing?" asked Hermosa.

"I mean it now and always will," Alberto said firmly.

It was a moment of shared discovery. They stood apart, awkwardly looking at each other, a reddish-tinged blush on Hermosa's creamy cheeks, an enamored look in Alberto's eyes. It was a reaching out with neither knowing exactly what to do next with Alberto's declaration of affection. The silence, like the feeling, seemed interminable until a voice in the distance called.

"Hermosa! Hermosa! . . . Are you down there?" yelled Dr. Pinto. Hermosa pulled herself away from the table and towards the ladder. She looked up and answered, "Yes, Father, I'm here."

"What's taking you so long?" shouted the physician, "The pot on the brazier is beginning to boil over."

"Yes, Father, I'm coming right now," said Hermosa.

Hermosa ran back up the ladder and into the living room. She quickly snatched up a long iron rod with a hook on it. Next she went to the brazier, its hot coals emitting heat and crackling noises. A sizzling pot placed over the coals was spilling its liquid contents. Hermosa lifted the pot away from the brazier by hooking its handle and carrying it into the kitchen.

Since she did not see her mother there, she assumed that was the reason the pot had been allowed to boil over. This was a common occurrence because Regina was accustomed to servants handling the cooking duties. To avoid suspicion, she usually gave the servants the day off on the Sabbath and on Sunday as well. But this only made matters worse, as far as household matters were concerned. In fact, there were often at least one or two such mishaps each weekend caused by her mother's ineptness in the kitchen, and it was left to Hermosa to fill in the gaps.

Hermosa put the iron rod away and walked into her father's study, its walls lined with many leather-bound books and medical pamphlets. She walked around to where he was sitting, head bowed, evidently engrossed in reading some abtruse Latin text on herbal medications. Ever since his medical school years at the famed University of Salamanca, Hermosa knew her father as a perpetual student, always studying, always learning, always seeking to know about new discoveries and insights. He was forever looking through all sorts of tomes for clues about how best to treat a puzzling ailment. It seemed to Hermosa that no amount of knowledge could ever satisfy her father. She admired him tremendously.

Hermosa bent over, kissed her father on the temple, and whispered, "Sabbath peace, Father."

Marco Pinto raised his head slowly from between the pages of the book, smiled, and said, "Sabbath peace, my daughter."

Marco looked lovingly upon his beautiful daughter who had grown and blossomed into captivating womanhood. She was a joy, a fragile flower that needed delicate attention and cultivation which, it seemed, only the garden of his home could provide. He loved to gaze upon her countenance, to take in the kindness of her smile. He took satisfaction in knowing that this was an extension of himself, that he was a part of her just as much as she was a part of him.

A series of knocks on the door interrupted Marco's reverie. He put his book down and walked to the bolted door.

"Who is it?" Marco asked.

"It is I, Enrique Domínguez de Córdoba," said the voice.

Marco and Hermosa were both startled by the unexpected response.

Neither had had any advance notice of this impromptu visit by the Hermandad officer. The physician, his usual calm gone, frantically signaled to Hermosa to shut the secret trap door. Hermosa understood, and she hurried off towards the kitchen.

Another series of knocks were heard on the door.

"Just one moment, señor," said Marco, "I'll be right with you."

Hermosa went quickly to the trap door. She whispered, "Shhh," and hoped that Alberto overheard her. There was no time to go down and explain to him what was going on. She shut the trap door quickly, covered it with a rug, and then moved the kitchen table squarely on top of the rug. Then she sprinted to her room and wrinkled the sheets and blankets on her bed and ran into her parent's room. There she found her mother half-dressed and combing her hair in front of a mirror. Regina angrily said, "Hermosa, please! Knock before you enter!"

Hermosa gasped, "Mother, it's the Hermandad officer Domínguez. He's here!"

Regina bolted up from her chair and began running about wildly, looking through her clothes for something suitable. She jerked a blouse from the rack and pulled it roughly over her head. She fastened the blouse to her dress with a knot, and grabbed for a bonnet to cover her head. Hermosa, meanwhile, made a total mess of her parent's bed by piling the pillows and blankets in its center. Regina hurried through the door and walked into the reception room.

"Dr. Pinto! What's going on?" boomed Domínguez. "Open up. I must talk with you." A series of hard, pounding knocks followed.

Regina, gasping slightly for air, took her position next to the spinning loom. As the spinning wheel began to turn ever so slowly, Regina signaled to Marco to open the door. They were ready.

Marco Pinto unbolted the door and angrily opened it "Yes? What is it this time, Dominguín? Oh! . . . Oh, Señor Domínguez, oh, my profoundest apologies. I had *no* idea it was you. Oh, my! I thought I heard you say that your name was Dominguín. He is a pest of a patient, one with no genuine illness. He never gives me any rest. Week in and week out, he bothers me, and I have to invent new ways to keep him out. If I had known it was you, sir, I would have opened it immediately. Oh, please, please accept my sincerest apologies, Señor Domínguez."

Domínguez, exasperated by the wait, looked straight into the physician's eyes and said icily, "Please, Don Marco, no apologies are called for. The apology is mine for being so forthright in inviting myself in this manner."

Domínguez was in the forest green uniform of an Hermandad officer. He wore a peaked green cap and pantaloons to the calf.

Domínguez doffed his hat in the direction of Regina, whom he saw in the far corner of the room. Regina stopped her spinning and came over to meet the uninvited guest.

"Good evening and welcome, Don Domínguez. What a pleasure, indeed, what a surprise it is to see you," said Regina courteously.

And good evening to you, Señora Pinto," said Domínguez, doffing his hat and kissing her hand. "Pardon my intrusion at such a late hour."

"Nonsense," Regina countered, "We were just about to have supper. Allow me to take your coat, Don Enrique."

Domínguez held her off, "Please, no matter. I shall only stay a while. May I ask — are you going someplace? You look so well attired."

Marco answered, "Why no . . . of course not. As my wife said, we were just about to have supper."

"In fact, why don't you join us?," Regina asked, "Yes. I insist. You simply must sample some of my mutton stew."

Domínguez was looking distractedly around the house, "Thank you, no. I myself am on my way home for supper. Why . . . why, this house is absolutely sparkling. I realize that I am already too bold but, if I may, would it be too much to ask to see more of your home?"

"My pleasure, Don Enrique," the physician said, "My pleasure. Come this way, please."

Marco led Domínguez into his study, the books neatly arranged on the wall racks, a few strewn atop his desk.

"My study . . . in its usual state of mild disarray," Marco indicated with a wave of his hand.

"Very impressive," said Domínguez, raising an eyebrow at so many books.

From the study, Marco wanted to lead the way to the bedrooms, but Domínguez followed Regina, who had wandered off into the kitchen.

"Is this the kitchen?," Domínguez asked, "Ahh . . . and the lady has prepared some wonderful dishes . . . marvelous, simply marvelous!"

"Are you quite sure you won't join us, Don Enrique?" Regina repeated. Domínguez walked next to the small table atop the trap door rug. He sniffed curiously and glanced about.

"Quite sure, thank you . . .," Domínguez said belatedly, "Is it my imagination . . . or do I smell candles burning?"

Doctor Pinto said, "I do not smell candles. You know what? It could be the stew . . . Darling, it could be you burnt the stew again."

Regina responded with a frown of disapproval. She said nothing as Domínguez hovered over the table, sniffing at the air about him.

A brief series of tinkling sounds came from the trap door area underneath. Regina's eyes flared frightfully wide-open, and she marched across the kitchen floor, making thumping footsteps as she went. Reaching a cabinet, she pulled open the cabinet door and pulled out a jar. She rattled the jar and shook its contents noisily.

"Oh, that jar of *panezicos*," she muttered, "the top is so shaky . . . you know, it's always doing that. I really must fix it."

Regina shook the jar again in order to reproduce the rattling sound. She opened the jar of cookies, took out a bread roll, and offered it to Domínguez.

"Here, take one, Don Enrique. You *must* try my *panezicos*," she said emphatically. Domínguez was puzzled, and he looked about carefully. Somehow he felt strange. He could not explain why, it was just a feeling that something strange was going on here.

"Uhmm, most delicious," said Domínguez as he ate the *panezico*, "A treat, a real treat."

Marco Pinto went up to Domínguez, took him by the arm, and led him away, "Nothing but the best. Come this way, Señor Domínguez, and allow me to show you the rest of our home."

They went into the bedrooms — first Marco's and Regina's, Marco apologizing for the mess on the bed. When they entered Hermosa's darkened room, they found her on her knees next to her bed, hands cupped in prayer and holding a rosary, praying in front of a wall crucifix and a small lit candle.

"My daughter Hermosa," Dr. Pinto whispered, "she's very religious . . . as we all are."

Domínguez was pleased to hear this.

"Don't disturb her," Domínguez said. "I'll meet her some other time."

"Very well," said Dr. Pinto. "This way, please."

When the tour of the courtyard and other rooms was complete, Domínguez returned to the central living area.

"A most enjoyable visit, Don Marco. You must invite me sometime . . . really, your wife's cooking is divine."

Regina said, "Why, thank you kindly, sir. I assure you, I do not put candles in my stew."

Domínguez guffawed loudly at this remark.

Marco added, "It was a pleasure to have you over. I hope we will be able to meet again soon."

Domínguez nodded, "Perhaps we will, under less hurried circumstances next time, I hope. That reminds me of the reason I came here in the first place. Our Hermandad has discovered some Judaizers in this city, and the Holy Office of the Inquisition has tried them and found them guilty of the grossest heresies . . ."

Dr. Pinto noted, "Go on. I am listening."

Domínguez continued, "Well, this Sunday at the central plaza after morning mass, we are going to have our first Auto-de-Fe. I wanted to let you know and to remind you. You are coming, aren't you?"

Marco answered, "I and my family have every intention of being there. Thank you for informing us of the event. Such heretics must be swiftly brought to justice, and it is to your credit that your Hermandad has already discovered some Judaizers. I will most assuredly be there, Don Enrique."

"*Adios*, Dr. and Señora Pinto," said Domínguez as he left.

"*Adios*, Don Domínguez," said the two Pintos.

As Marco closed the door, he went quickly to the window to make sure that Domínguez was indeed leaving. Regina came to his side. As they saw the Hermandad officer mount his horse and slowly ride away, Regina sighed with relief and rested her shaking head on his shoulder. She was drained from the encounter, totally and utterly drained. Dr. Pinto also felt a sudden release of tension. The doubts, the self-recriminations, the suspicions returned. It did not require great diagnostic acumen to conclude that the Pintos were objects of suspicion, but the physician was not yet ready to draw any conclusions.

As head of the local Hermandad, Don Enrique Domínguez de Córdoba carried out his duties as befitted a loyal servant of the crown. And yet, he knew he would never be admired by the local townsmen he so dutifully served, regardless of how well he performed his duties. It was a thankless task; everyone admitted it needed to be done, but no one wished to do it.

The Hermandad was "the brotherhood," the permanent police force of the King and Queen. It had been resurrected by Isabella in her militant bid for succession to the Castilian throne. A nation-wide league of such brotherhoods, loyal to the queen, had been formed during the war of succession to fight for her cause. Once the monarchical succession was decided in Isabella's favor, she retained the league of Hermandades to serve as her own permanent royal militia. Each local Hermandad was composed of a trained unit of mounted crossbowmen and skilled archers whose principal purpose was to maintain the peace in the rural and even the urban areas. And, of course, its members punished any and all individuals who dared to rebel against the crown. In time of peace, the duties of the Hermandad were to capture and punish criminals, especially those responsible for highway crimes, robbery, murder, and arson.

Every city and village was obligated to join a brotherhood, and its citizens were taxed to maintain the local militia. Many complained bitterly about the tax, which ran up to 18,000 maravedis per hundred households, not to mention the miscellaneous excise taxes on food and other merchandise. But these taxes were barely enough to outfit one light horseman. Had the issue been left to the local town councils, the Hermandades would have been eliminated long ago. Some prominent cities, such as Burgos, at one point refused to pay their share for the brotherhood expenses, but resistance collapsed when the King and Queen threatened them with economic and physical reprisals. The Catholic sovereigns insisted on having their own standing royal army. Thus it was that Don Enrique Domínguez, protector of Segovia and head of its local Hermandad, saw himself as an unloved and unwanted police officer, a protector-at-arms who did not even receive the respect given to a common foot-soldier.

Although the Hermandad league had committed a contingent of ten thousand infantrymen to the war effort against the Moors, Domínguez had somehow been bypassed in the selection process. He protested this decision, but his appeal to the governing council was denied. Like many of his countrymen, he heeded the call to battle under the banner of his King and Queen and longed to fight for the glory of Christendom and Castile. But this was not to be his fate. Instead of fighting the infidels, he was assigned the mundane task of tracking down highway brigands and other common criminals. He was second-best fighting material, even if he was the local Hermandad head. He knew it, and the townsmen in the area knew it. Because if he were indeed a soldier with great fighting skills, he would have been summoned to the battlefront, and not squandered fighting the petty thieves of Segovia.

There were, however, minor compensations. What he was denied in civil respect was offset in part by other rewards. For each capture of a criminal by one of his men, he was entitled to no less than one thousand maravedis as his rightful share. Furthermore, he learned the value of assisting the Inquisition as one of its familiars, which entitled him to a sizable percentage of any revenues from confiscated properties and estates. Segovia was teeming with *Marranos*. Of that he was sure. If he could but ferret them out and expose their heinous crimes against the Church, he could quite easily become a very wealthy man. And the wealthier the victim, the greater would be the reward . . . on earth, Domínguez would say, as it would be in heaven. Already, the first Inquisitorial Edict of Grace resulted in several informers coming to him.

On the basis of their testimony, Domínguez set out to trap a few *Marranos* in the forbidden rites. He turned the unlucky ones over to the Holy Office of the Inquisition for further interrogation and, as the forthcoming Auto-de-Fe seemed to indicate, to receive the swiftest of justice. He had done his job well, and the local tribunal decided to reward him generously with five thousand maravedis upon the liquidation of the estates of the captured *Marranos*. Things seemed to be progressing exceedingly well, Domínguez admitted, and the prospect of filling his pockets at the expense of the remaining *Marrano* vermin was most gratifying.

But it was not sufficient to Domínguez that he become rich in the process of confiscating Converso fortunes. He wanted respect. And if people were not going to treat him with respect, he would make them pay for their discourtesy. He would make the name of Domínguez synonymous with dread and fear.

Those who fell in Domínguez's hands were treated in the harshest way imaginable. A thief who stole less than five hundred maravedis was given a hundred lashes. He ordered that those who stole between five hundred and five thousand maravedis should have an arm or leg hacked off with an axe. Others were beheaded or killed in some manner, as Domínguez's vengeful judgment indicated. Sometimes he would have the victim tied to a post, and allow him to bleed to death slowly after ordering his archers to pierce the fastened body with a multitude of arrows.

Domínguez was judge, jury and executioner . . . and he meted out his justice however he saw fit. There was no one to stop him. While some local officials protested to the crown about Domínguez's cruel penalties, nothing came of it. Now that he joined forces with the Holy Office of the Inquisition, he was confident he was unassailable.

Yet he was not totally beyond account. It was irksome to Domínguez that a Jew, the Jew they called Don Abraham Senior, had been appointed the Secretary-Treasurer of the Hermandad governing council. It was Senior who would control his funds, pay his salary, and make him run about town collecting the taxes. He detested taking orders from a Jew, but he had no choice. Senior was so powerful that Domínguez was compelled to mask his feelings and to comply with Senior's orders. He would have loved nothing better than to flay the old Jew alive with his bare hands, but it was not possible to realize this vengeful fantasy.

While Jews were officially outside the official jurisdiction of the Hermandad, Conversos were not, so Domínguez concentrated on them. After compiling a list of wealthy individuals of reputed Converso origin, he assigned undercover agents to monitor their daily activities. The wealthier the Converso family, the more influential it would be and, therefore, he had to be especially cautious with them. But time was on his side, and with the entire city now bent on uncovering deviant religious behavior, sooner or later Domínguez or one of his men would be informed of any heretical activities. Then he would pounce upon the Judaizer and collect his due.

As to the Pinto family, there were intimations of peculiar behavior that did not allow his suspicions to subside, but there was nothing definite yet. As he rode back toward the Hermandad tavern, he wondered if the Pintos were *Marranos*, and if they were, how much their capture would bring.

After Domínguez's visit, Regina Pinto was in a state of hysterical panic: she screamed, she moaned, and continually went to the window to stretch her head out and look both ways down the street, expecting to see Domínguez or an Inquisition officer coming to take them all away. At the dinner table, she pushed away the food that was served to her. At night, she would either thrash about in bed or get up and pace the floor, waking everyone. When Sunday finally came, she was trembling with fear; her eyes were bloodshot from two nights of sleeplessness, her face was pale and ashen with heavy rings under her eyes, and her mind was a restless jumble of fears and imaginings.

"I can't take this anymore, Marco," she screamed at her husband, "I tell you, I can't take it. For the love of God, Marco, get us out of this country before it's too late. *What are you waiting for?* Don't you see what's happening? They're burning us, Marco . . . they're burning us alive. Don't you see that? Don't you have eyes? How long will you wait before it's too late and they come to burn us too? How long? Marco, *now* is the time to leave. For God's sake, Marco, please, I beg of you, get us out of here!"

The physician put his arm consolingly around his wife and placed her head on his chest. Caressing her hair, stroking it with gentleness and understanding, he would assure her repeatedly that they were safe.

"I'm working on leaving," he said. "We've all been making preparations: the tailor, myself, our friends in the royal court. They have connections in Antwerp, and I hear they're arranging a ship, a secret ship to take us out of here."

But Regina was disconsolate. "Oh, Marco, I just can't take it any more. I'm telling you, Domínguez is on to us. Please, get us out of here. They're on to us."

And she would begin to sob fitfully again, her piercing cries once again shaking the air. Dr. Pinto held her even tighter, patting her comfortingly, and smoothing out her hair. Hermosa was startled out of her uneasy sleep by her mother's shrieks, and she rushed into the living room to find out what was the matter. She, too, was on edge.

"Mama, control yourself. Someone could hear you."

Marco reinforced his daughter's plea, "Yes, you must control yourself, dear. It's extremely important . . . as important as finding us a ship. I'll do my best to get us out of here as soon as possible."

Regina sighed deeply. She had heard it before, and she wondered if perhaps this time her husband would do as he promised. She sighed again, slowly and deeply, her sense of composure gradually returning. "Very well, I'll do my best to control myself. Come, let us get ready for the Auto."

The preparations for the day had exacted their toll. Marco Pinto, too, was feeling its ill effects — the sensation of ominous foreboding, the drooping of spirits that came with carrying the weight of an invisible burden.

To Marco Pinto, physician and healer, deaing with difficult medical problems took up much of his time, yet these were problems that were limited to particular patients, or that were described in an abstruse treatise. The problems he routinely dealt with were definable, and usually amenable to solution. And now, almost without precedent, he had come to face a problem of a higher order that went beyond his ordinary method of rational analysis. His wife sensed the problem, and while her intuition led her to a quick practical response, she had no real solution either. Her response was to flee from the danger immediately. Perfectly understandable, thought Marco. While he sensed the appropriateness of the response, he questioned any rash move that might complicate their already precarious situation. He decided to move slowly, calculating every action until he and his family were ready to make their escape to freedom. The right time would come, if one but had the presence of mind to wait for the proper moment. He would not be influenced by hysterics, nor forego careful planning for any major alteration in his life. And now, even as he held his wife in his arms, he knew that he would resist the impulse to flee at the first sign of danger. He would console her for now, making comforting promises that would effect her pacification. But then, acting in the apparent best interests of the family, he would do as he pleased.

The Pinto family stepped out into the main street. Hermosa and Regina both wore dark blue-black dresses and draped their heads and shoulders in grey lace scarves. In contrast, Dr. Pinto was in somber, dark reddish-brown vestments from head to toe, covered by an academic robe. As they walked, Marco would occasionally extend his robe and cover his high-strung wife and daughter with it. This had a calming effect on his wife, and to a lesser degree on his lovely daughter, whose unnatural curiosity about the Auto was not to his liking.

"Please, Father, what do they do at the Auto?"

"You'll see," he answered.

"Yes, I know I'll see," Hermosa would reply, "but can't you give me some idea as to what takes place there?"

Dr. Pinto shook his head, but did not offer to explain further. There was no need to elaborate on what little he knew about Autos to his daughter. He did not need a second hysterical woman on his hands and, as far as he was concerned, the less said the better. He looked about at all the people on the street and was taken aback by their sense of frivolity and excitement.

The streets were full of people, many of them peasants from the countryside. When they heard of the upcoming spectacle, the curious rustics came to town in droves. The Pintos joined the tide of rural folk streaming toward the central plaza. In the distance, the incessant clanging of church bells guided the faithful. The Pintos weaved in and out of these human waves from the fields. As they approached the plaza, the crowds became denser and more raucous; they were shoving and pushing to get a better place to watch the Auto. Marco felt he was losing control: he was being caught up in the human flood, swept along by a torrent of unstoppable forces. He grabbed hold of Hermosa's hand, and she in turn clutched his. Together, they were propelled forwards by the mass, as was Regina somewhat ahead of him. He could see her scarf and headdress bobbing in the air. The jostling and shoving became worse at the narrowest point of the thoroughfare. Suddenly, the three of them broke through the crowd and found themselves on the periphery of the central plaza. They were free of the mob.

At the entranceway, a child rushed up to them, shouting, "Ten maravedis for prime seats on the scaffold. One maravedi for the list of dignitaries present, including the Duke of Abonedo and the Count of Cuellar. Only one maravedi . . ."

Pinto paid no attention to this scroungy-looking lad. Instead he looked in the direction of the scaffold reserved for the use of town dignitaries. But the child tugged insistently on his robe and would not let him go.

"Prime seating for the ladies, sir? Just ten maravedis each."

"No!" said Marco emphatically.

"How about a list of the dignitaries?" rattled the hawker.

Marco angrily raised his voice, "I said *no*. Now run along."

The young ruffian sneered at the threesome and walked away disgruntled.

As Marco looked about, he saw two major scaffolds: one was full of clergy — priests, bishops, and nuns; the other, at the other end of the plaza, held secular dignitaries — counts, dukes, knights, businessmen, and their wives. At ground level, around the scaffolds, was an overflow crowd of common people — farmers, apprentices, maids, and the like, gawking at the nobility and eating noisily. Mounted guards patrolled the plaza to keep the commoners from getting too close to the central platform.

Suspended on poles between the two scaffolds was a lush orange-red decorated canopy. Under the canopy sat the local Inquisitor, Diego Lucero, his head partly shaven in the manner of the Dominicans. He wore his black priestly tunic over a white robe. To Lucero's right was Segovia's own bishop, Juan Arias Dávila, renowned throughout the region as the archenemy of Conversos.

Pinto recalled only too clearly the event 20 years earlier, when Bishop Dávila burned and hanged 16 Jews for participating in an alleged ritual murder of a Christian child. He shuddered upon recollecting the event.

Everywhere Marco looked he saw tiered patios of the surrounding buildings crowded with onlookers. Everyone was waiting for the spectacle to take place. As he started to thread his way through the multitude, a roar went up. Suddenly, Dr. Pinto found that they could advance no further through the standstill crowd.

Someone in front shouted, "Here they come!"

The penitents marched slowly past Marco's vantage point. Each wore a pointed hat in the form of a mitre as well as a *san benito* cloak. On the cloaks of those who had confessed were painted images of flames. Those condemned to the fires of hell wore cloaks with images of devils driving heretics into the fires. With arms tied behind their back and nooses around their necks, each penitent was being pushed forward by guards. Two or three Dominican priests accompanied each penitent as they made their way to the central platform The dejected penitents, their faces tortured and agonized from shame, were paraded in front of the crowd amid its continuous jeering and taunting.

"Swine! Burn in hell!" yelled one crowd member.

Another ruffian spat on one of the penitents and shouted, "Take that . . . Jew . . . *Marrano!*"

"Filthy Jew," clamored another.

Regina drew close to her husband, curling her arms inside his. Terror-stricken, she squeezed his arm tighter while Dr. Pinto patted her comfortingly.

Hermosa looked straight into her father's eyes, and they exchanged a prolonged glance accompanied by an understanding nod. The glance and the nod, in a manner more effective than words, communicated what needed to be said.

As the guards pushed the penitents to the central platform, the insults and taunts persisted. The Dominican priest who led the procession raised his crucifix high in the air. The crowd was still.

He intoned, "Our Father, who art in heaven, hallowed be Thy Name, Thy kingdom come, Thy will be done on earth as it is in heaven.

"Everyone raise your right hand and repeat after me. We do so execute Thy will today — I swear before God Almighty and our Lord Jesus Christ, that I will defend the Catholic faith in all of its particulars, and that I will support the Holy Office of the Inquisition in its sacred task."

The crowd murmured its version of the prayer, and then Inquisitor Lucero stood up to speak: "Call forth the first penitent and read the charges."

Lucero sat down. A guard thrust the first penitent in front of the Inquisitor. The prisoner, thin and wan, hung his head. Two Dominican priests, one at each side, grabbed his arms while a scribe read the charges.

"Pedro Amado, New Christian, age forty-eight, resident of Segovia, guilty of the sins of practicing Jewish rituals, sentenced to two years imprisonment, and to the perpetual wearing of the *san benito* by you and your descendants. Your children and descendants, for all generations to come, are forbidden to hold public office, to engage in the professions, to enter Holy Orders, or to wear cloths of gold or silver."

Lucero signaled with his right arm, and the first penitent was taken away. A second one was brought in front of Lucero. It was an innocent-looking adolescent girl, her hair disheveled, and with tears flowing down her cheeks. Neither did she look up as the scribe spoke.

"Isabel Amado, age seventeen, daughter of Pedro, guilty of the sins of Judaizing, sentenced to the same punishment as your father, and sentenced to perpetual wearing of the *san benito* by you and your descendants.

Regina turned toward her husband and, closing her eyes, she whispered weakly, "God help us." Marco clutched her hand tightly, and brought her closer unto him.

The third penitent was brought out. She was a gaunt middle-aged woman who looked beaten and beyond caring. The scribe read the charges:

"Angela Amado, age forty-five, native of Segovia, guilty of blasphemous insult against the image of our Lord, unpenitent of her Judaizing practices and refusing to cooperate with the Holy Office in its sacred duties . . . sentenced to be burned at the stake without garrotting."

Angry outcries came from the crowd.

"She's the one that insulted our Lord! Burn the bitch!" shouted one. Another noisy crowd member next to Hermosa yelled in a similar manner, "Aya! Burn her! Burn the Jewish bitch!"

Hermosa turned toward this boisterous onlooker and asked, "Tell me, sir, what do you think about all this?"

The unshaven peasant next to Hermosa, a toothless grin on his face, answered, "I will tell you . . . I have seen better Autos in other cities where they burn Jews by the dozens . . . Take Valladolid, for example, or Toledo . . . but for Segovia, tiny little Segovia, it's the first of its kind, and that . . . well . . . that makes it something very special."

"The first of its kind?" replied Hermosa flatly.

"Yes," said the spectator, ". . . and there'll be more. There's lots of them secret Jews here in Segovia. Believe me, I know."

"You don't say," Hermosa said. Her body stiffened as she looked in the direction of the central platform.

Angela Amado was tied to a stake, with a rope around her neck and feet. Then an attendant piled many small pieces of wood at her feet, and stripped her of her clothing except for a few pieces of shabby underwear.

A rotund Dominican priest came up to her side and thundered:

"Angela Amado, I implore you in the name of our Lord Jesus Christ to confess to your ungodly sins, to receive the Holy Catholic faith at this last moment of oneness of your soul and body, and to humbly receive the holy sacraments."

She lifted her head for the first time and stared coldly into the priest's eyes, saying nothing.

Raising his crucifix again, the priest continued, "By the bowels of our Lord, I implore you for the last time to accept the truth of our faith."

Once again, the woman at the stake remained silent.

Hermosa watched the scene intensely. She strained to hear every word the priest said, to see every expression on the martyred woman's face.

The toothless peasant at her side added, "Stubborn, those Jews, aren't they..."

Hermosa nodded indifferently, "So I hear." She paid him little attention, inasmuch as her attention was riveted on the woman on the platform.

The priest lowered his crucifix and walked away from the stake. Putting the crucifix down, he took a burning torch and walked toward the scaffold. Planting himself in front of the dignitaries, he proudly announced, "The honor of carrying out the sentence is delegated to the head of the Hermandad of Segovia, Don Enrique Domínguez de Córdoba."

The priest handed the torch to the man who had brought the heretics to justice. Applauding and cheering, the crowd watched as Domínguez stepped forward to perform the honor. Dressed in a green uniform, white hose, and a pleated ruff, with a large cross painted on his vest and a sword dangling from his waist, he looked impressive as all eyes focused on him. He strutted to the platform, torch in hand. Domínguez was the hero of the day, commanding the attention, admiration, and respect of all.

Domínguez approached the prisoner on the stake. While he had participated in many executions, ordinarily he delegated this duty to his subordinates. Now, however, it was an honor to perform the deed himself.

Domínguez lowered the torch, touching the fire to the kindling wood at the feet of the condemned woman. As the heat of the torch set the wood on fire, the prisoner was aroused from her morbid state. With increasing intensity of the flames, she tried frantically to shake off her bonds. She shook and trembled as a cloud of smoke rose from her feet. Her horrid shrieks were almost drowned out by the crackling blaze. The flames of the death fire leaped into the air, roasting both wood and flesh and producing billows of smoke that enveloped the thrashing victim.

Regina looked away from the spectacle, covering her face, gulping deeply for air. She clasped her husband even tighter, while Hermosa looked on, transfixed, scarcely believing what she was seeing. Dr. Pinto was no stranger to the many faces of death; he had seen people die before, from disease or accident, but even for him the death pyre was incomprehensible. The physician studied the faces of the spectators about him. Many were open-mouthed, gaping like buffoons; a few were smiling, others looked on indifferently. The Inquisitor Lucero was observing the event matter-of-factly, while Domínguez was beaming with pride at his accomplishment. Sickened by what he saw, Pinto was concerned about the effect of the spectacle on his tender daughter. It did not take much to realize that, but for the grace of God, it could be the Pinto family up there at the stake.

The smoke-engulfed victim was swooning in place, her head whipping wildly. As the flames lashed out and singed her hair, she began to stammer, "Hear O Israel . . . the Lord our God . . . the Lord . . . is one!" Then she was swallowed up by the flames and she lost consciousness. Her limp, lifeless body remained tied to the stake as the blaze continued, incinerating her charred flesh and giving rise to a cloud of ashes with a lingering acrid odor.

Regina fainted and slid to the ground. Marco supported her and was able to break her fall. The crowd nearby watched as he tried to reawaken his wife. He nudged her gently. As they hovered over Regina, Marco whispered to his daughter, "Did you hear what she said at the end?"

Hermosa responded softly, "Yes, Father, I heard . . . Here, let me help you."

Marco said, "It's all right. I can manage."

Regina came to slowly, but her mind was still confused. She allowed herself to be helped back to her feet by Marco and Hermosa, who supported her at either side. She was still dizzy. Cautiously she put one foot in front of another as they walked carefully through the crowd. There were more burnings scheduled to take place that day as part of this Auto-de-Fe. But this was enough for the Pintos. It was time to go home now.

As they left the plaza, they saw Juan de Gonzalo, Hermosa's handsome Christian suitor. "Hermosa! I've been looking all over for you. Wasn't that something? I've never seen anything like it."

"Juan, I must help bring my mother home now," she answered. "She is not at all well."

"Please . . . let me help," Juan said as he gestured to help carry Hermosa's mother.

"No, we can manage, thank you," Hermosa said firmly.

Juan persisted, "If I cannot help, at least let me show you around. Are you going to the celebration in the field after the Auto? I would be honored if you would accompany me."

"Wait, Father," she said. Letting go of her mother's arm for a moment, she turned to face Juan. "We must go home, Juan. Leave us alone, please."

Juan was startled by her tone, "What . . . what's the matter? Have I offended you?"

Hermosa vented her resentment, "I do not believe there is any need to see each other again."

Bewildered, Juan shook his head and shrugged his shoulders. "But . . . but why? I do not understand. I want to see you, to be with you."

"But I have no need to see you . . . *ever*." With that, Hermosa turned away and returned to her parents' side. She put her arm inside Regina's, supporting her still shaky mother.

Juan considered her behavior to be a fickle woman's impromptu whim, and he was not about to let such a beauty slip out of his grasp. No, he would not lose her. He shouted for her to hear, "Hermosa, you cannot do this to me. I will not permit it. I love you, Hermosa . . . I love you forever and ever, and I will not take *no* for an answer."

Juan stood there alone in the street as the three walked away into the distance. He wondered if Hermosa heard him. It mattered little. Women were strange, whimsical creatures prone to a spur-of-the-moment capriciousness, and it was wise to be patient with them. If not tomorrow, then sometime soon, her mood would change and she would smile and look at him adoringly. He would bide his time, he would wait for her, he would give her the chance to change her mind, and then he would have her.

Chapter 5

During one of their many underground conversations, Dr. Pinto raised the question, "Tell me, Alberto, can a Jew be chivalrous?"

Alberto answered, "To be chivalrous, one must be brave, honorable, and virtuous, among other qualities. To the extent that Jews exhibit these qualities, they would certainly be considered 'chivalrous.' However, I must admit, when I think of chivalrous knights, I do not think of Jews."

"Ah! Thank you for an honest answer, Alberto. Why are Jews not considered chivalrous? Because they cannot be knights! And why can they not be knights? Think for a moment, and you will realize it is because they cannot bear arms. According to the laws of 1412, Jews cannot carry weapons. Without weapons, a Jew cannot defend himself at home, much less demonstrate his valor as a knight on the battlefield. Indeed, a knight defends his homeland, his people, his religion. But what are Jews allowed to do nowadays, except plead and whine for the physical protection of the authorities. It is true everywhere in this land: without arms, one cannot become a complete Spanish gentleman.

"In ancient Palestine, Jews were great fighters, like King David, Samson, and Simon Bar Kochba. Even here in Spain, as recently as a century ago, Jews served as warriors in the armies of Castile, or as guards in the fortresses of the kingdom. With the new legislation, in the eyes of some, Jews have become calculating bystanders during wartime who allow Christians to shed their precious blood while they, the Jews, sit safely at home and limit their war involvement to the payment of taxes."

Alberto spoke up, "But the Christians made these laws restricting the rights of Jews to bear arms. How can they now blame the disarmed Jews for not contributing to the war effort?"

Dr. Pinto chuckled, "Since when does hostility toward the Jew make logical sense? As long as such unreason abounds, we Conversos must learn to use weapons while we still can. Who knows what they may want to do to us? Despite our tough talk, we still know very little about weapons, and I doubt that we would be very effective with them if the need arose. You are the exception, Alberto, in that you are a trained cavalier. I am sure you would much rather be an armed Converso than a disarmed Jew."

"Absolutely," replied Alberto. "If I am to perish, I wish to take my enemies with me to the grave."

Dr. Pinto continued, "Among knights, glory gained in the battlefield adds to one's honor. Certainly whatever deeds you performed in Málaga were for the greater glory of Castile and Christianity, not for the sake of Jews or Conversos. But the original question that I posed, as to whether Jews can be chivalrous, is not simply a matter of *individual* honor, but of *national* honor.

"The Jews of Spain are dishonored daily here in Spain. They are denied the right to engage in certain professions; they are forbidden to be tailors, butchers, and carpenters, and a host of other things. They are forbidden to wear gold thread or silk or other expensive items. We Conversos can live wherever we please, but the Jews are restricted to the Jewish quarter. In some cities, the Jews are not even allowed to shave their beards, making them look dirty and unkempt. As long as Jews are treated this way, it does not matter how chivalrous a single individual Jew might be. Because however great the accomplishments of that single individual, no one will regard the downtrodden Jews as exhibiting those same traits.

"So in answer to my own question, yes, the individual Jew can be chivalrous, but only in the guise of a Christian knight. But the Jewish nation as a whole, segregated and dishonored, unable to gather an army to engage in epic battles in defense of their religion or their national territory, as the Christians and Moslems do, cannot presently be regarded as chivalrous."

Alberto seemed to agree with this assessment. "What you are saying rings true."

Dr. Pinto responded, "Is it? True for whom? I will now argue the opposite case. My analysis is faulty because you see, Alberto, I have been judging Jews by Spanish standards. Now, let us turn the question around and let us judge the Spaniards by Jewish standards as we understand them. Tell me, Alberto, who is most admired by Jews: the soldier or the scholar?"

"I would have to say . . . the scholar."

"Tell me, Alberto, how many Spanish soldiers read books?"

"Practically none. Most of them do not know to read and write."

"And, Alberto, what about the simplest Jew?"

"Everybody knows that the Jews emphasize learning and scholarship."

Dr. Pinto concluded, "So, judging Jews and Christians as a whole, the Jews are a literate people, whereas the Spaniards are ignorant and illiterate."

Alberto added, "The churchmen respect scholarship, but otherwise what you have just said generally holds true."

"You see, Alberto, the Jewish people were forced centuries ago to give up the sword. When the Romans destroyed the Temple in Jerusalem and scattered the Jews throughout the world, Jews were forced into a weaponless existence. Jews responded to the challenge by creating a new method of survival — living by their wits, by pursuing the peaceful paths of learning and scholarship, whether it be in scripture or science or business. In the process, Jews became aware of the tremendous power that great knowledge and learning can confer upon an individual and, even more so, upon a close-knit community composed of highly learned individuals. It is the power of the word, the greatest weapon ever devised, that Jews have rediscovered and armed themselves with in their continuing struggle.

"But what has happened to Christianity in the meantime? Christianity has become a militant, warlike religion just like that of the Moslems. Forget the nonviolent nature of the early Christians. Forget the lip service paid to brotherly love and turning the other cheek. No Christian of today, not even the Pope, turns the other cheek, although they expect the Jew to do so. In the Christian mind, only one thing counts: Power! Honor! Might! The Christian cause is nothing but a paltry excuse for the pursuit of one's self-glorification, the coveting of honor for its own sake at all levels — from the lowliest foot-soldier to the King and Queen. Christianity may work at the level of a single individual, but it is a total failure as a means of regulating an entire society. In Spain, as best as I can tell, the values of the cavaliers are non-Christian values taken from their Roman pagan forbears. The belief in this country is nominally Christian, but everybody behaves like a pagan. Christianity is the veneer, paganism the essence."

"That is a strong statement, Dr. Pinto," said Alberto uncomfortably.

"Indeed, it is! The sword still dictates what will be considered as the truth to the conquered. Just as our ancestors were converted by the sword a century ago, the Holy Office is the latest barbaric weapon devised against us, making sure we Conversos remain faithful. Strange, is it not? Being *forced* to believe in something? But force rarely succeeds in changing the mind of a thinking individual. That is why all the force employed by the Christians in bringing our forefathers to the baptismal font has been in vain. We, the grandchildren of the first Conversos, are the living proof that beliefs imposed by force are not very believable. Indeed, the greater the force applied, the greater the likely falsity of the belief. A truth is either self-evident or it is not. It does not matter how many millions of people espouse a certain belief; in the end, all that should matter is what *you* think about it."

The physician concluded, "I do not pretend to be a profound thinker, but I appreciate the importance of not lying to myself. If something is true, I will say it is true. If it is false, I will not say the opposite just to please others, except under circumstances when my family and I are somehow physically threatened. For this reason, limited as my understanding may be, I have concluded that the truth is closer to our faith than it is to theirs."

"You could not have chosen better words to express my sentiments. Dr. Pinto, thank you for a most interesting visit. I hope to see you again tomorrow."

"Most certainly," answered Dr. Pinto as he returned upstairs.

"Your documents have arrived," Hermosa said softly, an excited look on her face as she stood over the sleeping cavalier inside the underground cavern. Alberto looked up droopily to see the angelic bearer of the good news. Her smiling face slowly came into focus. The full import of her message took a while to penetrate his consciousness; he smiled weakly and went back to sleep. Hermosa placed her hand delicately on his shoulder and gently nudged him back to consciousness.

"Alberto, your documents have arrived," she repeated.

Alberto turned around and opened one eye. "My documents have arrived?", asked Alberto, a puzzled look on his face. Hermosa nodded with a beaming smile.

"Bravo! Bravo!," Alberto shouted as he bolted happily out of bed. He jumped jubilantly in the air and was about to take Hermosa in his arms, when he suddenly checked himself.

"Hermosa, forgive my impulsiveness. I thank you deeply for the privilege of receiving these documents from your soft and gentle hands. I would gladly do without these documents and suffer instead the empty darkness of this cave, if only I knew it would mean the continued brightness of your presence. Yet I am aware of the change in circumstances that these documents bring. I thank you for your companionship and your warm smile during the past few weeks, and I hope you will not think it too bold of me to kiss the hand of one so lovely and so dear."

Hermosa smiled and extended her hand.

Alberto kissed her hand and then held it. "Hermosa, I am content with this sign from my lady. In time, I hope my actions will merit further signs of your affection. A tender smile from you is . . . "

"Perhaps we had better go upstairs," she whispered.

Alberto took her hands and squeezed them gently. Hermosa smiled tenderly, squeezing his hand in return. As they looked into each other's eyes, never for a moment letting go of one another, they felt this moment was a harbinger of an everlasting connection, a bond that would tie them together.

"Very well, as you wish," said Alberto.

Hand in hand, they went up the stairs, Hermosa leading the way. Shafts of light illuminated Alberto's face: the brightness of day had come again into his life, and the brightness of Hermosa had now dispelled the darkness. Step by step, the shine on his face waxed with the knowing joy of more wonderful days to come, days that he would share with his beloved. Step by step, they would find happiness together.

Alberto had a new identity: his new name was to be Alberto de Molina, the sole surviving son of a Burgos constable whose family was unblemished by any Jewish blood. His mother had died in childbirth, and his father had perished soon thereafter in the performance of his duties. Baptized into the church, he had been brought up as a pious Christian from infancy and educated as a youth in a local Franciscan religious school. A close friend of the Molina family, one of unimpeachable lineage and a witness to the child's Old Christian upbringing, signed his name to the impressive document Alberto held in his hands. It was to be a written testimony, a certification of *limpieza de sangre*, of purity of blood. Purity could be purchased, pasts could be reconstructed, identities could be altered — if the price was right. Alberto marveled at the pompous parchment document that claimed to clear his name of the slightest trace of Jewish ancestry. It was purchased for a goodly price. Nay, Alberto noted, the penurious Old Christian who had signed this document was the one who had been bought. Money could buy breeding and the semblance of religious orthodoxy but, most of all, it could buy people.

Although his past had ostensibly been washed away in writing, Alberto still had to contend with the contingencies of the present. He had no means of supporting himself, no profession or skill that he could barter for income. Dr. Pinto offered to place him as an orderly in the infirmary. But Alberto declined the offer, feeling ill at ease among the diseased and infirm, however ennobling the attending to their ailments was deemed to be.

Besides, after having tasted the adventurous life of the cavalier, after having sought glory and honor in the battlefield, Alberto longed for a return to that life, with a sword at his side and a song in his heart. To be anything less was a surrender to the drabness of ordinary life. What was to become of him? He was not suited to the passive life of scholarship as the good doctor was. Nor could he demean himself with a menial occupation like a tailor or blacksmith. Such chores would have been unbecoming a cavalier. In any case, he was too old to be an apprentice, so most trades were out of the question.

Of all the activities he considered, only that of the spice-merchant attracted him. Somehow, the knowledge that his father had been a spice merchant made the idea of selling ginger and cinnamon honorable as a business activity. As his father had done, so would he do. Those spice merchants who arrived on Spanish shores came from many different lands. Perhaps this would enable him to find his father through the personal contacts and travels that he was bound to make. Perhaps, by emulating his father, Alberto would also be able to find a new path for himself, to recover the spirit of adventure that he felt was now sorely missing from his life.

If Dr. Pinto would lend him some working capital to begin the enterprise, he would be on his way. But it would not be easy; Regina was a problem. She did not care for vagabond warriors living in her household, distant relative or not. It was enough that she reluctantly allowed Alberto to sleep in the underground basement. It was enough that, against her will, her husband paid a handsome sum of money for the documents declaring Alberto to be of Old Christian lineage. And, more than any other reason, it was really too much that this good-for-nothing "cavalier" was playing amorous games with her innocent daughter.

"Enough," Regina told her husband, "enough of this Alberto. We've given him food and shelter for close to three weeks now. He appears to be a pleasant young man, but he must be informed that there is nothing more that we can do for him. It is not unreasonable to ask him to find another place to live in as soon as possible — in Segovia, or wherever else he wants to settle, but definitely not in our home. Am I right or wrong?"

"He likes it here," Pinto said cautiously, his eyebrows bent with anxiety.

Regina roared with surprise, "He likes it here! Marco, my God, what kind of answer is that? Since when does he decide whether to stay or not?"

"Regina, calm down. Of course we decide, you know that," the physician said worriedly.

"Then he must be informed of our decision that we wish him to leave. He can make living arrangements elsewhere . . . the sooner, the better. Do you not agree, Marco?"

"Yes, of course," Marco said half-heartedly.

Regina's voice tightened, "Your 'yes' does not sound very convincing, my dear doctor. Do you want him out or not? Have we not given him enough, documents and all? Did he not jeopardize our security during Domínguez's visit? Have you forgotten all that? Marco, I have given all that I can. What more do you want from me?"

Marco looked softly into his wife's eyes, sensing her agitation. Rubbing his chin curiously, he asked, "What about Hermosa?"

Regina snapped angrily, "What about her? Are you suggesting that I give her away to him too?"

The doctor replied, "No, I was merely saying that we ask her opinion on the matter."

"Why?", balked Regina.

Doctor Pinto said, "Why? Because the two of them like each other, or haven't you noticed?"

Regina countered, "So? Is that a reason for keeping him inside the house? On the contrary, it is all the more reason for keeping him out of our house . . . keeping his lecherous eyes off our daughter, keeping him away before we have a social embarrassment on our hands, if you know what I mean. Marco, I insist that this Alberto Galante . . . "

"Molina . . . Alberto Molina . . .," Marco corrected her.

Regina continued, "Alberto Molina, or whatever his name is . . . I want him out of my house by this weekend, or I, personally, will see to it that he is thrown out of the house. Are you going to tell him or not . . . because if you will not, I most certainly will."

Doctor Pinto sighed heavily, uncomfortable at the ultimatum but seeing no way of avoiding the decision

"I shall tell him," Marco agreed resignedly and left the room.

Alberto's and Hermosa's fondness for each other made the separation difficult.

"Will you miss me?" asked Hermosa.

"Everywhere I go, my heart, the moment of our parting will be as if it never was. In the fragrance of the cinammon, I will taste your sweetness. In the mellow odor of ginger, I will sense your delicate softness. The perfume of the red rose of the fields, as the one in your hair, will bring back to me the scent of my beloved. In my work, in my travels, you will always be with me. Be sure of this, Hermosa, that you are the ultimate spice, priceless beyond compare. You are the most precious flower which, God willing, it will one day be my fortune to have. Be well, my darling, for I will return for your hand if the Lord smiles on my endeavor and fortune comes my way."

With these tender words, Alberto made a deep bow and kissed Hermosa's hand. His body erect, his head held high, and sword at his side, he walked toward his horse. Mounting the animal, he doffed his plumed hat to Hermosa, who stood silently at the doorstep. She waved a sad goodbye, and Alberto urged his steed through the streets at a gallop, disappearing quickly from sight.

Chapter 6

It had gone well with Alberto in the intervening years. His spice business was growing. He was a respected merchant, in part owing to contacts facilitated by Dr. Pinto. He was known throughout Segovia as someone who knew how to obtain what one wanted when it was wanted: curry, black pepper, and ginger from India, sesame seed and cinnamon from the Middle East. His warehouse was stocked with fragrant and pungent goods to tantalize and excite the senses. The "prince of spices," as he was popularly called, became a favorite of the local nobility. He became their prime dispenser of oriental delicacies, valuable as gifts and whose worth was enhanced by their scarcity.

Alberto's activities took him to local marketplaces, to annual regional fairs, to the palaces of the nobility, to every square and city where business presented itself. In the port of Valencia, he befriended the Genoese merchants who controlled the trade with Asia Minor. They operated a network of caravans that connected the Far East with Europe. It was their tight control of the spice trade that prompted Spanish and Portuguese entrepreneurs to explore alternative trade routes for these lucrative goods. Because the efforts were so far unsuccessful, Alberto, like the other Iberian merchants, was forced to pay the prices demanded by the high-handed Genoese.

In his travels through Spain, Alberto was always wary of being recognized by someone who had known him previously. He grew a beard, hoping that this would serve as an effective disguise. Now that the war was over, and the soldiers were returning home, there was even greater risk that one of his former comrade-in-arms would spot him, disguise and all, and report him forthwith to the Inquisition. It was time to move on. Alberto developed close relationships with some captains of foreign vessels, discreetly testing their reactions to the possibility of transporting people who might need to leave Spain without official sanction. He inquired about the cost of a journey to various distant locations. But he did not approach just any captain; this came only after Alberto had made careful investigations into the man's background: his character, his honesty, the value of his promises. Only then would he consider the man. The Genoese captains, for example, were notorious for their unscrupulousness — not all of them, it was fair to say, but enough had earned the unsavory reputation, so that Alberto was forced to take every conceivable precaution before approaching a foreign captain. It was important not to make a mistake. The Inquisition had agents at every port, paying substantial amounts for information about would-be escapees who approached captains as Alberto had done. Thus, an incautious suggestion to the wrong captain could be fatal. Nonetheless, Alberto found a few captains he could trust.

It would not have been difficult for someone like himself, a spice trader of documented Old Christian lineage, to set sail from Valencia for some faraway destination on a business trip, knowing he would never return to Spanish soil. Although he considered such a journey to seek his family, whose whereabouts were still a mystery to him after all these years, Alberto hesitated. It was not that he was afraid to go; it was that his beloved Hermosa would not be permitted to join him in such a journey. At times, Alberto felt trapped between two conflicting commitments, torn between two loves. At times he blamed himself for his indecision; at other times he praised himself for honestly admitting that neither took precedence in his heart. Finally the long overdue decision was made, but by someone else

Regina Pinto, his one-time host who had thwarted his love through her vigorous opposition to his courting of Hermosa, decided it was time to put an end to the situation. Regina's hostility to Alberto seemed to remain unalterable. Despite his many gifts of spices and flowers to her, despite his willingness to please her and to perform one extraordinary favor after another for her, she seemed to be unmoved. Yet it was not so. Regina had actually come to enjoy the company of the dashing young cavalier from Sevilla, who had distinguished himself on the battlefield and who now was making a name for himself in the spice trade. The young man, she realized, had much ability and would assuredly make her Hermosa a most wonderful husband. And it was also important that he was a Converso, as they all were. Yet she never divulged her high opinion of him; not to her daughter, who was finding her mother's contrariness insufferable; not to her husband, who perceived his wife's adamantine resistance as incomprehensible. Regina sought to hinder any new family entanglement because she still dreamed of their escape, the three of them together. She believed that a marriage such as this would only add an unnecessary complication. And, placing the overall longterm security of the family above the short-term happiness of her daughter, she justified her antagonism.

Possibly it was a feeling of punitive spite against her husband who, with one lame assurance after another, continually put off their departure from Spain. She would give her husband no excuse for avoiding his responsibility which was to take the family away from the danger of the Holy Office. In matters of life and death, Regina reasoned, one did not add avoidable complications. One did not surrender on an issue of vital principle, and the only incontestable principle, below which all others paled in significance, was the principle of their own survival. If she had her way, they would all have left Spain immediately. And, if Alberto were truly in love with their daughter as he claimed he was, the young man would either accompany them or join them shortly. As far as she was concerned, only one person was to blame for the present situation: her hard-headed husband, the illustrious two-faced Dr. Pinto, whose procrastination was driving her to irrational spite.

But it was becoming apparent to Regina that, however noble her end purpose, she could not continue to use her anger at Marco and direct it instead towards Alberto. If she continued, Regina knew it would cost her the respect and love of her daughter. Was freedom so valuable that it should be purchased with the tears of her distraught Hermosa? Was not the uneventfulness of the last five years an indication that she had exaggerated the dangers that lurked in the city about them? She began to question her position. Indeed, she began to develop doubts about her dream of escape and about the terrible price she would have to pay to achieve it. As her doubts increased, her resistance collapsed. As her dream retreated into an illusory hope, so did her opposition to Alberto. Whatever pangs of regret she may have experienced from abandoning her dream were more than compensated by the pleasure she derived from seeing her daughter so ecstatically happy. Starting this year of 1492, she allowed her daughter to see

Alberto; she would no longer stand in their way. Amid profuse kisses and hugs and tearful expressions of joy, Regina welcomed the reconciliation in her own heart as much as her daughter did. She was tired of resisting.

Alberto was as surprised by Regina's change of attitude as he had been by her initial recalcitrance. The year augured well for him. And with the surprise came rapturous joy, as he payed court to his loved one. Immaculately dressed in sleek pantaloons and ruffled silk shirt, he would ride to their doorstep atop the Arab stallion that he had bought, a cavalier in search of his lady, a man in search of his woman. Hermosa, her laced fluffy skirt bouncing with each step she took, would climb carefully behind Alberto on the huge horse, put her arms around Alberto's muscular chest, and signal to him that she was ready. Then they would rush into the countryside, the wind slapping at their laughing faces, their hair flailing wildly, their carefree hearts filled with exhilaration. Ride and ride they did.

The powerful steed hurled itself against the road, plunging through rock-strewn grassy ravines, taking the two of them to neighboring mountaintops from which Segovia could be seen in all its splendor. The smell of pine was in the air, and the undulating range of the Sierra Guadarrama was laid out before them like some vast unexplored playground. It was theirs alone, a labyrinthine world of winding mountain passes and rocky escarpments, a hilly expanse dotted with crops of wild lilies and lined with tributary streams that meandered their way down to the central riverbeds. A flower in her hair, a happy sigh of relief in her heart, Hermosa was escorted across the land like a fragile blossom, her supple body bending like a floral stem with each turn of the road, her soft arms pressed tightly around the shield offered by Alberto's torso, her love for him in the fullness of bloom.

Alberto would come to a bubbling brook, dismount, and carry her in his arms across the frothy stream. Then, in an area on the opposite side of the riverbank, they would sit silently on an outstretched blanket to watch the blue-white roll of the sierra's water and to listen to its soft, crashing gurgles. Or they would saunter across to a nearby wood, at times dashing through it in a playful chase, only to end as one in each other's arms, their lips bound to each other in moments of repeated caress. It was heaven, or so it seemed, as they walked in the airy heights of the Iberian mountains, the fluffy clouds above them at their fingertips, the grassy earth beneath them as their footstool.

In the midst of this exhilaration, he could feel the fullness of her breast against his chest, her satin-smooth olive skin warmly touching his. The impulse grew stronger and, as their bodies met, so did their lips — cautiously at first, then a swirl of soft exploration as they glided and meshed their lips with one another. They were overtaken by a newfound electrifying passion sweeping through their bodies; the two of them were wrapped in a vortex of their own creation, their bodies and minds ignited by the spark now become wildfire.

Propriety dictated that Hermosa reject Alberto's advance, but instead she allowed herself to linger in the grasp of his muscular arms, powerful arms that lifted her and brought her towards him. She could feel the hard strength of his body, the rippling of his sinews. Yet his touch was soft. Here, she thought to herself, was a man she could love, did love without reservation. She returned his passion, kissing him on the lips and cheeks, prolonging this moment of ecstatic encounter. She could not control herself, she had never felt this way before. Something so beautiful, so tantalizingly wonderful could surely not be wrong.

"Oh, Alberto, it feels so good to be with you."

Alberto held her tighter.

"It is marvelous to be with you, Hermosa. I cannot believe you feel the same for me as I feel about you. Will you marry me, my beloved, and share the rest of your days with me?"

"Oh, yes!" gasped Hermosa as she embraced her sweetheart. "Oh, yes!"

"Then you have made me the happiest man in the world."

Alberto kissed Hermosa on the neck, deliciously savoring the sweet taste of her creamy textured skin, delighting his nostrils with her perfumed aroma. Hermosa, electrified by passion, yet fearing loss of self-control, gradually brought her emotions in check.

"Alberto, my sweet, I love you with all my heart, but until we are married, we can only go so far."

Alberto withdrew as she requested, the tension ebbing slowly from his arms, the dreamy look on his face fading. He allowed himself one more whiff of her presence, permitted himself one more delectable kiss on her rosy cheek, as he finally pulled himself away from her.

She said, "Hermosa Galante. I like the sound of the name."

Then they sat down and dreamed about their future and about the secret Converso wedding that would inaugurate their new beginning.

"Whom shall we invite to the wedding?" asked Alberto.

Hermosa let her fingers glide through his hair, tossing it into curls of her devising, then smoothing them out.

"Oh," she would say, "All the members of our secret society . . . you know, the tailor, the merchant, the blacksmith and their families. There are a few others in town who are Conversos like ourselves, but they are unaware of our secret meetings, and it is perhaps just as well. The fewer people at our wedding, the better."

"I agree, Hermosa. If it is all right with you, I would like Hacham Alhadeff to conduct the wedding ceremony."

"Oh, that would be wonderful. It would be an honor to have him marry us."

"And then?," asked Alberto, his mood turning serious. "What happens after we are married? Do we stay here in Segovia and go through the formality of a church wedding so that we will be able to live together as man and wife?"

Hermosa's eyes darted about nervously. "I am tired of pretending to be a Christian. I do not believe that I could go through such a make-believe church wedding and all of its hypocrisy. My marriage to you, Alberto, is something pure, something special, and I do not want the purity of my vow to you to be in any way compromised. I will marry you, my darling, only for what you are, a Jew. There will be no Christian wedding."

"I was sure you would say that, my beloved. If such is your wish, and I want you to know that it is mine as well, then we have no choice but to leave Spain."

"Leave Spain?" Hermosa answered, a disturbed look on her face.

Alberto continued, "It would be no problem at all. I have taken every precaution. I have checked with captains, spoken with foreign emissaries about the conditions in their countries, done everything imaginable to find out how to get away safely. The safest country to go to is Turkey, the land of the Ottoman Turks. Their unquestioned power in the Eastern Mediterranean enables them to be magnanimous to foreigners. They will welcome us in their capital of Constantinople, which they now call Istanbul, for they are tolerant and have no quarrel with the Jews. I have heard from a reliable source that they even desire Jewish merchants and artisans to come and settle there. Their empire is growing day by day, and their naval fleet is unchallenged in the Bosphorous. Already, several Jewish merchants from Spain have made the voyage to Istanbul and set up their business there. I thought perhaps that I too could set up a spice trade business in Istanbul. In Istanbul, there is no Inquisition, and from all that I hear, it is a safe place to bring up one's family . . . as Jews. We could live as Jews, identify as Jews, pray as Jews . . ."

"We would set up a kosher home," Hermosa added, "and we would have children, as many as God would bless us with."

"We would send our children to the Hebrew day school in Istanbul. Our children would receive the education that we never got. They would learn the laws of the Torah, they would speak Hebrew, they would put on tefillin . . . they would be married in a synagogue."

"Alberto, it sounds too good to be true. Can such a country exist where Jews are free to practice our religion without restriction?"

"Spain was once such a country," Alberto remarked, "until the spirit of fanaticism infected its being. As Spain has changed, so must we. It is no longer a place for us to live in. We must leave here quickly. Now that Granada has fallen, I fear the situation will get worse before it gets better. Jews can no longer be spice merchants. Next it will be the Conversos. It will become worse for us as it has for the Jews.

"Already, as a result of the Niño de la Guardia trial, Jews and Conversos are being accused of plotting to commit ritual murder. Four New Christians, by the name of Franco, are accused of cutting out the heart of a Christian child with the help of a sorcerer named Tazarte so as to desecrate the host and to make black magic against the Christians. Tazarte is among those being tried, and the charge is being made that the Jewish and Converso physicians all want somehow to kill Christians. Even your father, Hermosa, has admitted to losing some of his best patients because they are now afraid of being treated by a Converso sorcerer physician. What better reason than this for your father to leave now?

"Since the beginning of this year, I have seen an increase in the number of Inquisition officers at Valencia interrogating people who seek to leave Spain. It is the same at other ports, so my friends tell me. The longer we wait, the harder it will be to leave. If we are agreed that we no longer want any more of this Converso existence, then we must get out of Spain while we still can."

"What about my parents?" Hermosa asked worriedly.

"When they see that we are leaving, they will be forced to join us. As Conversos, they would be immediately suspect if their daughter suddenly disappeared only to turn up some weeks later in Turkey living as a Jewess."

Alberto placed his arm gently on hers. "It is an idea whose time has come. Lately, it has become even more difficult to escape. If we wait any longer, it will be impossible. In the end, I must admit, it is your mother who was right all along."

"It's my father. What can I do? He refuses to move."

"There is no time left, Hermosa. He has had years to get accustomed to the idea. Besides, has not the recent trial of the Niño de la Guardia shaken him somewhat?"

"Yes, it has. Still . . . I am asking you, beloved, for more time," said Hermosa sweetly. "Do it, please, for me and my father."

"I will do anything you say, my darling. Even if there were no time left in the world, I would create some for you if that was what would make you happy. Tell me, how much time?"

"Till Passover," answered Hermosa. "The festival of freedom . . . freedom for our people, freedom for us . . . yes, in Turkey. That is when I want to marry. I want to marry at the end of Passover."

Alberto sighed his resigned acceptance, smiling as he shook his head.

"Passover is two months away," he said. "It is a short time as time goes, but in these days, it is a very long time to wait. Having to wait for you, Hermosa, is to wait an eternity, an eternity made doubly long because I have to wait while we are not yet free."

Hermosa put her arms around Alberto's shoulders and kissed him softly on the neck.

"Your wait, beloved, will be doubly rewarded. You will then possess me completely, and we will have the freedom that we seek."

"Passover, eh," Alberto asked, returning the kiss.

"Passover."

Chapter 7

Regina was exhausted. Preparing for Passover was an arduous task, with many chores and duties, all to be performed according to ritual. First, the house had to be scrubbed clean for the holidays — cabinets, furniture, pots, fireplace, shirt pockets, bedrooms, everything. Not a single household item was omitted, no area neglected. The tile floors were washed clean with buckets of water, the walls were scrubbed till they shone. Cupboards were emptied of plates, and every single nook and cranny was fastidiously cleaned until Regina was satisfied that there could not possibly be any trace of leavened bread. The daily utensils were put away, and a special set of eating utensils, cooking pots, and iron ladles brought out. These were never used during the rest of the year, and before they were declared fit, they had to be boiled to a state of cleanliness. All through the house, from room to room, Regina and Hermosa scoured every possible area for remaining crumbs, washing and wiping, ritually purging their abode of the slightest remnant of leaven. It had been only a week ago that the two, seated together in the underground cave, had attended the secret session given by Hacham Alhadeff describing the laws of Passover. And now they wished to attain the state of ritual purity that he described.

"The laws of Passover are clear and simple," Hacham Alhadeff had said, "we may not eat unleavened bread for seven days. Whoever does not fulfill this law is to be cut off from the people of Israel. Your entire house, every single corner and place, must be rid of all unleavened bread — not one crumb of it should remain in the house. A Jewish home must be spotless when Passover arises, so that we may eat only of the bread of affliction that our ancestors ate in Egypt under Pharoah. The only bread that we can eat is this . . ." At this point, the Hacham held up the baked rounded flat cakes for them to see . . ."*Matza*, the *pan cenceño*, the unleavened bread of Passover. This is the only bread that we can eat. I will teach you as much as I can about the Passover service so that you can observe it in your home . . . Listen carefully to what I have to say."

They listened carefully. Regina and Hermosa learned about the order of the *Seder*, the ritual meal. They learned the order and the contents of the dishes, from the bitter herbs called *maror* to the traditional four cups of wine. They received instructions on how to prepare the dishes as well as explanations about their symbolic significance. Along with other Conversos, they received freshly baked cakes of *matza* and jugfuls of kosher wine smuggled in from the local Jewish quarter. Because most were unable to read Hebrew, they also received bound sheets containing the handwritten translation of the Passover Haggadah into Castilian. Thus instructed by the Hacham, the two returned home by way of the underground passageway, eager to begin the necessary preparations for the holiday. The *haroset*, the thick brownish paste symbolizing the mortar that the ancient Israelites had used to lay the bricks for Pharoah's pyramids, had to be ground out of apples, nuts, dates, and grapes. Heads of romaine lettuce, to be used later as the symbolic bitter herbs of slavery, had to be obtained from local market-place vendors; this had to be done without attracting the attention of the roaming agents of the Inquisition who were on the look-out for characteristic shopping patterns. Lamb shank-bones, symbolizing the paschal lamb of old, likewise had to be obtained, as well as several other items. After all was prepared, Regina stored everything safely below in the cave until Passover eve.

Regina and Hermosa could hardly wait for the holiday or, for that matter, for the wedding that would follow soon after the Passover celebration. The invitations to the wedding of Hermosa and Alberto had been extended to the members of their exclusive Converso circle. The nuptials would be one more cause for holiday joy. Hermosa and Alberto, whose faces were wreathed with beams of happiness, were the recipients of everyone's well-wishes.

Beyond the Passover holiday and the wedding, the Conversos were thinking of their forthcoming flight to freedom, the long planned escape that would culminate a decade of unfulfilled dreams. As in the exodus of old, their ancestors' flight from Egypt that was soon to be retold, they were about to embark on their own exodus. It would be an event in their lifetimes that they could tell their children and grandchildren about in the years to come.

Passover arrived, and the cave was full of life and light again. Its interior was brightly lit by the smoking torches on the wall and by the dozen candles on the oblong central table. Sparkling silver wine goblets, decorative plates, the large silver *Seder* tray set with the required foods — all were elegantly displayed on a white linen tablecloth to create a special festive atmosphere.

At the head of the table was the tailor, Señor de Aguilar; to his right was Dr. Pinto, to his left the Converso merchant Armando de Fonseca. Wives and children were eager for the celebration to begin. The tailor's twin six-year-old daughters were giggling and so were the merchant's two older children. The blacksmith snorted loudly every now and then to silence the twins, but it did no good. Hermosa and Alberto sat at the opposite end of the table, hand in hand, exchanging tender glances and hushed words of afffection, provoking the tailor's twin daughters to giggle even louder with each moment.

The tailor rose from his chair, as did the others. There were blessings over the wine, the washing of the hands, and the eating of celery (the *karpas*). Taking the *matza* into his hand, the tailor held them in the air and recited from the instruction sheets:

"*Tomarán las tres matzot shamurot. La del medio partirán media por media. La media meterán entre las dos, y la otra media meterán debajo de los manteles para afikomin ...*"

"Thou shalt take the three whole matzas. The middle one thou shalt break into two halves. One half thou shalt place between the two remaining places, and the other half thou shalt place under the tablecloth for Afikomin ..."

As Señor de Aguilar recited, he placed the portion of *matza* called the *afikomin* in a beautifully decorated bag and handed it to Dr. Pinto. "You begin, Doctor." Using his left hand, Marco Pinto placed the bag over his right shoulder and arose from the chair. He reached out for a large staff in a nearby corner and addressed those at the table.

Pinto commented, rod in hand, the bag with *matza* on his right shoulder, "It is said that on this night of the Passover, in every generation, each Jew must feel as if he or she were to be rescued tonight from the hand of Pharaoh. Today, we are still in Egypt and we are ready to set forth on our journey to freedom . . . Regina, Hermosa, we leave Egypt, we leave Spain as a family . . . will you join me?"

Regina, Hermosa, and Alberto stood and joined Dr. Pinto. Regina placed her arm inside her husband's and whispered softly, "Ah, yes, my dear, another one of your imaginary trips." Hermosa and Alberto joined hands and stood off to the side. Together, as a group, they started walking slowly in a semi-circle in the open area next to the table, with Dr. Pinto leading the way. He struck the ground sharply with his rod every time that he took a step. Marco said playfully, "Isn't this a wonderful trip, my dear?" Regina answered tongue-in-cheek, "Oh, yes, simply unreal . . . the kind that you always like."

The group completed its circular promenade and returned to the main table. Those at the table then asked: "Where are you coming from?"

Dr. Pinto and his retinue replied, "From the land of Egypt."

The others continued their questioning, "And where are you going to?"

"To Jerusalem!", was the hearty reply of the Pinto family and Alberto.

Dr. Pinto then handed the bag and rod to the tailor, Señor Aguilar, who with his family enacted the same scene. Aguilar then passed the bag and rod to the Converso merchant, and then to the blacksmith who each did the same.

The *Seder* service continued, the tailor leading the chanted recitation with the *matza* bag draped over his shoulder:

"*Hincherán los vasos de vino y dirán la Haggadah . . .*
Este el pan de la africíon que comieron muestros
padres en tierra de Egipto,
Todo el que tiene hambre, venga y coma
Todo el que tiene de menester, venga y pascue.
Este año aquí, a el año el viñen, en tierra de Israel
Este año aquí, a el año el viñen, en tierra de Israel
Este año aquí siervos, a el año el viñen, en tierra de
Israel, hijos foros."

("Thou shalt fill up thine wine glasses and tell the story of the Exodus from Egypt.

This is the bread of affliction

That our forefathers ate in the land of Egypt.
Whoever is hungry, let him come and eat.
Whoever is in need, let him come and join us.
This year we are here
But next year we shall be in Israel
Next year,in the land of Israel, we shall be free men.")

Alberto raised a wine glass and toasted, "Freedom . . . to believe and to live as we please. That is our wish this Passover."

The merchant Fonseca added, "We shall escape on a secret ship and leave this new Egypt that oppresses us so. This year we will be free men."

"Amen, amen," intoned the blacksmith.

Regina could tolerate no more delusions. "The same old wishes every Passover. I hope this time the ship that you find will not be a phantom ship like the one last year. Ha! All of this is idle talk, gentlemen. I want action, not empty words. I want a real ship, not the stuff of your fantasies."

The merchant's wife chimed in, "Regina is right. Why do you men just talk, talk, talk and never do anything? Why do you not do something?"

The tailor, silent thus far, interjected, "We *are* doing something. We have found a reliable captain through Alberto, a captain who has given us a good price. We will be acting shortly after Passover on the matter."

Regina waved him off. "What nonsense! You can hardly expect me to believe such babbling. Indeed, I will not believe . . . not until I am on that ship myself, on my way out of Spain."

Marco Pinto tried to calm down his wife. "The time will come, dearest. Everything in its due time and place. You know what our plans are."

Regina shook her head violently and remained quiet. She had heard that too many times before.

The merchant's wife continued the harangue. "Ha! . . . You men. You're all the same: dreamers! You build castles in the air . . . but you end up like this, with caverns under the earth to live in. That is what you do."

Marco frowned. "Enough!" he said. Signaling to his daughter, he said, "Hermosa, please get the water for the next ritual wash."

Hermosa left the group and headed back toward the house by way of the torch-lit tunnel. As she walked, the chanting became more distant . . .

> "Cuanto fué demudada la noche la esta más
> que todas las noches?
> En todas las noches, no nos entinientes afilu vez una
> . . .Y la nocha la esta dos vezes."

Hermosa proceeded down the tunnel and up the stairway into the kitchen.

Juan de Gonzalo had not forgotten Hermosa. He had not fogotten her soft textured beauty, the fine lines of her face, the sweetness of her soul, even her rejections of his amorous sentiments. His three years at the university, far from sapping his spirit with its ponderous discourses, gave him a new maturity. His blond hair was longer and his body more robust, his eyes still an intense blue. Juan was home for the Easter holiday with his family, but he also hoped to get a last look at the woman of his heart.

Spurned by Hermosa, Juan tried to extinguish his heartache and the memory of his loved one by devoting himself to his legal studies. But despite his efforts, her lovely face kept returning in his thoughts. In the study of turgid law tomes, in the serenading of señoritas with fellow student minstrels, he continually conjured up the image of his fair lady in the daydreams of his mind's eye. Unable to efface her memory, Juan had returned to Segovia one last time to see her. He was determined not to accept no for an answer. This time, he was sure he would win her heart. In this resolute mood, Juan de Gonzalo rode his horse to the Pinto residence. Much to his surprise, a guard was standing by the gate.

Juan announced himself. "Good evening, señor. I have come to see the young lady Hermosa Pinto."

The guard halted his advance by grabbing the horse's reins. "I am sorry, sir. I have instructions to keep all visitors out."

Juan was upset. "I do not understand. What is the meaning of this?"

The guard continued to hold onto the reins. "Doctor Pinto has an illness that is spreading to the other members of the family. It may be contagious. All visitors must stay away until there is no longer any danger."

Juan became even more distressed. "Hermosa . . . is she sick too?

No? Then I wish to see her, if only for a moment. I tell you, my good man, I must see her. I must see Hermosa."

With his other hand, the guard unsheathed his sword, and answered firmly, "No, sir, you shall not. My instructions are clear. No exceptions are to be made."

"You are being very unreasonable," said Juan, irritated.

But realizing that arguing with this armed oaf was useless, he added, "Very well, I shall leave, and come again some other time."

The guard let go of the reins, and Juan angrily kicked his horse and rode off into the night.

Hermosa returned to the *Seder* table, carrying a large pitcher of water along with an empty basin. The tailor continued with the reading:

"*Se lavarán las manos y diran berachah.*
Porque? Porque vamos a comer matza."
("Thou shalt wash thy hands and say the blessing.
Why? Because we are going to eat *matza*.")

Hermosa then poured water from the pitcher on the tailor's hands. After saying the blessing for washing of the hands, the tailor nodded to Hermosa, who went on to others at the table who similarly washed their hands and recited the blessing.

As soon as Juan was out of the guard's sight, he doubled back toward the Pinto home, using a narrow back alley that led to the rear wall. He advanced slowly down the alley, taking care to avoid being detected. As he reached the high stone wall, he dismounted and took a rope from the saddle. Juan shaped the rope into a lariat and tried to throw it over the wall. After a few attempts, he was able to get the rope to latch onto a hook on the uppermost portion of the wall. He tugged at the rope to make sure that it was taut. Assured that it was safe to proceed, he began to climb slowly up the wall, gripping the rope tightly as he went, digging his boots into the narrow crevices between the stone blocks. Slowly he pulled his body upward, one arm in front of the other. When he reached the top, he was flushed with excitement that soon he would see Hermosa.

Flipping the rope over the wall, he let himself down slowly into the inner courtyard. Crouching low, and tip-toeing as he went, he cautiously approached one of the windows.

Through the window, Juan saw Hermosa in the kitchen. She was not sick as the guard had said; indeed, she was as radiant as ever, and his face lit up with the gladness of heart-felt relief. But then he noticed that Hermosa and her mother were busy gathering trays and foods from the kitchen and carried them below via a trapdoor. Juan was puzzled, yet curious. What were they doing and where were they going? Was this the reason for the guard? He began to feel that something was terribly wrong. But what the wrongness was about, and what his beloved Hermosa had to do with it — all this remained a mystery. Yet he had not come all this way to allow his passion to be transformed into puzzlement. He came to see Hermosa, and no guard or mystery could stop him from seeing her.

As soon as Hermosa and her mother disappeared from sight through the trap door, Juan slipped into the house by a window. He crawled cautiously to the trap door and bent his ear to it. He heard noises below, and unable to contain his curiosity, Juan decided to penetrate further. He lowered himself through the trap door into the subterranean tunnel system, his heart pounding, his brow sweaty with anxiety over his illegal entry into the Pinto household.

In the distance, the tailor intoned the next blessing:

"*Y tomarán la lechua y entinierán en el haroset y dirán
Baruch Atah Adonai Eloheinu Melech Ha-Olam, Asher
Kidishanu Be-Mitzvotav Ve-tsivanu Al Achilat Maror.*"
("And thou shalt take of the bitter herbs and dip into
the mortar sauce and say: Blessed art Thou, O Lord our
God, King of the Universe, who has sanctified us through
His commandments by the eating of the bitter herbs.")

Everyone at the table dipped a leaf of lettuce into the vinegar and winced at the taste.

Juan began to advance cautiously down the tunnel, staying close to the slimy, soot-covered walls of the passageway. Guided by the muted sounds of the celebrants, he made his way down the corridor, advancing a few soft steps at a time. Every few minutes he glanced over his shoulders to make sure no one was behind him. Was the underground passage a smuggling center, a hiding place for political conspirators? He walked on until he was at the periphery of the central cave. The indistinct murmurings now became clear, and the deception was revealed to him in a flash of understanding: *Marranos!* False Christians! *Marranos.* Jew pigs. The word shook him as he thought it. *Marranos,* secret Jews, the worst of their kind, putrid Jewish swine, that was what the Pinto family was. Hermosa was a *Marrano,* too. Everyone at the table was one, practicing their Jew rituals underground so that no one could see them. Swine, *Marranos,* Jews — the whole lot of them. He hated them all. And he hated Hermosa.

Juan watched with disgust as the tailor made some kind of unintelligible blessing over a flat cake with lettuce on top and dipped it into a dark sauce,

> *Tomarán la matza de abajo que esta sana y de la lechua*
> *y de las verduras y entinierán en el haroset y dirán . . .*
> *"Zecher la Mikdash ke Hillel Ha-Zaken."*

Those at the table did the same, dipping their cakes in the mortar sauce. Juan shook his head in bewilderment, wondering what this was all about. He saw cups filled with red wine. This was surely the blood from the veins of innocent Christian children such as the Niño de la Guardia. And Dr. Pinto, was he not then an evil wizard who prepared magical potions to poison the Christians? His apprehensive eyes bulged at the thought, and a quiver of fear went down his tense throat. To add to Juan's dismay, the young man sitting next to Hermosa put his arm around her shoulder, hugged her, and kissed her on the cheek, a kiss that Hermosa returned with affection.

Juan de Gonzalo hated her even more. His rage was total. His face turned red with anger. He detested Hermosa and all her wretched kind. He hated her with a passion equal to, if not greater, than the love he had once held for her. Just as he had sworn to love her, now he swore that he would punish her and her family with his hate. She had made him suffer, and now it was her turn to feel pain. He vowed to kill her, to mortally punish the woman who had broken his heart. He started to back away slowly.

> *Y aparejarán la mesa y cenerán!,"* shouted the tailor.

("And thou shalt prepare the table and dine!")

They were finally going to eat.

"Bravo!" shouted the merchant.

"On to the food!" added the blacksmith.

"On to the land of the Ottomans, and to freedom!" said Alberto, holding a wine goblet high in the air. The others at the table joined him in the toast.

"To freedom!" joined the others. They drank the wine amid much warmth and merriment.

Regina and Hermosa rose from the table to bring the food from the kitchen. They walked unhurriedly down the tunnel.

Juan heard footsteps approaching his way. He backed up more quickly now, stumbling as he heard people coming down the passageway.

Regina squeezed her daughter's hand, looking into her soft blue eyes with maternal benevolence. The dispute over Alberto had long been forgotten: all was well between them again.

"Things are going to be good now, Hermosa," said Regina.

"Yes, Mama, they are going to be wonderful. I cannot begin to tell you how happy I am."

Regina nodded her head understandingly and gently squeezed her daughter's hand again. She was happy for her daughter, she was happy for herself. She wiped a tear from her eye and continued walking down the tunnel. Things were going to be good now.

Juan scrambled his way down the tunnel until he reached the ladder. Quickly he climbed up the ladder and bolted through the trapdoor, his heart pounding wildly, his arms shaking with fear. As soon as he pulled his feet up and out of the trapdoor, Hermosa arrived at the ladder and started climbing. Regina was right behind her.

Juan dashed to the open window, and in panic, he hurriedly tried to climb onto the sill. He slipped as he did so, loosing his grip and his footing in the process. Someone was coming up the ladder. Again he lurched forward to reach the window sill, but this time he fell head first through the window and landed on the flowerbed below. Hermosa, emerging from the tunnel, noticed the open window immediately. "The window is open, Mama. I will get it."

Juan again heard the footsteps coming his way. He crawled from the flowerbed and rolled next to the wall, his back pressed flat against the building, his breathing restrained and noiseless. Petrified beads of sweat slowly rolled down his forehead.

Hermosa came to the window. Juan held his breath, his body motionless. Hermosa looked briefly from side to side, but noticed nothing unusual. Satisfied all was well, she closed the window, bolted it, and pulled the curtain closed.

Juan sighed with relief. He was safe. He got up out of the flowerbed and crawled away. In a recessed part of the courtyard, he dusted the dirt from his pantaloons and wiped the leaves and twigs off his shirt. Using his rope as before, he hauled himself over the wall and hastened to perform his Christian duty.

Don Enrique Domínguez slept well. His large body dwarfed his wooden bed, and the pair of heavy, quilted blankets enveloped him like a cocoon. Only his large head was visible. His attendant had to call him several times and then nudge him before the head of the local Hermandad could be woken. Domínguez half-opened his eyes. The attendant, a lad of twelve, stood at his bedside.

"Yes, what is it?" Dominguez demanded, his eyes still squinting.

"Pardon me for waking you up at this time of night, sir. But there is a young informer waiting to speak with you. He refuses to speak to anyone but an authorized familiar of the Inquisition."

Domínguez rubbed his eyes wearily and yawned. "Only me? At this time of night?"

"He says it is urgent," the attendant explained. Domínguez pulled himself from underneath the mass of blankets and sat up in bed. He slipped his feet into a pair of slippers and covered himself with a heavy wool robe.

"Hmmm . . . it is Passover night, is it not. Perhaps I will be the exterminating angel after all." He signaled to the attendant. "Very well, bring in the informer."

The attendant led Juan in, and Domínguez invited him to sit down and speak. At this hour of the night, Domínguez thought, he had better have a good reason for waking him up!

Juan related the details of the story: the guard at the gate, his secret entry into the Pinto household, the trap door, the cave, all those who were present, and the strange Jewish rites. Domínguez needed to hear no more. Within moments of Juan's revelation, Domínguez dispatched orders to round up the Hermandad guards. He sent a special messsenger to Inquisition headquarters to inform the local Inquisitor, Fray Diego Lucero, about the violation. While he had long suspected the Pinto family of Judaizing tendencies, he had never been able to secure any evidence against them. Now the missing testimony had been supplied by this sincere Christian youth. If the account were true, and there was no reason to dispute the veracity of the youth's report, the arrest of such a noteworthy physician would bring honor and fame to Don Enrique Domínguez de Córdoba, the head of the Hermandad of the city of Segovia. Domínguez thought of how people would refer to him — as the "catcher of *Marranos*," or as a glorious defender of the Catholic faith, or perhaps as the pride and glory of the Hermandad brotherhood. All he had to do was bring the *Marranos* to justice. Of course, there were always the gold ducats he would get for services rendered to the Holy Office of the Inquisition. Wealth and honor, he sensed, would soon be his.

The assault group met at Domínguez's residence: 20 armed guards, two Inquisitorial aides, Fray Lucero, Domínguez himself, and Juan de Gonzalo, anxious to lead the way. As they advanced upon the Pinto residence, they discussed the strategy of the attack: how they would encircle the Pinto household from the front and the rear, unsheath their swords, take the guard at the front gate, enter through the trap door, and surprise the Converso gathering. The action was to be swift and coordinated, with Domínguez giving the attack signal.

Juan led Domínguez and Lucero to a nest of trees overlooking the Pinto estate. They crouched low and studied the surroundings. Juan described the plan of the house and its walls, concluding . . . "and over there, behind the rear wall, is the kitchen area where you will find the trap door."

"Good work, my son," Lucero intoned. "God will bless you for what you have done today." Lucero patted Juan appreciatively on the shoulder.

"Thank you, Father," replied Juan, his voice still hushed. "I was only doing my Christian duty."

Domínguez motioned to his men to advance. "We can begin the attack. Soon we will have them completely surrounded."

Hermandad soldiers crept slowly through the brush and along the alleyways. While five guards covered the rear wall, the main group advanced stealthily toward the front gate, taking their positions first at one corner, then another, until they came to the periphery of the Pinto residence itself. As pre-arranged, one Hermandad soldier suddenly came out of the brush to engage the guard at the gate in conversation. When the guard came up to him, he was attacked from his blind side by another Hermandad guard. Other Hermandad men came out of the brush to gag and bind the guard.

The Hermandad guards opened the front gate and advanced to the house. Juan, followed by Domínguez and Lucero, ran up to the house to join them. The front door was still locked, so then Juan ran to the window and forced the bolt loose again. Opening the window, he lifted himself through it as before. Once inside, Juan rushed to open the front door to allow the others to enter.

Led by Juan, with Domínguez at his side, the Hermandad soldiers quietly advanced to the trap door and descended through it. With swords unsheathed and ready to battle the enemy, they began their deliberate move down the tunnel. They could hear the ringing sounds in the distance, a rhythmic chanting from deep inside the tunnel:

> *"Quien supiense y entendiense?*
> *Alabad al Dio creense, cualos son los trece?*
> *Trece son los Ikkarim*
> *Doce hermanos con Yosef*
> *Once hermanos sin Yosef*
> *Diez mandamientos son*
> *Mueve mezes de la preñada . . ."*

Closer and closer the soldiers came toward the central cave. Domínguez raised his arm above his head, as a signal for the men to prepare for combat.

> *". . .ocho días de la mila*
> *Siete días de la semana*
> *Seis libros de la Mishna*
> *Cinco libros de la Ley*
> *Cuatro madres de Israel*
> *Tres muestros padres son*
> *Dos Moshe Y Aron*
> *Uno es el criador*
> *Baruch-Hu u-Baruch Shemo."*

Domínguez brought his arm down quickly. The attack began: the Hermandad guards surged forward into the cave. Alberto, aroused by the peculiar rustling sounds he heard, looked down the tunnel. In a fraction of an instant, he recognized the forest green uniforms of the Hermandad, and shouted "Hermandad!" The others at the table sat transfixed by his yell, not knowing how to respond.

Alberto bolted from his chair and reached for his sword. Quickly, he pulled Hermosa up and forced her behind him into the tunnel that led toward the blacksmith's home.

Domínguez bellowed, "You are all under arrest. Put your hands in the air and do not move. You heard me, hands in the air!"

Everyone at the table began to scream. Marco and Regina Pinto raised their hands obediently and stood up, their faces stricken with anguish. The tailor's twins stopped giggling and blinked worriedly. The blacksmith shook his head in disbelief, cursing and snorting under his breath. It was over. Everyone, everyone knew it was all over. The end had come.

Alberto lashed out with his sword against the Hermandad guards, holding them temporarily at bay. But he was outnumbered, at least a dozen to one. Hermosa screamed hysterically behind him, and she made an effort to get back to her parents. Alberto grabbed her and thrust her back into the tunnel behind them.

"Run, Hermosa! Run into the tunnel," Alberto shouted. "Get out of here!"

Alberto swished his sword aimlessly against the five Hermandad men who were approaching him. But, Hermosa, paralyzed with fright, did not move. She stood behind him — terror-struck, stupefied.

The five guards advanced cautiously toward Alberto as he retreated step by step. Alberto shouted out again, "Run, Hermosa! What are you waiting for? For the love of God, run!"

Hermosa, confused and distraught but finally responding to Alberto's plea, began to run. She ran as fast as she could, plunging deeper into the darkness of the tunnel, running breathlessly as never before.

Alberto made his move. With lightning speed, he unleashed a series of crashing blows that felled the lead Hermandad guard to the ground. Within the narrow confines of the tunnel, the other guards now came at him, two at a time. The first pair fell on him, but Alberto parried their blows without difficulty. With uncanny ability, he countered with a flurry of his own, striking his opponent and drawing blood, then recoiling in time to parry the blow of the other opponent. It was a matter of moments. The wounded Hermandad pair was forced to withdraw. One had a puncture of the chest, the other a deep gash across his face. They were no match for such a highly experienced swordsman.

Alberto, sensing an opportunity to escape, now started running backwards down the tunnel.

The lead Hermandad soldier, together with the remaining pair of guards, rushed headlong through the tunnel in pursuit of Alberto. Domínguez and Lucero now turned their attention to the *Marranos* that had been taken captive.

The Inquisitor announced, "You are all under arrest by order of the Holy Office of the Inquisition."

Domínguez came up to Dr. Pinto. The physician, eyes downcast, head bowed, was uneasy. Domínguez, however, was elated. The prize catch, Dr. Marco Pinto, was his!

"Well, surely you have not forgotten my dinner invitation, Don Marco Pinto, my good doctor. But, pray tell, what is all this? A dinner party . . . and I was not invited? Not very gracious, Don Marco. Please excuse, if you will, my intrusion into this splendid affair. Not very gracious, Don Marco, most unbecoming of someone such as yourself."

Dr. Pinto's expression remained unchanging. Domínguez laughed at his attempt to force humor out of the situation, and let the man be.

The Inquisitor, wishing to observe the legal proprieties, informed the prisoners: "The Holy Office hereby declares that your property and belongings are under our control. They will be used to pay the cost of the trial and for the ongoing investigation of Judaizing activities.

"You mean our property is confiscated?" asked the tailor.

Domínguez smashed a fist into the tailor's mouth, hitting the tailor again and again until the blood gushed down his chin and onto his shirt. Domínguez placed the tip of his sword at the tailor's neck, "Hold your tongue, Jew . . . or I will cut it off. Understand?"

The tailor, whose courage was suddenly gone, humbly nodded his head, while his twin girls and wife sobbed fitfully.

Fearing that the worst was yet to come, Dr. Pinto whispered softly, "*Se para uno en sus trece . . .*" The message, meaningless to the captors, had been communicated to each of the Conversos present.

Lucero looked at the physician, trying to make sense of the statement. Then he examined at close range each of the *Marrano* prisoners, feigning admiration at their subterfuge.

"Very clever, this underground system of tunnels," he noted. "Devilishly clever."

As the Inquisitor passed him, the blacksmith suddenly let out a series of loud snorts, his face glaring with contempt. "Damn your Holy Office, you murderers in cloaks of piety." The blacksmith spat in the priest's astonished face and pushed him to the ground.

Domínguez roared into action as if he were a caged animal sprung loose. He slammed a fist into the blacksmith's face and ferociously threw the man against the stone wall. Then he kicked his knee into the blacksmith's abdomen, which caused the injured man to collapse on the ground. Clasping and moaning in agony, the blacksmith seemed finished. But his pain was not to end there. Domínguez kicked him once again in his face, snapping the blacksmith's head back. Again and again Domínguez kicked the blacksmith's head, until his face was unrecognizable — his nose swollen and gushing blood, his forehead and cheek cut, his eyelid split open, and his front teeth buried in his upper lip. The worst was a steady stream of blood coming through his ear onto Domínguez's boots. Domínguez kicked the motionless head one last time and then spat at it.

"*Marranos*, what awful manners they have!" And Domínguez walked away, wiping his hands clean and acknowledging an appreciative nod from his Inquisitorial accomplice.

Alberto raced down the tunnel that led to the blacksmith's shop. His legs churned rapidly, beads of perspiration streaming down his face and neck, his chest heaving as it drew in the smoky tunnel air. He heard noises behind him, which meant the Hermandad soldiers were not far away. He pushed on, sword in hand, until he arrived at the ladder that led up to the blacksmith's shop. A terrified Hermosa was there, waiting for him.

Alberto, in a gasping voice, signaled to Hermosa. "Quick! Up the ladder!" Hermosa did as she was told, her body trembling as she went. When she reached the top, she opened the trap door, and Alberto tried to follow her. Hardly had he stepped on the first rung when three Hermandad guards emerged from the tunnel and attacked him.

Alberto jumped off the ladder and readied himself for the onslaught. The lead Hermandad guard swung his sword at Alberto. Alberto ducked. The guard swung again from above, but this time Alberto met the sword with his own, neutralized the blow, and drove the opponent's handle backwards and up against his chest. Using all the force at his command, Alberto shoved the guard back into the two men behind him. In the confusion, one of the rear guards broke free and drew Alberto into a one-on-one contest. It was not a contest. Alberto slammed his sword through the man's chest, and the man fell quickly, his hand clutching at his mortal wound. The lead guard jumped over his fallen comrade and resumed the assault, as the did the other guard at his side. Together, they came steadily at Alberto, slowly driving him back. Cornered, Alberto made a furious series of slashes at the two, which caused the guards to hesitate. In that moment, Alberto spun around and dashed toward the ladder. He jumped, reaching as high as his free arm would take him, and his feet landed squarely on the third rung.

The Hermandad guards were right on top of him, slashing away at his feet. Fearing for his life, Alberto swung his blade this way and that, trying to keep their steel away. He climbed up one rung. As he did so, the rear guard swung fiercely with his sword and sliced through Alberto's boot, cutting the flesh underneath. Alberto was hurt, and he was bleeding. Blood gushed from his boot. The guard grabbed the boot and tried to pull Alberto down, but Alberto wrested his foot free, and kicked the guard in the face. When the guard fell back, Alberto climbed another rung, putting his feet beyond their reach. Now only one guard at a time could meet him on the ladder. The lead guard rushed up the ladder and engaged Alberto in a duel, fighting blow by blow, rung by rung. He went after Alberto's injured foot, hoping to disable him. Slowly, up the ladder, the two of them went, Alberto content to keep the guard from hurting him further, the guard concentrating on drawing second blood from the elusive bleeding extremity. Finally, Alberto reached the trap door, and he flung himself through it into the blacksmith's shop.

While Alberto struggled to close the trapdoor behind him, the guard's sword stuck through the opening, preventing him from shutting it. Alberto threw all his weight on the trap door. He could feel the thrusts of the guard underneath as he tried to force the door open. Hermosa, trembling and deadly pale, stood alongside him. Alberto motioned to her with his face and arm to bring him the torch on the wall. Finally, Hermosa, comprehending what he wanted, gave the torch to him.

Alberto readied himself. Placing his sword against the protruding blade so that the opponent's weapon would be forced in a corner, he suddenly lifted the door and thrust the torch into the face of the guard. Screaming, the guard fell down the ladder, with his sword falling after him.

Alberto slammed the trap door shut and bolted it. Limping as he walked, his foot almost giving out under him, he dragged a heavy anvil onto the trap door. Once again, he could hear the renewed banging of the guard on the door, but this time to no avail. They were safe.

Alberto saddled one of the horses and put Hermosa on its back. His foot aching with pain, he then mounted the animal himself. Together, they emerged into the street, looking for attackers, but there were none. On the eve of Passover, in the middle of blackest night, they rode out of Segovia.

Chapter 8

Hermosa was overcome with tears. The escape from Segovia, harrowing as it was for her and Alberto, was worse for her family. As they fled in the moonlight, Hermosa began to comprehend the magnitude of her loss. She looked back one last time, dimly seeing the the outline of the Segovian aqueduct in the distance, her hometown blanketed with nightfall and receding into the blackness. She had lost all that she had. Neither she nor Alberto had anything they could call their own except for each other. She clung to Alberto's body tightly, pressing her head against his back.

They rode through the night, resting little, to put as much distance between them and any pursuers. As the sun cast its first rays, a tired and weary Alberto directed his horse to the top of a small hill overlooking the valley below. It provided an excellent vantage point, allowing them to keep a look-out for pursuers. In the shade of a pine tree, they finally rested. The flesh had been cut deeply, but he would be able to use the foot. Hermosa washed the wound with fresh water from a nearby spring and bandaged it with her scarf. The cut would heal if protected properly.

She let Alberto rest and walked about the grassy hilltop to ease the pain in her heart. But tears welled up repeatedly; she was unable to contain her sorrow, unable to believe that this was happening to them. What tomorrow would bring was less of a question than how they would survive the day, having no food or money. Yet their problems seemed as nothing when compared to those of her parents and Converso friends caught in the prison cells of the Inquisition. By comparison, her lot was enviable. She thought of her parents under-

123

going unimaginable tortures, and she broke down into tears again. She reflected on whether she could live without them, and remained puzzled over why God had seen fit to spare her and Alberto. As she looked out into the distance, she spotted a small isolated monastery, and she suddenly realized where she was. Pleased to have found a ray of hope, she ran back to Alberto to tell him.

Later that morning, Alberto and Hermosa advanced to the monastery gates. Hermosa stayed on the horse while Alberto dismounted and banged on the gate. A hooded monk came to the gate and greeted him, "Good morning, my child. How can we help you?"

Alberto spoke, "We are pilgrims from Segovia en route to Santiago de Compostela. May we stay here for the night? My sister and I are tired and hungry."

The monk responded favorably. "Of course, my children, you are most welcome. Come in. Spend the night with us, refresh yourselves, join us for vespers. Then tomorrow morn you can set out once again on your holy path."

Alberto accepted, "Thank you, thank you most kindly."

Taking the horse by the bridle, Alberto pretended to be off balance to disguise the limp in his walk.

The monk continued, "I myself was in Santiago just a year ago. It was a glorious visit."

Alberto walked on. "It is our first pilgrimage to the shrine of St. James."

"You must be very excited," said the monk.

"Oh, yes, very," concurred Alberto, as the monk led them into the monastery proper. It was a massive stone structure, simple and solid in construction, its hallways poorly lit and the arched wooden doors in need of repair. Alberto followed the monk to his small, dusty room. Its one piece of furniture, a hay-filled sack, served as a bed.

"This is your bed," the monk indicated. "Your sister will sleep in a room next to the cloister."

Alberto thanked him. "Good, it is all we need . . . Tell me, Father, do you by chance know of Bishop Dávila? I hear he often visits these parts. He is from Segovia and used to be the parish priest for our parents."

"My dear young man, how can I not have heard of him? He comes often to visit us here in times of spiritual retreat. In fact, he is here with us now."

Hermosa jumped with excitement. "Oh, it is a blessing from on high. Truly, the Lord has brought us here to deliver a message."

"Message? What message?" the monk asked, puzzled.

Hermosa said, "Please. I must speak with him."

He put them off. "Bishop Dávila has come here from Segovia to rest and to meditate, and I cannot disturb him without good reason."

Hermosa insisted. "My message is of the utmost urgency. His sister is deathly ill. I am sure he would want to know about it immediately."

The monk eyed them suspiciously. "I was not aware of any such illness. Surely the diocese office would have informed us of any grave illness in the family."

Hermosa took affront at this. "This happened *yesterday*, Father. The bishop's sister is very ill — almost on the verge of dying. If you wait until the diocese office informs you, it may be too late."

Perturbed, the monk remarked, "That is dreadful. Is it really so bad?"

Hermosa made the sign of the cross. "Yes, I swear to you ..."

The monk raised his hand to stop her. "There is no need for swearing like that. I will inform the Bishop that you are here; however, I cannot guarantee that he will see you. Does he know you personally?"

Hermosa answered quickly. "No, he does not. But we live on the same street as the Bishop's sister. Everybody knows each other there, and that is why I know what has happened to her. The Bishop *must* be informed."

"I see," said the monk, still suspicious, and walked away.

A short while later, the Bishop arrived. He was a man of 70 or so, slender in face and body, his garments hanging loosely on his frame. Serious and soft-spoken, he wasted no time. "Good day, my children, I am Bishop Dávila. I understand that you have information concerning my sister's health."

Hermosa came up to the Bishop and whispered in his ear. "I am the daughter of Dr. Pinto, your nephew. Have the monk go away so that we can speak alone."

The Bishop instructed the monk to leave the room. Turning to deal with Hermosa, the Bishop whispered, "You little fool, are you out of your mind? Are you not aware that I am to be used only in case of extreme emergency?"

Hermosa interrupted him. "It is an extreme emergency. My father and mother have been caught by the Inquisition ..."

"The Inquisition! Oh, my God!," the Bishop exclaimed softly under his breath. "Whisper, child. Someone may hear you."

Hermosa continued. "Last night, as we were observing Passover, they caught all of us by surprise. Had it not been for Alberto, they would have caught us too."

Turning towards Alberto, the Bishop said matter-of-factly, "I assume you are Alberto."

Alberto nodded in agreement.

"A friend?" asked the Bishop of Hermosa.

"More than a friend," whispered she. "Alberto is my fiancé. We were supposed to get married next week, but now this disaster has occurred."

"And you want me to help you, is that it?" queried the Bishop.

Hermosa said, "Yes . . . and my parents too, if you possibly can."

Alberto now spoke up. "We need to get out of Spain, one way or another. The Hermandad will be looking for us. We need food and clothing. We could also use a little money if you can spare it."

The Bishop said, "I will do what I can, but I want both of you to understand one thing. Even though I am a Bishop, there are limits to what I can do. There is absolutely no way I will be able to obtain the release of your parents from the Inquisition, Hermosa. The security is impenetrable. And do not think that I can influence a reduction in their sentence. That is also not within my power to do. The Holy Office has its jurisdiction, and I have mine. Nonetheless, I will do what I can. I can give you food, clothing, and some money to help you on your way. This I will do."

"But what about my parents," Hermosa said angrily, her eyes wet with ears. "You mean, you cannot do anything, not even so much as to let them know we managed to escape?"

"Too risky," said the Bishop. "A few people know I am of Converso descent. It would arouse suspicions if I were to get involved."

Hermosa persisted. "But my father was no ordinary person. He was the physician of the nobility. He was a prominent member of your church in Segovia, as was Mother. It would look suspicious indeed if you did *not* take an interest in the Judaizing activities of such a prominent individual. Besides, and pardon me for reminding you of this, but he is your nephew."

The Bishop reflected upon Hermosa's remark. "You may have a valid point, young lady. Very well, then, I will go to Segovia."

"Thank you, Bishop," said Hermosa, sighing with relief.

The Bishop continued. "In the meantime, stay here until I return. Guard your tongues, and pray like faithful Christians. By the way, is my sister ill?"

Hermosa winked at him, and the Bishop smiled weakly. Dávila walked out the door and down the hallway to locate the monk. When he found him, Bishop Dávila told him, "Brother Pedro, my sister is ill. I must go to her. Saddle a horse for me for the long ride, along with two days' provision. I wish to set forth before noon."

Wanting to help, the monk said, "Perhaps one of us should accompany you, Bishop, in this hour of need. We would be most honored."

The Bishop put his hand comfortingly on the monk's shoulder. "Thank you, Brother, for your kind and considerate offer. But on this occasion, I would prefer to journey alone. I am sure you understand. In any case, I much appreciate your offer."

The monk withdrew and went to saddle the Bishop's horse. Dávila went to his office, packed a few things, and readied himself for the trip. He had a mission to fulfill.

Seated at his desk, Fray Diego Lucero, the Inquisitor of Segovia, was pouring over the records of the procedural trials of certain Judaizers, hoping to find some thing he might have overlooked in their testimonies. He held up two documents of confession, and looked from one to the other, comparing the statement of one prisoner with that of another, searching for contradictions. As he studied the statements, he heard the door open and a shuffle of footsteps. It was an aide, he thought, coming to disturb him in another moment of concentration. Lucero was conscious of the presence of a figure looming above the documents; nonetheless, he continued to concentrate on the documents. Finally, after a while, Lucero looked up, wondering what the latest problem was. He put the documents down when he saw who it was, and rose respectfully from his chair.

"Dávila! By the cross of Calatrava, it is really you."

Dávila extended his hand. "Yes, Fray Lucero. How good it is to see you. Pardon me for interrupting you."

Lucero motioned him to sit down. "Please, Bishop Dávila, it is always my pleasure to see you again. We rarely have time nowadays to talk about the years we spent together at the seminary. Those were the good days when we were both students. So many years have passed since that time."

The Bishop answered, "Many years, good years in the service of our Lord. You with the business of the Holy Office, I with the diocese of Segovia."

Lucero chuckled. "Each of us in his own way, eh? How amazed I am to see you. Tell me, what brings you to me here . . . here in the building of the Holy Office?"

Dávila said, "Church matters. I wish to examine the files of certain New Christians recently imprisoned, and I wish to request that I personally be allowed to interrogate them."

"Why?," asked Lucero.

The Bishop replied, "I have reason to believe that they may be links to suspected Judaizers in my diocese."

"By all means," said Lucero. "I am delighted to learn that people like yourself are finally becoming involved in the activities of the Holy Office."

The Bishop spoke, as if explaining his visit. "In years past, I did my share against the heretics in Segovia. But now I have been deceived most grievously by some I thought that I could trust. I thought that Dr. Pinto was a faithful Christian, a person beyond reproach. How mistaken could I have been! Now I have been informed that he was caught practicing the depraved Jew rites of Passover. My outrage at this man is so great that, with your permission, I wish to be given the opportunity to interrogate him and to punish him, as well as his entire nest of lying accomplices, so help me God!"

Sympathetically, Lucero asked, "Uh . . . forgive me for asking, Bishop, but have you ever interrogated a prisoner?"

Dávila stammered, "Why . . . uh . . . no, not recently . . . but in years back, 20, maybe 25 years ago, I did do something of the sort."

Lucero asked on. "And you think that these prisoners, these Judaizers or New Christians will tell you, just like that, everything you want to know?"

The Bishop answered, "Why, yes, it is not inconceivable. Why not?"

Lucero shook his head in dismay. "Ay, Bishop Davila, you are still the same naive seminarian as ever. Come with me. Let me show you how we get at the facts. Come, Bishop. My aide will get you the files that you request."

The two rose from their chairs, Lucero leading the way from his office. They walked out into the hallway, and went down two flights of stairs. Ultimately they arrived in a cold, dark basement, protected by a large stone door. In the semi-darkness, Lucero pushed hard to open the massive double-bolted door, causing it to creak noisily on its hinges. Having dislodged the door sufficiently, Lucero stepped inside and reached for a torch. Dávila followed him. Once past the door, it was apparent that they were at the top of a long winding stone staircase, the individual steps roughly hewn and covered with dust and grime. Even with the aid of the torch, it was not possible to see the bottom end of the staircase, immersed as it was in darkness. Carefully watching their steps, Lucero and Dávila went down the steps. Muted screams mixed with sharp, intermittent clanging noises came from the distance, noises from iron instruments being used somewhere in the darkness below. As they continued, the sporadic sounds, at first heard faintly, became steadily louder. Attentive as he was to each potentially perilous step, Lucero spoke not at all until they both had safely reached the bottom of the darkened staircase. It was then that the Inquisitor said, "Our function here is not only to punish crime, but also to save men's souls. For this, a full confession must be made. If the Judaizer does not wish to be saved, if he does not voluntarily confess his sins, then he forces us to use very means at our disposal to extract from him a full admission of guilt."

Lucero then opened another door, and they entered a large dimly-lit underground cavern, its acrid air assaulting their nostrils. The smell was terrible.

A horrid shriek was heard. Dávila looked about, wondering where the scream came from. They heard another shriek, and this time Dávila saw a scrawny, half-clothed man hanging from the ceiling of the cavern. The man's wrists were tied behind his back and attached to a rope from which he dangled in the air. A pulley had been placed in the ceiling, so that the rope extended through it and down to the level of the ground floor. An aide on the ground held the rope so that he was able to raise or lower the prisoner. The emaciated figure turned slowly in the air, his face contorted with pain.

Lucero explained, "This is the *strappado*. It is our first mode of treatment." The Inquisitor signaled to the aide to strap the prisoner. He pulled on the rope, and the prisoner began to rise slowly. Aware of what was to happen to him, the prisoner mumbled, "No, please . . . no more, no more, please, no, no, no . . . ." Up the man went, higher and higher, until he was at the very top of the cavern. Suddenly, the aide released the rope, and the man fell rapidly through the air. Just before the prisoner struck the ground, he was yanked to an abrupt stop in mid-air, as the rope would go no further. With the sudden halt there was a horrible tearing sound, the sound of muscles being torn and of bones being pulled out of sockets. The prisoner writhed in agony two feet from the floor, his shoulders deformed and dislocated, his wrists and feet raw and bloody. It was a grotesque sight, and Dávila's face turned pale with horror. Lucero, impressed with his own work, cooly stated, "Effective, at times. Come with me, Bishop."

The Inquisitor and Bishop Dávila walked slowly down a low-ceilinged passageway that led into another hall in the underground prison complex. Here they found a female prisoner, scantily clad, her limbs bound tightly to the sides of a wooden trough. The trough was tilted so her head was lower than her feet. A priest stood calmly next to her, exhorting her to confess, while at the same time he gave directions to the two aides operating the trough. Another priest, seated at a table a short distance away, recorded the interrogation.

Lucero told Dávila simply, "Watch."

Using a wooden implement inserted between the cords that bound the victim's limbs, the aides tightened the cords by slowly turning the implement. They turned it again and again, and still yet another turn, causing the terrified woman to scream wildly.

"Mercada Mazon, tell us the truth," said the priest calmly at her side.

The victim, in pain, stammered, "I have told you all I know. How can I tell you more?"

The priest signaled with his head, and another turn of the cord was ordered. The victim's arms turned a darkish blue, and it seemed as if every vein was about to burst.

"My arms," she screamed, "I cannot feel my arms. Señores, please, I have said all that I can . . . my arms, señores, please, for the love of God, no more, señores."

Another turn of the cord was ordered, and the woman screamed in place. "Ay, my arms! It hurts! My arms, ay, my arms! No, ay, ay ,ay, my arms! Tell me what you want me to say, and I will say it."

"Tell us the truth," the priest instructed her.

The woman cried, "I have told you the truth. I have told you everything. What more can I say?"

Another turn of the cord was ordered.

"I advise you to tell the truth, Mercada Mazon," said the priest.

The woman screamed in one loud frenzied wail of pain, her arms limp and discolored.

The priest motioned to the aides. The cords were loosened. One aide pulled on her hair with one hand, and, using the other hand, pushed hard against the victim's forehead so she could not move her head. The other aide forced open her mouth, jamming a strip of linen down her throat. The woman resisted but to no avail. She choked as more of the linen was forced into her mouth.

Then they put a funnel in her mouth, forcing water down her throat and nostrils. The victim choked and gasped, straining for breath as the two jars of water were forced down her. Finally, they pulled the linen out of her mouth, and she gasped and coughed. The priest at her side resumed the questioning.

"Mercada Mazon, tell us what it is you have done."

"I have done nothing," said the hapless victim, still coughing.

"Do not bring false testimony against yourself," answered the priest. The cords were tightened again, and the victim screamed again in pain. Again and again the cords were tightened, and the victim broke out into another piercing wail.

The tormented woman on the trough said, "Tell me what you want me to say, and I will say it. Tell me."

The Inquisitor repeated himself, "Tell us what you have done."

The victim stammered, "I . . . I do not know what I have done. Is it because I lit candles on Friday night to observe the Sabbath day?"

A short distance away, Lucero turned towards Dávila and said, "She is coming around. She will confess, this one. You will see."

Dávila, half-dazed, said nothing, but kept on observing the interrogation.

Another turn of the cord was ordered. The victim continued to screech.

"God, help me! Take me away from here. Please, señores, what is it you want me to say? My arms, señores, you are breaking them. Oh, how they hurt! Oh, please, señores, my arms, they hurt, my arms, how they hurt, oh, ay, ay, ay . . . my arms . . . stop it, please, señores, do not hurt me anymore."

The Inquisitor ordered another turn of the cords. He told the woman calmly, "Tell us the truth, and we will stop."

"Oh, señor, stop now and I will tell you everything. Yes, everything. Stop, please . . . ay, my arms, my arms, my arms . . ."

The woman seemed to become incoherent.

Losing his patience, the Inquisitor said, "Strip her."

The aide tore the remaining garments off her body. The woman lifted her head from the trough and saw herself completely naked. She began to sob in short fits, her glassy eyes laden with tears.

"Oh, señores, cover my nakedness. Why have you done such a thing, señor, that you put a woman to shame. This is against the Law of God."

The Inquisitor ordered another turn. Her sobs, her wail, her pain — all became jumbled in a torrent of anguish.

"What Law of God?" asked the Inquisitor.

The only response was a litany of moans and sobs.

The cord was twisted another time. The aide reported the cord was turned fifteen times, but the Inquisitor ordered one more turn.

The victim yelled, "Ay, my arms, ay, ay, my arms . . . Señor, stop. I will tell you . . . the Law . . . the Law of God is the one given to Moses. Yes, that is the Law, but I know little of it. Now, please, señor, untie my arms, untie me, I beseech you, I have told you all I know. Untie me and cover my nakedness, good señor, please, I beg of you, cover my shame."

The Inquisitor continued, "Mercada Mazon, who told you to keep the Law?"

The woman, seeking a respite from her torture, answered feebly, "Let me go and I will tell you all."

The cord was tightened further.

The Inquisitor persisted, "Who told you to keep the Law?"

The woman shrieked in pain, but could say nothing intelligible. Her blue arms squeezed to the bone, she squirmed to get loose, but it was pointless.

The Inquisitor said, "Tell us who told you to keep the Law, or we shall pour the water."

The victim screamed, "I have told you everything, you servants of the Devil!"

The woman screamed and screamed again. One aide grabbed her head as before, and the other aide again jammed the linen down her mouth. Again a jar of water was poured down the victim's throat, followed by still another jar, as the victim choked, thrashed, and gasped for air.

Lucero led Dávila away from the area. "This one is almost on the verge of breaking. It will not be long." They continued walking through the stone complex, Lucero elaborating on the success of his methods, proudly boasting of how many Judaizers the Holy Office had brought to confession and repentance. Bishop Dávila, listening quietly, finally said, "Impressive as the methods of the Holy Office may be, dear Fray Lucero, I still wish to question the prisoners alone."

Lucero was indignant. "I really cannot understand this folly of yours, Bishop, in wishing to interrogate the prisoners yourself."

Dávila spoke forcefully, "Folly or no folly, I insist. Is that clear?"

Lucero said, "But our methods are so effective. You saw with your own eyes what success we are having."

Dávila did not budge. "You have your methods. I have mine. Let me remind you that I have executed my share of *Marranos*. Let me also remind you that I am the Bishop here. I shall speak to the prisoners *alone*."

Lucero agreed with poor grace. "Pulling rank on me already, dear friend? I do not appreciate those who take advantage of my hospitality, nor does the Holy Office forget those who do not honor its protocols of interrogation. Very well, Bishop, if that is your wish, then so be it. The guard will go with you for your protection."

Bishop Dávila answered, "Thank you, Fray Lucero. When I am finished with this interrogation, I will provide you with a full report for your records."

Lucero replied sarcastically, "Yes, Bishop Dávila, whatever you say."

The guard and Dávila walked into the dungeon. The cold of the underground area chilled Dávila, and he pulled his cloak tighter to keep warm. In the dungeon, it was difficult to see. It was dark, with only a few slivers of light from distant torches, and the Bishop wondered how it was that the guard could find his way about with such faint illumination. Yet he wondered more about the effect of the imprisonment on the starving victims — caged in a cold dark cell, subjected to torture with the *strappado* and the *cordeles*, isolated from friend and family, reduced to shadows of their former selves. He wondered about his imprisoned relatives, wondered how they would stand up to the Inquisition's instruments of pain. It was not humanly possible, he thought, for anyone to resist such cruel afflictions. Sooner or later the victims, including his relatives, would be broken in spirit and body. The time of reckoning was here. And if someone revealed his identity through a forced confession, would he not soon be joining his brothers and sisters in their misery?

The Bishop entered the first cell. Almost overcome by the stench of urine, he clutched his chest as if every breath was an effort. In the lightless cell, a guard gave him a candle to light his way. He now saw the narrow confines of the cell and the straw on the floor. In one corner, a sudden flurry of noise attracted his attention, and he saw a rat scamper into a crevice in the decaying wall. One figure crawled into the opposite corner, cringing with fear, head buried between the knees, hands covering the head, passively trying to avoid detection.

Dávila instructed, "I wish to see the prisoner alone."

"Yes, Bishop," said the guard, who then shouted, "You in there . . . on your feet . . . now!"

The figure stayed in place, unresponsive to the command.

Dávila said, "Let me take care of this. You may go."

"Yes, Bishop," said the guard, closing the door behind him. Candle in hand, the Bishop walked slowly through the cell. The prisoner, sensing his approach, withdrew further into the corner, covering its head with arms in expectation of blows. Without looking up from its fetal protective posture, the cowering victim sobbed, "No, please, no more . . . no more, please, no more."

The Bishop spoke softly. "Regina, look at me. Look at my face. I am not here to hurt you. I am here to help you. It is I, Juan Arias Dávila. Do you remember me?"

Regina's sobs turned to silence. After a long pause, she raised her head from between her knees and arms. In the flickering candlelight, her face, covered with dirt and grime, looked bewildered and confused. Her lips were cut, and her eyes winced from the unaccustomed light of the taper held at close range. Then, as her eyes adjusted themselves, and she was finally able to discern the features of the man in front of her, an expression of relief came over her face. She broke into tears and hugged Dávila.

The Bishop took note of his niece's wounds. Her upper arms were discolored in a hideous mass of black-and-blue welts, rope cuts, and scabs from the cords. The gruesome sight of her mangled flesh made Davila shudder. Unable to look at the festering wounds, he embraced his niece.

"Regina, Regina, what have they done to you? How could anyone do such a thing? How great must be your pain. In the name of God, how can people do such evil?"

"Uncle Juan, how good it is to see you. Even now, uncle, you have not forgotten us. Even now, here in Hell itself, you have remembered that you are still one of us."

The Bishop replied in a whisper. "Yes, Regina, I remember. I also came to tell you that Hermosa is safe in my monastery. A man named Alberto is with her."

Regina's relief could be no greater. "Thank God," she said, feebly hugging him tighter. "Thank God at least for that. I was afraid they might have been caught, my Hermosa and Alberto, too, and that they would suffer here as we do. At least they are safe. What about us, uncle Juan? Can you get us out of here?"

Bishop Dávila shrugged his shoulders, unable to tell his niece the hard truth. "I am working on it. There may be a way," he said, knowing it was not so. "In the meantime, I have brought something for you. It is a potion, a potion to make the pain more bearable."

The Bishop answered, "I will do whatever I can, Regina, believe me, I will do my utmost. But surely you understand that I must take every precaution to avoid suspicion. One mistake is all it takes, Regina."

Regina nodded her head in silent understanding, her eyes dazed and distant. She sluggishly pulled herself away from her uncle, now understanding the situation.

The Bishop said, "I must go now. Is there any message for Hermosa?" Regina weakly grabbed his arm. "Tell her . . . tell her that I need her, that I miss her so very much. Tell her to preserve whatever honor is left of our family name and to be true to the religion of our fathers. Tell her how much we love her . . . and that her love for us means more than anything else in the world. If all is to be taken from us, tell her that it is our love for her, our memory of her, that will sustain us while we still have life . . ."

Regina could talk no further. Tears mixed with dirt ran down her cheeks. She sobbed in erratic fits, resting her head on her uncle's shoulder, seeking some consolation. Her uncle, able to do little more, took her into his arms and caressed her hair sympathetically, plucking the bits of straw from her disheveled hair.

Regina's sobs ultimately subsided, and she was able to speak again. "You must ask Alberto to forgive me . . . for my petty spite, for all the obstacles that I placed in his way. He is to marry Hermosa with all my blessings. You must see to it that they marry soon, even if her father and I are still imprisoned. You must swear to me that you will tell them so."

"I shall tell them," said the Bishop.

Regina's voice cracked. "Juan Arias, my life is coming to an end. I will die soon, separated from the ones I love, a beaten old woman living out the last days of her life in pain and darkness. If there is any value left to my life, it is to warn others of the fate that may await them. We waited too long, uncle Juan, we waited until it was too late to get away. Hermosa, Alberto, even you, uncle, while you still have the chance, all of you must try to get away before it is too late. My life is finished, my life and my husband's, too. I thank you, uncle Juan, for all you have done for us, but it is not worthwhile for you to risk your life for us. Nay, let us say farewell, dear uncle. You have done your duty to your kin in need. Now it is time to save yourself, uncle Juan Arias. You must throw off your disguise and return to your people, now, before it is too late."

Dávila sat next to her quietly, thinking about what she said and wondering if it was already too late.

The Inquisitor Lucero walked toward the prison cells. He tiptoed cautiously on one of the upper rafters that lay atop the cells. Above each cell, there was a hole in the ceiling for listening to conversations underneath. Lucero crouched low to listen, but he had to loosen his robe first.

Down below, the Bishop said softly, "I shall tell her, Regina, every word you said. But now I must go. Be strong and of good courage. There is something else, however, that I must ask you to do before I leave." Dávila told her what it was he wanted her to do.

Lucero got down quietly on his knees, being careful not to make the slightest noise. Gripping the rafter firmly, he positioned himself silently on his side.

Regina, her voice faint, said, "Goodbye, Juan. Tell Alberto to take good care of my daughter. And Juan, one other thing, your identity is safe with me. Trust me. Now, let us do what we have to do."

Bishop Dávila stood up. "Ready?" he asked.

The prisoner nodded affirmatively.

Lucero finally put his ear against the hole. He could not see those in the cell, but he was able to hear them.

Bishop Dávila pretended to slap Regina across the face. Regina made a simulated scream, smiling weakly as she did so. The Bishop shouted, "I say to you, tell me who he is. Now! Do you hear?" Dávila feigned another slap, eliciting another simulated scream. Then another slap and another scream. The Bishop pretended to kick the prisoner, kicking instead the stone wall.

Lucero listened intently, a malicious smile on his face. It was obvious that the Bishop, crude as his methods were, had his own way of handling such matters.

The guard, hearing the commotion, rushed to the door thinking that the Bishop was in need of his protection. As the guard opened the door, Dávila missed a kick at the prisoner's head. Walking away from his sobbing victim, the Bishop angrily lashed out at her as he stepped out of the cell.

"Your impudence will not go unpunished, *Marrano* swine . . ." Then to the guard, he added, "Lock the door and do with her as you please."

The guard, looking inside, shouted, "You in there . . . I will get you later." He bolted the door.

The Bishop said, "She has had enough. For the moment, leave her alone. Come with me immediately. I want to interrogate the other prisoners."

"Yes, Bishop," said the guard, leading the way to another cell.

Lucero rose from his awkward position on the rafters. The Bishop's ways had not worked. He warned him they wouldn't, but the Bishop paid him no heed. Dávila, he concluded, was a stubborn seminarian of the old school who could learn a thing or two from the Holy Office. He would teach Bishop Dávila a lesson, and he would do so by forcibly extracting the confessions that Dávila was obviously incapable of obtaining. Returning to his office, the Inquisitor waited patiently to receive Bishop Dávila's admission of failure.

Upon his return to the monastery two days later, Bishop Dávila was welcomed at the entrance by the same monk who had seen him off.

"Welcome back, Bishop, thanks be to God," said the monk.

Dismounting, Dávila acknowledged the welcome. "Thank you most kindly, brother. This was a most difficult trip, very difficult, for reasons other than physical hardship."

The monk took charge of the horses's reins. "I understand, Bishop. Here, let me help you. May I ask how it goes with your sister?"

The Bishop cleared his throat. "What can I say? The fate of all humanity has caught up with her. She is but skin and bones. Truly her soul's departure is close at hand."

"With it, her soul will be free to enjoy eternal bliss in Heaven."

Acknowledging this, the Bishop sighed resignedly. "So it will be with my sister, if it please our Lord."

As they entered the monastery, the monk said, "Bishop Dávila, you look very tired. Allow me the privilege of preparing some soup for you."

The Bishop raised his hand in protest. "Please, no. Not tonight. I am fasting on behalf of my sister. Bring instead to my office the young man and woman whose pilgrimage I have delayed. I wish to thank them for informing me of my sister's grave condition."

"Yes, Bishop, I will do so immediately," said the monk, who promptly disappeared. He reappeared a short while later to escort the two pilgrims. Alberto and Hermosa, anxious to speak with the Bishop, found it difficult to suppress their excitement at Dávila's return.

"The young man and woman, Bishop Dávila," said the monk.

"Thank you. That will be all, Brother," said the Bishop. The monk obeyed the order and left the room.

Dávila spoke matter-of-factly. "Hermosa, your parents are alive and are as well as can be expected under the present circumstances. Your mother and father both send their love. They ask you to marry Alberto and to be true to the faith of our fathers."

Hermosa began to weep. "Oh Mama . . . Papa . . . I will, oh I will . . . and tell me, uncle, is there any chance they could be set free?"

Dávila, his eyes cast down, seemed embarrassed by what he had to say. "It could take months, perhaps even years, before the Inquisition passes final judgment on your parents. There is absolutely no prospect for a quick release. I did what I could to contact someone with inside knowledge of the affairs of the Holy Office, but so far I have had little success. The likelihood is that your parents will be in prison for several years to come."

Hermosa wept even more on hearing this.

Alberto put his arm tenderly around her waist. Hermosa could not stop crying. "O no! Not Mama, not Papa! I can't live without them!"

Alberto hugged her tighter, unable to bring his beloved's tears to a stop.

Dávila continued, "Time is short. You must leave the monastery immediately . . . certainly by tomorrow morning. I have extended my influence on this matter, perhaps more than I should have, and questions will certainly be asked. How much money have you?"

Alberto spoke tersely, "Not much."

Dávila pulled out a key from a drawer, unlocked the closet, and pulled out a large bag of coins.

"Here are five hundred maravedis for your needs. Go to Alcalá de Henares to the Inn of El Caballero. Ask for Mendoza. He will get you on a ship leaving the country."

Alberto said, "We thank you, sir, for all you have done for us. How can we ever hope to repay you?"

Dávila answered, "In such matters, one does not think of repayment. Survival is its own reward. Both of you, go to your rooms and ready yourselves. I will see you in the morning before you leave. You have a long ride ahead of you tomorrow.

Hermosa did not move, caught up in her own sorrow.

The Bishop walked over to Hermosa and grabbed her firmly by the shoulders. "Look at me, Hermosa," said Dávila sharply. Hermosa looked up, her eyes filled with tears.

Dávila spoke to her firmly. "Hermosa, your mother is a woman of valor. There is no woman more brave than she. If you wish to do your mother honor, you must be strong and of good courage. The road ahead of you is long and perilous, and there is no mercy for those who are weak and half-hearted. Conquer your tears, Hermosa. Spill them not on this land that consumes the downtrodden. Be like your mother — a proud lioness who is ever defiant of those who seek her harm, a lioness who will keep the hunters at bay while you, the cub, have an opportunity to escape. This is not a time for tears, Hermosa. This is a time for valor."

Hermosa wiped the tears from her eyes, bit her lip, and tried to smile. She was back to being herself again. She went up to her uncle, and kissed him on the cheek. "Trust me, uncle Juan. I will cry no more," she said, "I will be a lioness too, like my mother. Thank you for what you have done."

"May the God of Israel be with you, Hermosa and Alberto," the Bishop said in their parting. "May He be with you always."

The following morning, the Bishop bade farewell to his visitors. As Alberto and Hermosa rode away, Dávila stood silently at the window, feeling an impulse to join them. His life, his church career was at a point of no return, and the momentary hope of a fresh beginning was quickly suppressed with the weight of reality.

Choosing holy orders in his youth had seemed the best way to cover his Converso trail. Molding himself after those whose social approbation he sought, Dávila had out-Christianed the Christians. He became one of them, lived like them, believed like them, acted like them, till at times he found it hard to think he had been anything but a

Christian. But no man can completely forget the cradle of his origins, however humble they may be. Strangely, the more Christian he became, the more he yearned to understand where he had come from. In the pursuit of the alien, he found the familiar. In his escape from himself, he found himself. In the end, he found his beginning.

Reestablishing his ties with the past, Bishop Dávila sought long lost relatives, among them his nephew Marco Pinto, now a prominent Segovian physician. The association was not without risk, and Dávila took every possible precaution to avoid being detected. One encounter with Pinto led to another, the intitial suspicious exchange developing into shared intimacies and ultimately to friendship. They helped each other. Marco would supply Dávila with reports on the local Converso activities, and the Bishop would reciprocate by securing falsified certificates of purity of Christian blood. It was Dávila, through his connections in the higher echelons of the Church, who had obtained Alberto's certificate.

But any assistance that Dávila could offer his Converso brothers did not lessen his estrangement. While being a Christian distanced him from the Jews, his need for secrecy as a Bishop alienated him from his Converso brethren. It was clear that if his identity were to remain secret, only a select few Conversos could be entrusted with the knowledge of their secret church contact. Marco Pinto and the tailor had been the only ones who knew. And now, the only family he could call his own, the small family of Converso comrades who had shared his darkest secret, had been taken away from him by the very institution that he served. Dávila was once again alone in the world. Bereft of friend and family, he realized his only course was to continue his life as the Bishop of Segovia. It was a life he no longer wanted, but it was a life he could not bring himself to reject.

Dávila thought of what Marco Pinto had said in the prison cell. With unkempt beard and dirt-smudged face, the physician truly looked the part of one who had gone from riches to rags. But Dávila could not forget those softly rendered words that came from Pinto's bloodied lips:

"Uncle Juan Arias, listen to me. Of all the false confessions that I ever made to you as a would-be Christian, let this be my confession as a would-be Jew. I ask not for forgiveness. Only God can grant that. I ask for your understanding which you have always graciously given.

"As I sit here rotting away in the blackness of this dungeon, with no one to speak to, waiting for my torturers, I compare the past with my present lot. I try to find a reason for what has happened, and I think I realize how this wretched situation could have been prevented.

"It is more than my not having left Spain soon enough. It is the culmination of a series of little mistakes, none of which produced any injurious consequence, that led me to foolishly believe I was somehow immune to calamity.

"How greatly I have erred! Indeed, so great is my error that I must forever suffer its consequences. Yet I would willingly bear all my afflictions, acknowledging them to be the rightful punishment for my misdeeds, if I could be assured that only I would be the sole victim of my miscalculation. But it is not to be.

"I, Marco Pinto, who have devoted my life to relieving the sufferings of others, have become the cause of pain to my beloved wife and to my friends. I, who have always cared about the welfare of others, have unleashed the forces of evil upon those whom I love. All because I failed to heed the signals of danger. What blindness kept me from seeing the unmistakable omens? What deafness kept me from hearing my wife's oft-repeated wishes? What was it, I ask you? Was it my arrogant pride, or perhaps my fear of losing my wealth? Had I left Spain when Regina urged, I would have lost far less than now. This is the needless suffering I have brought upon myself and others.

"Do not offer me your potion for my pain. I want no drug to lessen the pains of my torture nor to deprive me of my sense of guilt. I deserve to suffer. I want to feel the hurt. I want to punish myself for hurting my friends and family. And as the Inquisition consumes my body, I will let my conscience lacerate my soul for what I have done. Leave me, Juan Arias. Leave me alone to bear the consequences of my unpardonable mistake."

As requested, Dávila left Marco Pinto to wither away in the cold dark cell. Thus he remembered the moment of their parting, the physician languishing silently in a corner of straw and dust, he the Bishop returning to his cross-begotten cage of gold.

Fearing what had happened to Pinto would also happen to him, Juan Arias knew that his best security was within the bosom of the Church. He, Juan Arias Dávila, Bishop of Segovia, had long ago sacrificed his conscience for the security offered by the priestly cage of his own creation. As he had advised Alberto and Hermosa, so now he told himself: survival is its own reward.

Chapter 9

Shortly after Passover, the event everyone feared came to pass: the King and Queen issued an edict ordering the expulsion of all Jews from Spain. The declarations of the public scribes in every town and city made it painfully clear: all Jews and Jewesses, of whatever age, were compelled to leave the kingdom within three months. Any Jews who failed to comply with the edict, and who dared to remain in Spain after the deadline of July 31, 1492, would suffer punishment by death and confiscation of all belongings. Only those Jews who converted to Christianity would be permitted to stay.

Everyone talked about it. Alberto and Hermosa heard it on the lips of excited wayfarers whose paths they crossed. Over and over they heard: the Jews are being expelled, the Jews are being expelled! The horrendous news of the edict motivated Alberto and Hermosa to put even further distance between themselves and their pursuers. Now the Conversos, lacking the supportive presence of the Jewish community, would be annihilated. And if Jews still had three months to choose between expulsion or conversion, the Conversos had no options and no time. Whether you were a Jew or a Converso, the only sensible thing was to leave Spain as quickly as possible.

Alberto rode slowly as he entered the city of Alcalá de Henares. When he arrived at the inn of El Caballero, he carefully dismounted. There were a few horses outside the inn, and Alberto placed his alongside the others. Within the tavern, he could hear much raucous laughter and carousing. It was not a place for a woman, and he was happy that he left Hermosa safely behind with a farmer and his wife. He wondered if he would find Miguel, the man the Bishop told him to look for. He walked inside, hand at his sword.

The air inside was thick and musty, reeking of wine and straw. Standing at the bar was a small crowd of cavaliers and sailors, their goblets already half empty, many of them with one elbow resting on the bar and a boot placed on the underlying balustrade. A few were drunk. Alberto looked about the tavern. An agent of the Hermandad, identifiable by his uniform, sat quietly at one end of the tavern. At the end of the bar, a heated discussion was going on amid bursts of wild laughter. Curious as to the cause of the merriment, Alberto walked toward the group.

What he heard was a red-haired mariner trying to gain recruits for what seemed an unbelievable voyage. The man, however absurd his intent, was resolute in his convictions.

"And I tell you, according to my calculations, it should be possible to reach the Indies by traveling west."

A sceptical cavalier shook his head. "Bah! What nonsense! Have you ever heard such a thing?" Columbus explained. "My calculations are based on the works of Marinus of Tyre and Alfragan, Moslem geographers and scholars of the greatest reputation."

One of the sailors roared in disbelief, "Scholars? And Arab scholars at that! What do they know? Have they ever set out to sea and seen the restless ocean that lies to the west — the size of its waves, aye, the monsters of the deep, and its awful, dark mysteries?"

A young sailor joined in, "Aye, and from what I have heard, there is a sharp edge where a ship can fall off . . . and then . . . and then, there is nothing . . . nothing . . ."

Columbus, vexed by this reply, said, "How can you believe in such fables? Every scholar knows the world is round."

The sailor quipped, "Then take all the scholars you want and let them sail *around* your world. We know better."

As everyone nodded in agreement, the first sailor continued. "Besides, you are forgetting one thing."

"What would that be?," asked Columbus. The sailor reached into his belt and pulled out an object, which he held tightly in his hand. He looked knowingly at Columbus with a cunning smile. "The Jews. They are leaving the country, all of them. And you know what they have? They have this."

The sailor opened up his fist. There was a gold ducat in his palm. He shoved the ducat into Columbus' face.

"Gold ducats . . . Gold. Money. Lots of it. That is what the Jews have. And they will pay dearly for anyone to take them out of Spain. That, Captain Columbus, is where the money is. What you are offering for this pointless and dangerous expedition is hardly enough — especially compared to the sure money to be gotten from carrying the Jews to ports we already know."

The other sailor slammed his fist on the bar. "Aye, why should I risk my neck for an idiotic venture like yours . . ."

The cavalier joined in. "That is right . . . and maybe fall off the edge."

The captain was unruffled. "All right, I will match what the Jews are paying."

The first sailor took the ducat and bit it with his teeth. "Look, Columbus, why don't you look somewhere else, eh? I am not interested in pursuing your wild ideas, however much you pay me, understand? Not interested!"

Another sailor added, "Going west — to the Indies! What will they think of next?"

Everone guffawed and resumed their drinking and carousing. As Columbus walked away frustrated, Alberto stopped him.

"Excuse me, Captain, I heard what you were saying. You have ships, do you?"

Columbus nodded, thinking he had found a recruit after all. "Yes, I do. Three sound ships authorized by the crown of Castile. Three caravels that will open a route to the Indies, or so I hope."

Alberto's interest grew. "Will you be stopping anywhere else along the way?"

Columbus responded, "I am afraid I do not understand."

Alberto explained. "I am a spicetrader by profession, and that is why your voyage intrigues me. If you were to find a route to the Indies, it would be enormously profitable. But right now I have a different voyage in mind. I am looking for a ship to . . . to take us, that is, my wife and myself, to North Africa . . . that is . . . ahh . . . to explore the spice market opportunities there."

Columbus spoke peremptorily. "No women aboard my ship! Please, señor, do not waste my time. I need sailors, not burdens."

Alberto apologized. "Sorry, señor."

The mariner apologized for his outburst. "I am sorry, but there is no way I can help you. Interestingly enough, I have been asked several times today by Jews who want me to take them out of Spain on the ships under my command. Of course, I cannot tolerate any request that would divert me from my mission. You understand that, do you not, sir?"

"I am not a Jew," said Alberto nervously.

Columbus apologized further. "Please do not take offense, sir. I did not mean to imply you were a Jew."

"I should hope not," said Alberto. Out of the corner of his eye, he saw the Hermandad officer look up, pay his bill, and walk out the front door. Had the man's suspicion been aroused? Alberto was not sure. To switch the conversation to a different topic, Alberto asked, "By the way, do you know a sailor named Miguel?"

Columbus smiled and pointed to a humped figure on the bar. "Miguel? That's him, the drunk on the corner . . . a good sailor he is, when he is sober. I must leave now. Good day."

Alberto turned his attention to the man called Miguel. He was a disappointing figure of a man, his head resting on its side, like a dead weight on the flat surface of the counter. With goblet in hand, Miguel snored loudly through pouting thick lips, the smell of alcohol heavy on his breath, his decaying yellowed teeth filled with foam and brew. Alberto went to the unkempt figure, wondering whether he dare wake him up. He gave Miguel a gentle shove.

"Miguel?" he said, shaking the man by the shoulders.

Miguel raised his head slightly, first lifting an eyebrow, then partially opening one eye. "Huh? . . . Huh? What ails you, youngster?"

Alberto whispered, "Are you Miguel? Bishop Dávila sends his regards."

Miguel closed his eye quickly. "Oh, he does, does he? Well, send them right back." The drunk burped, gulped down the wine in his glass, and put his head back on the table.

Alberto shook the man again. He whispered, "He said you could help me."

The eyelid rose again, revealing a bloodshot eye. The eye studied Alberto. "I am really quite thirsty, you know."

Alberto said quietly, "He said you could help me find a ship to get out of the country."

The drunk's eyes opened wide. "Thirsty I am, are you deaf?"

Alberto got the message. "Bartender, a goblet of your best Valmaseda wine." The bartender brought the wine and served it.

The drunk closed his eyes and smiled happily. Miguel took a big swig of wine from his goblet and purred with satisfaction. "Ahh, the maroon sweetness of Valmaseda. With such good taste, youngster, you will go far. What is it that you want from me?"

Alberto said, "I must leave Spain immediately. The Hermandad is after me."

The drunk stared at the red wine in his goblet, swishing for his open eye's admiration. "Ahhh," he purred as he took another drink. "The Hermandad, eh? So why did you not say so in the first place?"

Alberto asked, "Can you help me?"

"No," came the answer quickly.

"What?" said Alberto, startled.

Miguel lifted his head from the counter, opening the other bloodshot eye, trying to be as alert as he could. "No more ships or sailors available for three months until the Jews leave . . . hic! . . . The Jews have all the ships tied up. Every one of them"

"But I . . . I . . .," said Alberto, surprised.

Miguel finished the sentence for him. "You are a Jew . . . hic! I know . . . a secret Jew in trouble . . . a New Christian as they say . . . I am very sorry, I still can't help you." The man gulped down the rest of the wine in the goblet. "Sorry," Miguel said, as he rested his head once again on the counter.

Alberto left the drunk to his stupor and walked down the tavern entrance. As he did so, two Hermandad officers entered through the door. One of them was the officer who had previously been sitting in the tavern. The other was an Hermandad guard, the right side of his face badly burned. Alberto recognized the man immediately; it was the guard who had fought with him in the underground tunnel and into whose face he had rammed the flaming torch. The guard, his disfigured face contorted in an expression of rage, recognized Alberto and drew his sword.

Alberto moved quickly. He smashed his boot in the first Hermandad officer's stomach, knocking the wind out of him. The scar-faced officer swung with his sword at Alberto one, two, three times, but Alberto managed to avoid them all. He pretended to slip to the floor as the second officer, his eyes wild with hate, lunged toward him. Alberto swerved at the last moment, and he sent the second officer flying, sending the man crashing onto a nearby table. By this time, the first officer had recovered and was ready to fight again. Alberto lashed out with a right hook and sent him tumbling to the ground. His scar-faced opponent, dazed by the fall but certainly not disabled, came roaring back. Alberto ran out the tavern door, waiting for the Hermandad guard to come out. As the guard emerged, he drove a fist into the man's midsection, followed by a blow to the man's head. The guard fell to the ground in a slump of forest green.

Alberto ran to his horse, unhitched it from the post, and rode away quickly. He had been right after all. It was no place for Hermosa.

Don Enrique Domínguez, head of the local Hermandad of Segovia, was furious. After the fiasco at the tavern, the sailors and cavaliers had spread damaging rumors about the ineptitude of the Hermandad officers. The incident was shameful to everyone associated with the Brotherhood, and he made it clear to those involved that he would not tolerate any further incompetence.

As the two Hermandad officers stood stiffly at attention in his office, he rebuked them severely for their disgraceful performance. "You fools! You bunch of bumbling fools! Can you do no better than this? Never have I heard of Hermandad officers being humiliated like this, by a *Marrano* of all people. He humiliated us at the Pinto residence, and he has humiliated us now at the inn of El Caballero."

The first officer, his left eye swollen and discolored, tried to speak, "But, sir, he was incredibly quick and strong."

Domínguez shouted him down. "No excuses, young man. You are an Hermandad officer under my command. Another mistake like this and out you go. I want to catch this criminal and roast him alive. He must be found and dispatched. No one can humiliate an Hermandad officer and live to tell about it. Do you hear me? No one!"

"Yes, sir," said the first officer stiffly.

The other officer spoke. "Sir, I want him as badly as you do. See this scar on my face? He did this to me. I will capture this dog, Galante, and I will chop off his head. We think we know where he is, or at least the direction he is headed. We made inquiries among the villagers; someone who fits his description was seen on a back road headed toward Segovia. A beautiful young woman is riding with him."

Domínguez smashed his fist into his palm. "Then that's him. Good, he is going back where he came from. We'll be waiting for him. Alert the authorities in neighboring cities."

The first officer replied, "Yes, sir, I will do so immediately." As the two men started to leave, Domínguez called out to them again, "One other thing . . . the King and Queen have given us secret orders concerning some of the Jewish leaders. I want both of you to report to me in the morning for this secret mission. No word about this to anyone.

Now go, get out of here."

"Yes, sir," said the first officer.

"It will not happen again," said the officer with the scar on his face, a determined tone in his voice.

Domínguez waved them off. Deeds, not promises, were what he wanted.

Chapter 10

Alberto and Hermosa wandered on, traveling at night to avoid detection. If they were too tired, they stayed a night in a traveler's inn and bought food at a local market the next morning. Still posing as brother and sister on a pilgrimage to Santiago, they continued to elude the Hermandad. But Alberto knew the continual traveling was too strenuous for Hermosa. Unaccustomed to sleeping on hard rocky ground and disturbed at the separation from her now imprisoned parents, the physician's daughter was troubled and exhausted. The physical hardship of the journey, the daily loss of sleep, and her mental anguish made her melancholic: she sighed often, and there was a wistful look in her eyes.

Alberto noticed these subtle changes in his beloved. Her striking beauty was undiminished: her blue eyes were as dazzling as ever, her nose sculptured to perfection, her eyebrows two finely drawn arches of silken brown. Yet the tender face with these flawless features bore an expression of episodic sadness. Whenever Alberto questioned her about her feelings, she maintained that nothing was the matter: she would smile her magnificent smile and banish the sadness from her eyes. Nevertheless, Alberto worried about her.

He knew they had to get out of Spain. But how? The seaports were full of Inquisition officials who checked out anyone seeking to leave the kingdom. It might be possible to sneak across the Portuguese border and settle there. There was no Inquisition in Portugal, and thousands of Jews were streaming across the border. Why not pose as one of them? Why not pose as Jews? Hermosa and he could put the red circular patch on their right shoulders, obtain the necessary documents, and flee the country. With all the disorder at the border towns, this should be easy. They would even be able to use the main roads and inns along the way. It would lessen the hardship on Hermosa. Most of all, Inquisition officials would be looking for Christians attempting to hide their Jewish ways; they would not be looking for crypto-Jews identifying openly as Jews.

As Alberto had once secured written testimony of his Old Christian lineage, so now he sought to obtain evidence of his undisputed Jewish background. In his wanderings, he heard that there was a famous leader of the Jews named Abravanel. According to popular reports, Abravanel had gone into hiding in the outskirts of Guadalajara at a country estate belonging to Don Iñigo López de Mendoza, the Duke of the Infantado. It was from this estate that Abravanel was reportedly supervising the exodus of the Jews.

It suited Alberto's needs perfectly. They would not even need to enter the city of Guadalajara to contact Abravanel. They could avoid attracting the attention of the ubiquitous Hermandad. Deciding this was what they needed to do, they set forth on horseback for Guadalajara in the dark of night.

After two nights of riding, Alberto and Hermosa arrived at the outskirts of the city. In a meadow close to the river Henares, they dismounted and slept the first untroubled rest they'd had in weeks. With eager excitement, they awoke ready to ride once again. For weeks they had been hiding from the sun; now, in the brightness of midday, they rode through the flat Castilian terrain in search of Abravanel.

The roads leading from Guadalajara were thick with Jewish refugees, their carts laden with valuables and other possessions. Hermosa, observing the traffic of Jewish exiles, commented, "You know, Alberto, I envy them. They have given up everything — their belongings, their homes, their land. They have given it all up for their faith, our faith."

"We will do no less," said Alberto, nodding in agreement. He directed his horse to the main road and asked refugees where Abravanel could be found. Everyone knew Don Isaac Abravanel, as this famous rabbi was called, and they told Alberto how to reach the isolated Mendoza estate two leagues to the west of the city. Since he was coming from the west, Alberto reversed his direction and passed once again into the brush-lined countryside.

A short while later, Alberto and Hermosa arrived at the secluded Mendoza estate in search of Abravanel. Crouching out of sight in a wooded area, they watched what was going on before making any rash move. The estate was surrounded by a high stone wall with only one point of entry, a wooden front gate protected by a guard. Alberto bided his time carefully. He waited to see if something might happen that could lead to his meeting Don Isaac Abravanel. He was not the only one who waited.

On a craggy hill overlooking the Mendoza estate, Don Enrique Domínguez, head of the Hermandad of Segovia, waited along with his two henchmen. Since dawn, they had waited to undertake the secret mission ordered by the King and Queen. They had been commanded to abduct the spiritual head of the Jews, Don Isaac Abravanel, and to bring him to baptism. The mission was complicated by Abravanel's hiding, which meant the Hermandad had lost the element of surprise and could expect some resistance. The protection offered by the Mendoza estate was considerable, and Don Enrique still had not found a way to penetrate its walls. It was worth the wait, because in bringing this spiritual leader of the Jews into the bosom of the Church, it would be another triumph for the greater glory of God, Spain, and Don Enrique Domínguez. Although the capture of the Pinto family brought Don Enrique some local fame, the completion of this mission would make him known throughout the kingdom. If Abravanel could be brought to his knees and to faith in Christ, it would break the resistance of many others. When informed that their great rabbi had submitted to baptism, many Jews would be inclined to do the same. Abravanel was the key: if he succumbed, the others would, too.

Domínguez knew that it was a difficult, perhaps an impossible task to bring the well-guarded Don Isaac Abravanel into custody. When he talked about it with his advisors, the Grand Inquisitor Tomás de Torquemada and the Segovian priest Diego Lucero, they agreed that any close relative of Abravanel would also be acceptable. But the relative also had to bear the Abravanel name. The Church must be able to proclaim to the world that the faith of the Abravanel family had been shattered from within. Of course, there was always the prospect that if a close relative had been converted to Christianity one way or another, Don Isaac Abavanel himself might be induced to do so; but even if this did not occur, at least the chief rabbi might delay his departure and thus fall into the Hermandad trap.

Domínguez waited patiently. In a thicket of pine trees, behind large boulders surrounded by dry brush, the three Hermandad officers observed the Mendoza estate. The elusive prey, Don Isaac Abravanel, was nowhere to be seen. The guard never strayed outside the stone walls; he spent most of his time at the observation tower next to the front gate. Only after a visitor was cleared for admission would the guard come down from the tower and unbolt the gate from within. The visitors were few — an occasional courier, a rabbi and his family come to give their parting greeting, a mule-driver bringing parcels of food. The only visitor of any significance was the Marquis of Cádiz who, accompanied by four cavaliers, was allowed entry. What business a Christian nobleman such as the Marquis of Cádiz could possibly have with the accursed Jew inside was beyond Domínguez's comprehension. The Hermandad head, anxious to flush the Jew out of his lair, continued to wait for the right moment.

On the estate grounds, the Abravanel belongings were packed and ready. For two weeks now Don Isaac and his wife Esther had been selling one household item after another. Don Isaac's vast personal library, account books, and mementos had been moved to this secluded country estate of the Duke of the Infantado. And practically all of it remained packed, ready to be moved at a moment's notice.

Don Isaac had squared away his tax-collecting affairs, transferring all debts owed personally to him over to the Crown for collection. The total amount exceeded one million maravedis. In exchange, Abravanel was allowed to take out one thousand ducats. Although it was not a great sum compared to the wealth he had once possessed, it was more than sufficient for his family's needs, and it would serve him in good stead in the Italian city-state of Naples to which he intended to flee.

Yet Don Isaac had more important matters to worry about than his own personal finances. Up to the last moment, he was busy overseeing the Jewish exodus from Spain, helping to assemble fleets of caravels at the various ports. He also protested the behavior of the custom guards at the border, who were reported to be charging an exit toll of twelve maravedis on each Jewish household, as well as half a real per person. Likewise, in Ciudad Rodrigo, each Jewish family was being made to pay first a real, then five reales total, along with an inspection fee of thirty-five maravedis per household. Abravanel dispatched a letter of protest to the local authorities and to the Crown, requesting that measures be taken to correct such abuses.

But there was only so much he could do. And as the Jews of nearby Guadalajara, his hometown for the last year, began to leave, Don Isaac felt it was time for him to leave as well. It was only two weeks more until the deadline for the Edict, when all Jews had to leave Spain, would expire. And with every passing day, the danger to him and his family increased.

His wife Esther likewise fretted over their welfare. Two of their sons, Joseph and Samuel, along with their families had already fled the country. Only Judah, the eldest son, and his family were still in Spain. Judah sent word he would soon be coming to the Mendoze estate on the outskirts of Guadalajara. Esther wished Judah would hurry. Having completed all her packing, she would pace nervously up and down the house, wondering when her first-born son would show up. Had Judah perhaps been detained as had Don Isaac's nephew, Joseph, on some trumped-up charges of not having satisfied all their debts? She feared it might be so.

"What is keeping Judah?" she asked her husband repeatedly. "Why doesn't he send us a message to let us know when we can expect him?"

"Judah said he would be here soon," said Don Isaac calmly. "I have never had any reason to doubt him."

"Yes, but how soon?" retorted Esther. "It is already one week since we heard from him. My God, two more weeks, Isaac, that is all the time we have. We cannot wait much longer if we are to catch that boat from Valencia. If we miss that boat . . ."

Don Isaac frowned. "We will not miss the boat, Esther."

"But, Isaac, we have so little time."

"We will not miss the boat, I assure you of that."

Despite her husband's assurances, Esther still worried. The prospect of being trapped in Spain terrified her, and she knew that her heart would know no peace until she and all of her family had forsaken this land of Edomites. Where, o where, was Judah and his wife and their grandson, little Isaac Abravanel? When would they come? Each time a visitor came through the gate she thought it might be Judah. But it never was. Esther would signal to let them come in. She would graciously welcome them all — most were close friends from Guadalajara — and wished them Godspeed and a safe trip. The visits were a welcome distraction from her worry, yet they did not put her mind at ease, waiting and yearning as she did to see her poet-philosopher son safe and sound.

She welcomed the visit of the Marquis of Cádiz, the great noble of Andalusia, who offered whatever assistance he could. The Marquis, accompanied by four of his best fighting cavaliers, offered to escort

Don Isaac and his family to the seaport of his choice. But Don Isaac and his wife assured him that adequate security measures had already been taken, thanks to Don Iñigo López de Mendoza, and that an escort party had already been arranged. Nonetheless, they thanked the Marquis profusely for his magnanimous offer of protection as well as for his years of friendship. The Marquis regretted that he could be of so little help; most of all, he came to deliver a parting apology to his friends.

The Marquis said, "Don Isaac, Señora Abravanel, I am ashamed of my countrymen that this abomination has come to pass. Believe me when I tell you that there were many of us who tried to stop it. I only regret that our efforts on behalf of the children of Israel were to no avail."

It was Don Isaac who comforted him. "Your efforts will not be forgotten, Marquis. We respect you for having the courage to speak on our behalf at the Alhambra, against the wishes of your King and Queen. This took great courage. As the Spanish world knows you as its greatest cavalier, so, too, we Jews will remember you as our greatest defender, as a friend who stood by us in the time of our greatest need, a royal cavalier who lived up to the highest principles of his creed."

The Marquis was touched. "Your words do me great honor, Don Isaac, an honor for which I do not deem myself to be worthy, insofar as my deeds and words were insufficient to stop the Edict. Forgive me, dear friends, for my failings, as I trust you will. In the scroll of my heart, my failure is writ large with the blackest ink of the pain I feel within. Truly, it hurts me to see you go like this. But now, good and dear friends, since it appears my service to you has come to an end, it is time to bid you farewell. I, too, shall remember you always, Don Isaac and Señora Abravanel, as the finest examples of your people whom it was my pleasure and good fortune to know. Always I will speak of you with admiration and fondness. I bid you a safe journey, my friends. May the God of the heavens protect you wherever you may go."

As the Marquis came outside the front gate, Alberto was astonished to see the famous cavalier he had served in Málaga. As the Marquis alighted upon his horse, Alberto pointed him out to Hermosa. "Hermosa, look, see that one there, that man is the Marquis of Cádiz."

"Ohh," said Hermosa in a soft admiring voice.

Alberto whispered his amazement, "I do not believe it . . . the Marquis of Cádiz!"

Hermosa urged, "Approach him now, the Marquis, before he leaves."

Alberto shook his head. "You don't understand. I've told you before. The Marquis is a believing Christian. He would turn me in to the Inquisition without hesitation."

Hermosa said, "Maybe . . . maybe not. You saved his life, remember? At least that is what you told me."

Alberto shrugged his shoulders. "Yes, it is true. But when it comes to the Inquisition, even great nobles like the Marquis have to comply. I cannot afford to take the chance."

"Then you won't approach him?" asked Hermosa.

"'No," answered Alberto.

Atop his horse, the Marquis waved to Don Isaac and Esther standing at the gate. His friends waved back. "*Adios, amigos,*" said the Marquis, as he spurred his horse and rode off with his men. The guard closed the front gate, walling his wards off from the outside world.

The stillness returned to the Mendoza estate. Alberto continued to wait.

Distracted by a rumbling in the distance of a noisy mule-driven cart, the guard looked down the road. On one of the mules was a handsome, relatively young gentleman, about thirty years of age, with black hair and black beard, his coat spun of fine weave, his bearing distinguished.

On the other side was a young woman, comely of appearance, her skin pearly white, her hair hidden by the grey scarf about her head. She carried a one-year-old child in her arms. The threesome, who came steadily closer to the gate, were Judah Abravanel with his wife and child.

The guard announced them: "Judah Abravanel and his wife are here! Judah is here!" he shouted towards the center of the estate. Leaving his observation post, he scrambled down the steps to unlock the front gate. The gate swung open, and out came the guard.

"Judah! Judah my son!" shouted Esther Abravanel as she excitedly ran out the gate, followed by Don Isaac himself. "O Judah, I worried about you so," said Esther as she clutched her son to her heaving breast. "Ay, my son, if only you knew how relieved I am to see you again — you, your wife, and your son, little Isaac, yes, all of you, safe and sound here with us."

"It is good to be here, Mama," said Judah warmly, kissing his mother, . . . "and Papa," hugging his father.

Judah's wife, Hanna, stayed on the mule, holding on to the child. Esther came up to the animal's side. "Welcome, my daughter, and you, too, little Isaac. You little rascal, you are welcome, too," she said playfully, as she squeezed the child's cheeks. The child giggled.

Domínguez ordered, "Now, men, attack!"

The three Hermandad officers burst out of the thicket. Spurring their horses, they swooped down the hill toward the estate, their swords held high in the air.

From his vantage point in the thicket, Alberto was the first to hear the sounds of the impending attack. In the distance, he could discern the sound of hooves approaching, the thunderous trampling becoming more menacing with each passing moment. Alberto saw the three armed riders converging upon the Abravanels. He saw the guard appointed to their defense shout out, "Quick, everyone, inside the gate!"

As they tried to get inside the gate, the guard drew his sword and stood there alone to face the onslaught.

The Hermandad riders smashed their way through the entrance.

Domínguez struck the outside guard with his sword, killing him with the blow.

Alberto wanted to go help the Abravanels. But Hermosa clung to him and would not let him go. "Alberto, no! Don't! The Abravanels have guards. Let them protect them. Don't leave me, Alberto, I beg of you, don't leave me alone!"

Alberto Galante was torn between his urge to aid the besieged strangers and the supplications of his beloved; he gave in to Hermosa's plea, reluctantly agreeing to be a bystander.

Domínguez and his men closed in on the Abravanels. Don Isaac and Esther ran for their lives. Judah was tugging at the reins of the mule that was carrying his panic-stricken wife and his one-year-old child. But tug as he may, he could not make the mule go fast enough to escape Domínguez and his men. The scarfaced guard rammed his horse into Judah, knocking him to the ground. Domínguez came alongside Judah's wife, Hanna, who clutched the child tightly in her arms. Domínguez wrestled with her and tried to take the child away.

"No! No! No!," she screeched hysterically, as Domínguez got a hand on the child. Still she would not let go. Domínguez slapped her in the face. He slapped her again, but she still would not let go. Domínguez grabbed her arm and pulled it off the child, wrenching the child away. With outstretched arm and with outstretched body, Hanna tried to maintain her grip on the child as Domínguez started to move away, almost pulling her off the mule. The Hermandad head struck Hanna's wrist with his sword and broke her grip. Domínguez thrust the frightened, crying child in front of his saddle, leaving Judah's wife to her river of tears. He had Abravanel's grandson. Now he wanted Don Isaac Abravanel himself.

A petrified Don Isaac and Esther watched the kidnapping of their grandson from the porch. A second guard, hearing the commotion, emerged from within the house. Abravanel instructed the guard, "They have stolen my grandchild. In the name of God, stop them!"

The guard answered them, "Get inside, hurry, *inside*! And lock the door!" Against their will, the guard forced Don Isaac and his wife back inside the house.

The two Hermandad officers closed in on the front porch of the house. Inside the house, Abravanel and his wife Esther, their bodies shaking with fear, tried to bolt the door. While one Hermandad officer clashed swords with the remaining guard, the scarfaced officer dismounted and scrambled onto the front porch. Fumbling nervously with the lock from within, Don Isaac succeeded in locking the bolt in place as the officer began to kick at the door. One blow after another shook the door, almost jarring it from its hinges, but they could not force it open. Unsuccessful, the officer left the door and went off to the aid of his comrade. Together, they overpowered the second guard and slashed him to pieces.

Domínguez rode up to them quickly. "All right, let's get out of here." The scarfaced officer remounted his horse, and the three began to ride out of the courtyard.

After Domínguez had taken away the child, Hanna got off the mule and ran after him. Screaming hysterically, her arms flailing wildly in the air, she stumbled toward the riders. "No! No! No!" she sobbed fitfully, almost falling as she ran. Judah dashed boldly in front of her, as he made a last attempt to regain their child.

As the Hermandad kidnappers rode by, Judah lunged at Domínguez, hoping to wrest his child away. For a few seconds, Judah clung to the saddle with one hand, using the other to reach for little Isaac.

Domínguez rode on, dragging Judah along with him. Domínguez shoved his hand in Judah's face to push him away and kicked him hard in the pit of his stomach. Suddenly, Judah let go and fell backwards, his hands grabbing his abdomen, his body tumbling once again into the dust, as the riders rode off with his son.

Domínguez crowed with laughter and raised his arm triumphantly as he and his men stormed out the gate. They had the grandson of the chief rabbi, Don Isaac Abravanel, whose heart, if not his faith, would surely be broken. The mission was a success.

Hanna ran up to the front gate and watched the three Hermandad men galloping down the road, her sweet and only child in their evil clutches. Giving up all hope, she fainted. Judah, his face and clothes covered with dust, ran to her and took her in his arms.

Alberto and Hermosa emerged from their hiding place in the thicket and ran to the gate. Judah was on his knees with his unconscious wife, muddied tears streaming down his face, as he tried to rouse Hanna back to wakefulness. Hearing footsteps, Judah looked up to see two strangers, a man and a woman, standing next to him. Sensing the concern on their faces and perceiving no threat from them, Judah allowed himself to give vent to his sorrow. "My son Isaac . . . those men, they have taken him away. They have kidnapped him!" He wailed on. "O Isaac, my son, Isaac, Isaac, my son!" Unable to speak further, Judah broke down in tears, embracing his unconscious wife.

Alberto looked on helplessly. Why had he stood by and done nothing to prevent the kidnapping? Why, against his better judgment, had he listened to Hermosa's pleas not to intervene? What had happened to him, Alberto Galante, the cavalier, and to his code of ethics?

Alberto saw the elderly bearded gentleman and his weeping wife hurrying to the gate. Crying, Esther Abravanel stood next to her son Judah and raised her arms heavenward.

"I cannot, I will not, do you hear me, God, I will not leave Spain without little Isaac. Oh, God, how can you do this to us? *GOD OF ISRAEL, HOW CAN YOU?*"

Esther buried her face in her hands. Don Isaac Abravanel gently put his arm around his wife, trying to console her. His face, too, was stricken with grief. Don Isaac closed his eyes and whispered, "Little Isaac, come back to us. Please, dear God, don't take him away from us."

Alberto had heard enough. Without any further hesitation, he ran toward his horse. Hermosa again tried to stop him. "Alberto, no!," she shouted behind him. But this time her plea was in vain.

Alberto jumped on his horse and spurred it on. The animal, respond-ing to its rider's command, surged forward through the thicket and then broke out into the open. Hermosa's pleas were lost in the reced-ing sound of hoofbeats, as Alberto raced after Domínguez and his men.

The cavalier of Málaga was back in stride. Riding his horse down the winding road towards Guadalajara, he saw the trees on the road-side whip by. Faster and faster he pushed the powerful steed, its nos-trils flaring, its mane fluttering, its head bobbing to and fro as it raced on. The stallion's powerful legs churned up a trailing cloud of dust, as it hurtled through the air, propelling itself and its rider forward with the speed of a roaring wind.

Using his reins as a whip, Alberto drove the horse relentlessly down the dirt road in pursuit of the kidnappers of Don Isaac Abravanel's grandson.

During the pursuit, the young cavalier thought about how the Inquisition had hounded him since his days in Málaga. The unholy tribunal had caused him to lose contact with his family, thrown his beloved's parents in dungeons, postponed his marriage, and made him and his bride end up as exiles in their own homeland. And now, unable to run any further, he was giving chase to his pursuers. Unable to tolerate the evil the Inquisition did, he resolved to punish the evildoers once and for all.

On and on Alberto drove his horse till he was within sight of the kidnappers. Domínguez and his men had passed from the estate trail onto the main road that led back to Guadalajara. At the intersection of the two roads, Domínguez looked back and caught sight of a single rider pursuing them. Domínguez signaled to his two officers to deal with the approaching rider. Domínguez, holding on to the Abravanel child, galloped on down the main road as his two officers reversed direction and readied themselves to finish off the last guard.

As Alberto neared the two Hermandad officers, he drew his sword and geared himself for combat. The officers also drew their swords, expecting to finish off the foolhardy pursuer quickly. As Alberto drew closer, the scarfaced officer recognized him, the *Marrano* who had disfigured him and escaped. He now resolved to finish him once and for all.

The cavalier of Málaga and the Hermandad officers met head on. The officers took the initiative with a flurry of sword blows that

Alberto managed to parry. To counter his disadvantage at being atttacked from both sides, Alberto spurred his horse to the side of one of the attackers, making for one-to-one combat. Alberto pounded away at his opponent alongside, causing the man to twist and lurch further in the saddle. Alberto thrust his sword through the officer's defense and struck him in the chest. The officer slumped in his saddle and then fell to the ground.

The other officer, consumed with hatred, came from behind Alberto and swung at Alberto's head. But Alberto ducked, and the blade only grazed his hair as it went by in a loud whoosh. Then he backed away after such a close call and spun his horse around to meet his opponent face to face. Alberto slashed furiously at his attacker. But the Hermandad officer held his own, beating back Alberto's assault. Their deadly blades clanged against one another in the still air of the road, the steel instruments slicing at each other's flesh.

In a vicious sideswipe, the Hermandad officer drew blood from Alberto's left arm, causing a patch of red on his upper left sleeve. Alberto struck back at his opponent with a series of thrusts and jabs, driving the officer into a steady retreat. Alberto feinted with his head and shoulder, and the officer raised his sword in response to the threatened swing. Quickly, Alberto drove his sword under his raised opponent's, causing the officer to drop his sword and clutch his chest. The man fell headfirst from his horse and hit the ground with a loud thud. Alberto touched the blood of his wounded left arm. Relieved that it was a minor wound, he went off in pursuit of Domínguez.

Riding up to the main intersection, he slowed momentarily at the sharp-angled intersection and then sped his horse in the direction of Guadalajara. There were many Jewish exiles on the road, and Alberto had to avoid knocking them over as he sped down the dusty path. Determined to catch up with Domínguez, Alberto drove on.

Alberto stormed down the road on his fleet-footed steed. Blocked by a group of exiles and their mule-drawn carts, Alberto almost rode into them, but a merchant, spotting the onrushing horse and rider, shouted for everyone to clear the road. Men and women quickly ran to the sides of the road to avoid being struck by the charging animal. Alberto and his horse raced past, almost knocking the exiles down.

"Watch where you're going, you fool!" someone shouted to Alberto.

Down the road Alberto darted on, heedless to everything but his pursuit. His horse galloped down the road in response to his single-minded direction, its thundering hooves causing the frightened travelers to clear the way.

In the distance, Alberto caught sight of Domínguez and the child. Buoyed by the hope that they could still be overtaken, Alberto persevered as he drove his own horse at full speed, closing the distance between himself and the Hermandad head. As they approached the city of Guadalajara, the gap became even smaller, until Alberto was twenty horselengths behind Domínguez.

Don Enrique Domínguez could not believe his eyes when he turned around to see who was behind him. He expected to see his two guards coming to protect his rear; instead he saw that *Marrano* criminal who had eluded him on Passover. A concerned if not astonished look flashed across Domínguez's face, as he began to whip his horse viciously. His horse began to pick up speed, but his pursuer continued to gain ground. The child slowed him down, and its endless crying irritated his ears. Tempted to cast the child aside, the Hermandad leader nevertheless held on to him; after all, the infant was the grandson of the chief rabbi, Don Isaac Abravanel, and was his most important prize in the war against the Jews.

Domínguez rushed past the city gates, the wailing child in the saddle with him. Alberto, in close pursuit, had now closed the gap to four horselengths. The Hermandad head raced his horse through the alleys of the city, with Alberto right behind him. They dashed swiftly through the narrow streets, making a series of rapid turns — first to the left, then to the right, then to the left again — as they plunged forward. Suddenly, they came to the main plaza of the city, and the central church came into view. In front of the church stood Fray Antonio Lucero, waiting to see what Domínguez brought him.

Dismounting rapidly, he handed the crying child to Lucero. "Baptize him. Hurry!" said Domínguez as Lucero ran with the child up the steps and into the church.

Alberto dismounted in front of the church. Domínguez was ready for combat, his sword waving menacingly in the air. He said fiercely, "You escaped me once before, *Marrano*, but this is the last time. Today I will make your tongue taste the steel of my sword."

Alberto countered, "We will see whose tongue it is that will speak last, you Hermandad swine."

Alberto and Domínguez aimed their swords at each other's throats. Domínguez landed the first blows, but Alberto warded them off without difficulty. Up and down the length of the church steps, the two fought, exchanging blow after blow, fencing with courage and skill. Alberto took command as he drove Domínguez back with a volley of swift powerful strokes. On the top step, just as Domínguez was within his grasp, Alberto tripped and stumbled. Domínguez took his advantage and came in for the kill, holding his sword high, when Alberto, with catlike quickness, recovered his balance and stretched his sword out at the last moment. His sword caught Domínguez square in the chest. Alberto drove the blade clear through Domínguez, and then he pulled it out again. Domínguez, horror-stricken and open-mouthed, his hands grabbing at his bloodied chest, fell forward and rolled down the steps to his death.

Alberto sprinted into the church. In the dim light within, he stopped momentarily and looked about. Fearing he was too late, that his sword fight with Domínguez had cost him too much time, he saw Lucero next to the altar. Lucero, flanked by two bodyguards, held the hair of the Abravanel grandchild over the baptismal font with his left hand and the holy water in his right.

The priest was about to sprinkle the baptismal water on the child's head, when suddenly four men burst in through the side door. The bodyguards were disarmed, and a sword struck the priest's wrist, knocking the holy water out of his hand. Lucero screamed in pain and let go of the child as he held his injured hand.

Alberto stood incredulous. It was all over. The Abravanel grandchild was safe. And it was also clear that it was all over for Alberto Galante — because of his past, in spite of his past.

The Marquis of Cádiz and his men had everything under control. The arms of Lucero's men were raised in surrender, and the Marquis' sword was at the priest's neck. The nobleman said, "We can do without your kind of priest in Spain. Cavaliers, take him out of my sight, and place him in the prison of the Duke of the Infantado until we decide what to do with him."

The Marquis' men took Lucero away, while the Marquis picked up the crying child and patted him comfortingly on the back. "There, there, little one . . . everything will be all right now. Don't worry, we will get you back to your parents."

Alberto walked slowly to the altar. He stood in front of the Marquis, expecting as much punishment as praise from the man he had once served and then abandoned. Finding it difficult to speak, he managed to say, "Marquis . . . how are you?"

The lean-faced Marquis looked at the young man standing next to

him. He said, "Alberto Galante . . .," a look of surprise on his face.
"You still remember me?" asked Alberto.

"Remember you? My dear Alberto, I have been looking all over Spain for you — where have you been?"

The Marquis handed the child to one of his men. "Here, take this child and guard him well." The Marquis came over and put his arm warmly on Alberto's shoulder. "First, you save my life at Málaga, and then, before I have a chance to thank you — poof! You disappear. Why . . . uh . . . I never knew . . . never suspected up until now what made you leave. Come now, allow me to return the favor. Is there something you need? Please, allow me to help you."

The Marquis led the way out of the church, his arm still around Alberto's shoulder. "By the way, my cavalier, you are a bit rusty with that sword. It took you a little while to finish off that barbarian Domínguez, no? Anyhow, did you hear about what happened at Granada?"

Alberto shook his head and smiled. He was happy that it was not over between him and the Marquis.

"You haven't? Ahh, now, *that* was a battle," said the Marquis, delighted to see Alberto again, and equally eager to recount his exploits to someone he knew would be an appreciative listener. They walked away, two gallant cavaliers who exemplified the highest virtues of Spanish chivalry, two friends come together once again to vanquish the foe.

A shroud of darkness blanketed the estate. In the gloomy rooms of the residence sat Esther Abravanel with her daughter-in-law Hanna, burying their weeping faces in each other's breast, their sobbing become a perpetual lament. Benumbed and heartbroken himself, Judah Abravanel was unable to offer words of solace. He sat listlessly in a corner, bitterly contemplating the loss of his beloved son. Don Isaac Abravanel, reeling from the blow of losing his own flesh and blood, prayed quietly in a corner, concealing his torment in the movement of his lips and in the swaying of his body. Devastation had befallen them.

Hermosa, who was admitted to the estate, could not stand to watch the suffering. She walked out onto the front porch and worried that her beloved might never return to her, that she too would soon have equal cause for sorrow. She gazed at the road, waiting for Alberto to return.

Suddenly in the distance Hermosa spotted a rider, then five riders coming toward the estate. Excitedly, she seemed to recognize a familiar figure, and she rushed back into the house to tell the others. "Someone is coming!" she said breathlessly. "Someone's coming!"

The Abravanels, aroused to life by the announcement, came out to the front porch. They saw five horsemen — the Marquis of Cádiz and his men, and another cavalier, who carried little Isaac in his arms!

Esther and Hanna, Isaac and Judah, all joyfully rushed out to meet the group of riders. Hanna took the child from Alberto and smothered her son with kisses and tender caresses. Relieved, Esther put her arms around her daughter-in-law, kissing the child, mingling her tears of sadness with tears of joy. Hugging the child between them, the Abravanel women rejoiced, holding their most valued treasure.

As the darkness lifted, Don Isaac lifted his eyes skyward, grateful that his prayer had been answered. "Thank you, O Lord, for your everlasting kindness. Blessed be Thou, O Lord, King of the Universe, who has heard our prayer and delivered us from the enemy. May it be Thy will, Lord our God and God of our fathers to lead us in safety and to direct our steps in safety. Mayest Thou always lead us to our destination, happiness, and peace."

With outstretched arms, Hermosa ran up to Alberto as he dismounted. As they met and embraced, he swung her in a slow arc through the air. They kissed passionately. Hermosa gasped, "Oh, Alberto, I missed you so. I worried about you, my love. Promise me you will never leave me again."

Alberto said, "I promise, *querida*."

Hermosa pushed him away slightly as she noticed the blood on Alberto's sleeve. "You're hurt!" she exclaimed.

"It is nothing, Hermosa. Come, we have some business to attend to. Did you bring up the matter with them?"

Hermosa stammered. "I ... I ... just couldn't. They were so sad, so heartbroken I could not do it."

Alberto nodded his head.

The Marquis of Cádiz dismounted. He was received with heartfelt appreciation by the chief rabbi, who took the Marquis in his arms. Touched by the warm embrace, the Marquis said, "Isaac, old friend, we meet again."

Don Isaac said, "How can I thank you, Marquis, how can I ever thank you for the rescue of my grandchild?"

"Do not thank me, Don Isaac," said the Marquis. "The man you have to thank is this brave young cavalier, Alberto Galante. He is the one who saved your child."

Abravanel turned towards Alberto. "Alberto . . . . ." he said, extending his hand.

The cavalier of Málaga introduced himself. "Alberto Galante, at your command, Don Isaac Abravanel."

Abravanel said, "Alberto, our sages say, 'He who saves a life is as if he saved an entire world.' What thanks I can offer can in no way match the deed you have done. What price, what thanks can I possibly offer for an entire world, the world of my grandchild and his children to be . . . Alberto, God has blessed me with good fortune. On behalf of my family, allow me to offer you some recompense."

Alberto looked to Hermosa for assistance.

"Don Isaac . . . ," said Hermosa haltingly, "Alberto and I, we do not want money. We want something else."

Abravanel asked, "Yes, what is it? Name your reward and, if it is my power to do so, I shall do it."

Alberto spoke up. "We wish to return to the faith of our fathers. We wish to be married not as the Christians that we have pretended to be, but as the Jews that we have always been in our hearts. We ask of you, Rabbi Abravanel, if it is within your power to do so, to declare us to be Jews in name and in writing. If you can do this for us, though it be contrary to the laws of the kingdom, our gratitude would know no bounds."

Don Isaac stroked his beard curiously. "It will be my greatest pleasure to perform such a deed. As I shall soon declare you to be full-fledged children of Israel, so shall it be my great privilege to declare you man and wife according to the divine laws of Moses and Israel."

The Marquis added, "And, my good cavalier, it will be my privilege to escort you and your lovely wife safely to the city of Cádiz, which is under my control. At Cádiz, I will see to it that you find a ship heading in whatever direction your hearts desire. This, Alberto, as well as other things, will be my wedding present to you and your beautiful bride."

As he led the way back into the house, Don Isaac Abravanel said, "Welcome, my children, into the goodly tents of Jacob, welcome into the tenements of the House of Israel, and into the eternal covenant with the Holy One, blessed be He." Alberto and Hermosa followed him faithfully into the house.

Within a day, after proper witnesses had been summoned and the marriage contract drawn up, Alberto and Hermosa were formally married by Don Isaac Abravanel. As Alberto placed the ring on his radiant bride's finger, he uttered the traditional sacred oath to his beloved, saying with utmost tenderness, "Behold, thou art sanctified unto me with this ring according to the laws of Moses and Israel."

Their vows accomplished, their Jewish faith restored and certified by documents from none other than the chief rabbi himself, Alberto and Hermosa could not thank Don Isaac enough for his help. The Abravanels reciprocated with thanks for Alberto's heroic rescue and showered the couple with well-wishes and presents. They gave them an emotional farewell as the young newlyweds joined the Marquis of Cádiz on the journey south.

The following day, the Abravanels themselves began their journey to the port of Valencia. Sensing the time of reckoning, they joined the stream of exiles on the dusty Castilian roads, exchanging and receiving wishes of "*Caminos buenos!*", or "Good roads!", with one and all.

Two weeks later, Alberto and Hermosa were aboard ship in Cádiz harbor. The Marquis' wedding present was a magnificent reception at his estate, as well as a gift of one hundred ducats. The Marquis felt that he owed his very life to Alberto Galante, and as a nobleman who gave unto each cavalier his due reward, he sensed the inadequacy of any offered gift.

From the caravel, Alberto waved a final farewell to the Marquis on the dock. He doubted he would ever see again a man so virtuous, so true, and so noble. The Marquis of Cádiz, Rodrigo Ponce de León, would remain forever in his heart as the embodiment of the perfect cavalier, a man he would miss as much as Spain itself.

The caravel sailed out to sea. As people stood on the deck, Hermosa looked toward the shore. She rested her arms on the shiprail. "I think about my parents . . . being left behind in the prison, while I am making the escape to freedom they always dreamed of. Yet, I know they are happy for me, happy that one of us got away — to keep the tradition, the faith, with the one I love so dearly. Alberto, I love you."

Taking her arms into his, Alberto tenderly kissed her, saying, "And I love you, my princess, forever."

Chapter 11

Only a few more days, and they would set foot in Fez, the end of their wanderings. From Cádiz, Alberto and Hermosa crossed the sea to the Straits of Gibraltar and the land of the Moors. Soon after their arrival in Arcila, they were told that the King of Fez had sent soldiers to escort the Jewish exiles to the capital city. Alberto and Hermosa were thankful for the armed escort, particularly because of the horrendous tales they heard about others who had chosen the same path.

Arcila was teeming with two groups of Jews. There were those newly arrived who were going to Fez. And there were those who had already suffered too much in the land of the Moors and wanted no more of it. Those who had been able to return to Arcila were naked, starving, and full of fleas. By asking a few questions, Alberto was able to find out what had happened to them.

On the road to Fez, and on the way back to Arcila, bands of barbaric Moors had stripped the exiles of their clothes, violated their women, killed many of them, and ripped out their intestines in search of the gold that they were known to have swallowed. The Moors had thrust their hands forcibly into every human orifice, both from above and from below, with the same purpose in mind. These beasts of the field subjected the young Jewish men to all kinds of unmentionable sexual outrages, committing one humiliating indignity after another. Having suffered these countless abuses, the hapless Jews returned to Arcila to ask the Count of Borba to save them from further insult. In the name of Jesus Christ in whom they all now professed belief, they asked for baptism, and begged to be allowed to return to Spain. The Count of Borba agreed to their wishes. Because of the large numbers of Jews seeking to be baptized, the priests had to sprinkle their heads from above with hyssop dipped in holy water.

Alberto witnessed one mass baptismal ceremony with great alarm. Hermosa was fearful of what might happen to them if they continued on their way to Fez. But she was not alone in her fears: after hearing the tales of horror, many of the newcomers refused to disembark from their ship. Some, unwilling to risk their lives further, chose the route of baptism in Arcila. Hermosa felt her resolve weakening. She was tempted to turn back, to return to the fleshpots of Spain.

"There is no turning back," Alberto told her. "We are heretics in the eyes of the Church. In Spain, we are criminals. If we return there, we will be burned at the stake. Our fate, for better or for worse, is here in Morocco. If we make it to Fez, we will live. With these soldiers of Fez protecting us, there is a good chance we will make it to the city. It is our only chance, Hermosa."

Hermosa anxiously bit her lower lip. "O Alberto, I am so confused. When I see how much these people have suffered, I know I do not have the strength within me to suffer what they did. I cannot go on, Alberto. Let us stay here in Arcila. Others are staying behind. Why can't we?"

Alberto shook his head. "No, Hermosa, that is not for us. We did not come all this way to settle in a small Portuguese Christian fortress. There are priests here that are in correspondence with the Spanish Inquisitorial authorities. They may be able to track us down if we stay here too long. We must keep on going. We cannot stop here, my darling."

"But others are staying here," Hermosa said innocently as she pointed out the hundreds of Jews that were encamped nearby.

Alberto was insistent. "Hermosa, my sweet, please do not let me down. The Count of Borba is no angel, and he will not allow Jews who settle in Arcila to remain so undisturbed. Borba does not want us; and even if he did, the city of Arcila could not support such a large number of Jews. I tell you, Hermosa, Arcila is not the place for us ... Fez is."

Hermosa crossed her arms and took a deep breath. She was still unconvinced.

Alberto came up behind her and gently kissed her on the shoulder.

"I understand you, *querida*. Either way we go, danger, and perhaps even death awaits us. Yet for all the dangers, I know and you know that we have no choice but to continue onwards to Fez. I will always be at your side, my beloved, protecting and caring for you, and I swear to you that no hand but mine will ever touch your body. Trust in me, Hermosa, I can take care of you. I do not wish to die any more than you do. Yet if life is to be given to us, let us live a life of truth in Fez, and not one of pretense in Arcila. Difficult though the road to Fez may be, it is the only road open to us. It is what your mother, if she were here with us, would want us to do. If we die on the road to Fez, we die. If we live, we live. It is as simple as that."

Hermosa turned slowly around, a soft smile on her lovely face. She took hold of Alberto's hand and asked, "No hand but yours?"

"No hand but mine," said Alberto.

Hermosa took Alberto's hand and kissed it. She asked further, "No lips but yours?"

"No lips but mine," answered Alberto, as he lifted her gently towards him. Their lips met in moistened sweetness, their kiss became a renewed vow of commitment to their old-new dream and to one another. Their lips, their will, became once again as one. Hermosa allowed herself to linger in Alberto's caressing embrace. She felt herself buoyed in space, a free-floating flower lifted up by Alberto's strength, the power of his arms, the force of his love. Her love for Alberto also had a force of its own; it had the strength to overcome its wild fears. Hermosa felt comforted. She was ready to join her husband wherever destiny would guide them, for better or for worse, be it in Spain or in Fez. Live or die, she would be always at his side.

Alberto and Hermosa were part of a group of 30 Jewish exiles that set forth to Fez. The royal escort of ten soldiers led the way down the coastline toward El Araish, then turned inland to guide their party through the barrenness of the interior and up the banks of the Sebú River. The pace set by the soldiers was an acceptable one, particularly when the caravan of people and pack-mules had to traverse the arid, white-hot plain of the Sebú itself.

During this trek, Alberto became friendly with the swarthy, bearded captain of the party, a certain Hakim Hassan. The Berber captain wore a bright red tunic, an indication he was a royal soldier. Hakim was a proud and well-educated Berber, his manner marked by great reserve, his sense of caution indicated by the tight grip he kept on his sword handle whenever he spoke with anyone. Yet for all his formality, Hakim was willing to answer all of Alberto's questions concerning Fez.

Fez, he said, had been founded by Idris I at the end of the eighth century, and the city had become the capital of the Kingdom of Morocco under the rule of his son, Idris-Ibn-Idris II. Within two centuries, the fame and splendor of the city had grown so much that it came to be called the Mecca of the West. There were magnificent mosques and Islamic libraries. After Idris, first the Almoravids and then the Almohades held sway. Finally, in the thirteenth century, the Marinids took control. But whoever ruled, Hakim explained, Fez remained as great as ever. It was still the queen city of all the cities in Morocco. Her scholars were the wisest of all men, her eight hundred mosques the most ornate, her royal palace and gardens beyond compare, and her king the greatest of its rulers.

"Who is the King of Fez?" Alberto inquired.

"The King of Fez, may Allah protect him, is our great and wise ruler, Mulai Muhammed esh-Sheikh. He is a Wattasid like me and the rest of our soldiers."

Alberto asked, "A Wattasid? What is that, Captain Hassan?"

Hakim looked up at Alberto with his dark, penetrating eyes. He forgave the man's ignorance. "A Wattasid is someone who belongs to the tribe of the Banu Wattas. Our tribe is strong, but not as strong as some others. All of the Berbers in Morocco belong to a tribe. The three most powerful tribes are the Masmuda, the Sanhaja, and the Zenata. Every tribe is broken up into smaller clans, and there is much fighting between one tribe and another.

"We Wattasids have ruled in Fez for only 30 years, since the time of the great revolt. The other Berber tribes, especially the Masmudas, want to bring us down, as do many of the Arab tribes. I do not understand why our King has allowed so many of the Arabs from Spain to settle in Fez. The Emir of Granada lives in the royal palace in Fez. The Arabs, they think they are better than Berbers.

Alberto remained silent for a while, then asked cautiously. "And what about the Jews, Captain Hassan?"

Hakim glanced up again to give Alberto a cold, piercing look. He answered Alberto without any trace of emotion. "The Jews are no threat to the King. They do not want to overthrow him, as some of the tribes do. The Jews are faithful to the King. They are good in crafts and arms production. The Jews have suffered much at the hands of the Christian infidels, and they will be, I should hope, grateful to our King for his mercy."

"That is true," said Alberto. "We are all very grateful to your great

King."

Hakim said nothing as he continued walking. Questions, not statements, were what he responded to.

"One last question, Captain Hassan. How many people are there in Fez?"

"Well over one hundred thousand," said Hakim, a touch of pride in his voice.

Alberto said, "Thank you, Captain, for answering my questions."

"You are quite welcome, sir," Hakim answered stiffly, his stride unbroken as he marched toward the ascending horizon.

The mountains encircling Fez were now in full view, and Hakim's face seemed to light up with each advancing step. It was evident to Alberto that Captain Hakim Hassan was a man who loved his city and who loved his King.

Soon they were within view of the Bab-el-Tinca mountain gorge. The gorge was bordered on each side by a mountain whose flat faces, jutting sharply upwards at a perpendicular, flanked the narrow passage. Amid the scattered rocks and shrubs, the party of exiles wound its way down a ravine and into the constricted gorge itself. As the passageway became so narrow that only one person at a time could pass, the surrounding walls of stone engulfed them in sharp angled shadows of menacing blackness. Vertical shafts of feeble light penetrated the overhanging roof of the precipice, illuminating the clumps of jagged rocks on the worn path below. Progress through the gorge was possible but slow.

Alberto and Hermosa held on to each other as they followed their pack mule. They watched their step, stumbling at times, sharing an impromptu kiss when the privacy of sudden darkness gave them license. The sounds of the caravan, hushed voices mingled with unsure steps, filled the fissure. The sounds in the gorge were somehow out of place, their timbre harsh, their ringing echoes dissonant. The flanking mountains seemed to menace the caravan: any moment, the walls might crush the intruders who had disrupted the gorge's silence. After what seemed like an eternity, the anxious exiles came out the other end, relieved that the gorge was now behind them. The reverberation of the gorge gave way to the serenity of a barren valley. The channel of shadows gave way to an expanse filled with light.

The caravan moved on. The serpentine procession wound its way among the huge boulders that marked the exit from the gorge. The vegetation was sparse, the unyielding land dotted with low-lying shrubs and an occasional tree, the landscape bleak as ever.

The group had hardly gone a short distance from the gorge, when suddenly they were attacked by wild Berbers of the mountains. The raiders came from nowhere, some from behind boulders, others running out of ravines, still others riding horses. Their shrill cries curdled the blood and broke the silence of the valley. There were about 30 of them, wild primitive savages with scimitars, malevolent and blood-thirsty, who ravaged one caravan after another. Hakim regarded them as the foulest villains in the land. He stopped the caravan's advance. "Stop! Back to the gorge!" He signaled with his arm for everyone to get back. "Back! Back to the gorge!"

The exiles retreated toward the gorge, as much from Hakim's command as from an instinctive desire to distance themselves from the oncoming invaders. Hakim and his men, outnumbered three to one, braced themselves for the attack. Swords drawn, they stood in a protective arc around the exiles.

"We're going to die!" said Hermosa, "We're going to die!"

"No. We are not going to die," said Alberto calmly as he went up to their pack-mule. Reaching into one of the heavy cloth sacks, Alberto withdrew his sword. "Hermosa, we are not going to die, so help me God. Now listen to me, whatever may happen, you stand behind me at all times. Is that clear? *You stand behind me!*"

Hermosa, her eyes bulging with fright, nodded her head. She looked downcast, the spirit of struggle gone out of her. Alberto took her chin in his hand and lifted her face up.

"One last kiss," said Alberto. "Quickly!"

Hermosa placed her lips on Alberto's, the one last kiss that he requested now possibly become the last of all their kisses. In that final moment of contact, all her love for him flowed passionately through her lips. She wished to prolong this moment, but Alberto wrenched himself away and said, "Remember, my love, behind me at all times!"

As the exiles retreated toward the gorge, so did Hakim and his men. Alberto joined the soldiers at one end of the arc, with Hermosa right behind him. Surprised, Captain Hassan saw Alberto's sword and flashed him a smile. Alberto acknowledged the captain's rare smile with a tilt of his sword. They were ready.

A dozen Berbers on horseback smashed into the line of defense. One wild-swinging Berber tried to run his horse straight into Alberto. Alberto dodged the charge, moved off to the side, and slammed his steel sword against the rider's. Alberto's blow was delivered with such force that it spun the the Berber halfway around in his saddle, almost throwing him off the horse. The angry Berber turned his horse around and made another charge. This time, Alberto's swing did lift the Moor out of his saddle. The ferocious-looking Berber fell to the ground, but quickly got up again, brandishing his scimitar in front of him. Alberto sensed the man's lack of full command of his blade. This Berber could kill and maim defenseless travelers, but he was no match for a trained cavalier. The Berber made one wild swing after another. Alberto waited for the right moment and then skillfully made his move. The Berber swung crudely, leaving himself momentarily unprotected, and Alberto slammed his sword into the murderer's chest. It was no contest.

Alberto looked rapidly behind him and saw Hermosa. She was all right, but her fingers covered her frightened face. He went back to the battle.

One of the soldiers was having a difficult time with a mounted Berber. Alberto came alongside to help, adding his blows to the soldier's. The Berber, pummeled on all sides, succumbed quickly to the double attack.

Alberto wanted to help another soldier, but the Berber raiders on foot now set upon him. Twenty ruthless men, whipping their scimitars viciously, joined the fracas. The primitive shouts of the Berbers, the harsh clash of colliding metal, resounded in the air. Three Berbers came at Alberto, three wild barbarians against one cavalier, their blades lashing out against his. Alberto backed away from the approaching three. He shouted out, "Hermosa, get back! Get back to the gorge!"

Hermosa, responding to his order, started to run back.

Alberto stopped his retreat. He feinted a charge at one Berber, luring him out of position. The Berber swung and missed, but Alberto did not. The forceful swing of Alberto's blade drove deep into the Berber's arm, ripping into the enemy's flesh and bone. The man howled in pain, his arm dripping with blood.

The other two Berbers came after him. Alberto parried their blows and bided his time. He waited till an opening developed. In the flurry of exchanged blows, the opening suddenly came, and Alberto struck with lightning speed. His sword darted out with its superior speed, and found the flesh of his opponent's chest. The Berber fell head first, his life of pillage at an end. The remaining Berber, realizing he was fighting alone, ran, and Alberto ran after him. He would have continued to pursue the Berber had it not been for the shouts behind him.

"Help, Alberto! Alberto!"

It was Hermosa calling to him. Alberto spun himself around and looked back toward the gorge. The Berbers were spilling through the gorge, and they had Hermosa in their hands! One Berber had Hermosa by the arms, another had her by the legs, and they were hauling her back into the darkness of the gorge.

"Alberto!" she screamed at the top of her lungs. "Alberto, help me!". She twisted, she turned, she resisted mightily, but it was to no avail. The Berbers dragged her into the gorge.

Alberto sprinted back towards the mountain passage. Yet his legs could not carry him fast enough. His beloved was in danger. Her honor, her very life, was at stake. He ran breathlessly, his hatred for these Berbers driving him on. He was oblivious to all but the need to rescue his beloved Hermosa.

Alberto dashed headlong into the gorge. He could hear Hermosa screaming, her desperate yells for help tearing at his heart. In a poorly lit section of the passageway up ahead, he saw the vile Berbers force her down on her back. Hermosa struggled to get free, but she could not. One Berber pinned her arms behind her back while the other tried to take off her dress. The second Berber had barely touched the hem of Hermosa's dress, when Alberto's sword crashed through his skull, splitting his head in two. The other Berber quickly released Hermosa's arms and tried to get away by dashing down the gorge. Alberto jumped over Hermosa, caught up with the savage, and smashed his sword on the Berber's shoulder. The Berber fell to the ground, writhing in pain and begging for mercy. Alberto had no mercy for such slime. He drove his sword into the barbarian's chest and then cut off his head.

Alberto went back to Hermosa. She was crying but otherwise unhurt. He had kept half of his promise to her. He lifted her up and held her tightly in his arms. He kissed her soft cheeks and wiped away her tears. And with a firm hand around her waist, he led her back toward the exit of the gorge.

The battle was still raging. Alberto left Hermosa with the rest of the exiles huddled next to the mountain. Much as he loved Hermosa, much as he wanted to comfort her at this time, there was a battle to be fought. He ran back to the front line of battle at Hakim's side. Outraged by the attack upon Hermosa, Alberto fought with devastating fury. Those who dared to confront him were overwhelmed by the velocity and power of his shattering blows. No Berber could match his speed, no one could offer contest to the aroused cavalier of Málaga. One Berber after another fell by the wayside as Alberto cut down all who confronted him. His sword whirled mightily through the air, dealing death to all who challenged.

Then Alberto noticed that more Berbers were coming. They were obviously the reinforcements the others were waiting for. Fifteen attacking Berbers were still fighting against eight royal soldiers and Alberto. How could they possibly hold off another 40 assailants? Alberto saw the tide of battle soon changing. Hakim and he would be put on the defensive; overwhelmed, they would soon all die as Hermosa had foretold. Hermosa! He fell back for the first time, realizing the real threat to Hermosa and the end for both of them. If they were to die, he would be with her until the very end, keeping his vow, making sure no hands or lips but his would ever touch her.

The reinforcements arrived. Alberto, already retreating, was astonished at what happened next. The new band of Berbers began attacking the Berbers the soldiers had been fighting. He could not believe his eyes. What was going on? Did these other Berbers want the Jews for themselves? Surely that was the case. The new band of assailants was much more skilled in battle. Their leader, a tall, swift-moving figure, whipped his blade with blinding speed through the air. The leader ruthlessly chopped down one Berber after another. The bodies at his feet testified to an ability so dazzling, so magnificent, that Alberto feared to do battle with him. Yet the tall warrior kept on coming, yes, coming toward him! Alberto raised his sword, in anxious expectation. He prepared himself to do battle with the greatest swordsman his eyes had ever seen. The huge warrior, his face half-covered with a white scarf, struck down the last of the Berbers and came face to face with Alberto. Only the warrior's fierce brown eyes could be seen through the scarf and headdress. The chilling dark eyes studied the poised opponent, examining him from head to toe.

The warrior lifted his sword in the air as if to indicate the start of battle. Alberto moved to the side in order to be in a better attacking position. The warrior reached for his scarf and headdress and pulled them both off, revealing his identity.

Alberto was staggered: No, it could not be! But yes, it was . . . it was the man whom Alberto most feared. It was the man who Alberto knew wanted to kill him. It was the greatest of the Moorish warriors . . . It was Abrahen Zenete!

Ever since the two of them had fought to a draw in Málaga, Alberto harbored the fear that a vengeful Zenete would one day find him and blot out his name. The day had come. Zenete, the champion of the Moors, had finally found him. Zenete, his sword drawn, was ready to make Alberto pay with his life for what he had done at Málaga. It would be a battle to the death, Alberto's death to be sure.

Alberto was astonished even further when Zenete lowered his sword. The cavalier blinked his eyes and opened them wide again to make sure he was not seeing things. With a quick motion of his arm, Zenete drove his sword into the ground and said, "*Salam Aleikum!* Peace be unto you!" The champion of the Moors extended his hand in a gesture of friendship.

Alberto was frozen. He thought for a moment: was this a trick? A trick to get him to put down his sword and leave him defenseless? Yet Zenete was an honorable warrior. He had heard of how the noble Zenete was the only Moor at Málaga set free by Ferdinand and Isabella. During a skirmish, Zenete on horseback had overrun the Christian camp and had come across a group of Christian children whom he could have easily killed. Rather than do so, Zenete slapped them lightly on the head and said, "Move on, young ones, and get back to your mothers!" His fellow Moors argued with him for letting them go, but he responded, "I did not kill them because I did not see beards." When Málaga was conquered, the King and Queen remembered this chivalrous deed of great virtue, even though committed by a Moor, and Zenete was granted his freedom.

Yes, Alberto realized, Zenete was an honorable warrior. Besides, the great Moorish warrior did not need a trick to defeat him. The gesture, he realized, was a sincere one. Alberto, too, drove his sword into the ground and answered, "*Aleikum Salam!* Peace be unto you!"

"Galante," said the Moor, identifying the man in front of him.

"Zenete," said Alberto in like manner.

They approached each other and shook hands. Then Zenete embraced Alberto as if he were a long lost brother. It was an emotional reunion between two invincible warriors, one the champion of the Moors, and the other the pride of the cavaliers.

Alberto spoke first, "Thank you for coming to our rescue. We are most grateful."

Zenete answered in perfect Castilian. "You had little need for my help. I watched the battle from the top of the mountain. My eyes were amazed when I saw one of you fight with the grace of a leopard and the strength of a wild bull. And the more I watched, the more I realized that I had seen such a one fight before. In my heart, I knew there was only one man who could fight that way. That man was the only one whom I had fought and never beaten. That man is you, Alberto Galante."

Alberto confessed, "Ever since that day at Málaga, I have had terrible dreams. I dreamed that one day I would have to fight again the great Abrahen Zenete, the greatest Moorish warrior of Al-Andalus. In my dreams, I fought you many times, yet I always lost. When I saw you again today, it was as if my dream was coming true. I was ready to lose to the great Zenete. I was ready to die."

Zenete answered, "I am content to win in your dreams what I could not accomplish in battle. Galante, there will be no more battles between us. Our fight is over. We are both outcasts from Spain. We have to join forces. We have to fight together."

Alberto added, "We have to be brothers, Abrahen, brothers-in-arms."

Zenete smiled for the first time, realizing that was what he wanted to say. "Yes, brothers."

The Jew embraced the Moor. "My brother Abrahen."

The Moor returned the embrace. "My brother Alberto."

Peace had come unto them.

While one of Alberto's dreams was to remain an imagining, another dream had come true. They were in Fez! After winding their way through a tortouous, hilly path, the procession of Arabs and Jews finally made its way to the Magreb metropolis in the mountains. Alberto rode one of Zenete's magnificent stallions into the city alongside Zenete and Hassan. Hermosa joined him in the saddle, her arms around her cavalier's waist.

The city came into view, a silhouette of elongated minarets soaring against the azure Moroccan sky. Arched gates and cobbled streets were lined with white houses glistening in the sun. Battlement towers loomed high above spacious squares, gardens teemed with vines and foliage, orchard trees encircled bubbling fountains. Handsomely turbaned men rode steeds and camels, while a rabble of barefoot, grimy urchins noisily greeted the caravan. Nearby were vendors hawking their wares as well as a squad of royal soldiers on the march, Arabs and Berbers in a continuous mix and motion. Dark-eyed women, their faces covered with scarves, watched the caravan from terraced windows as it made its way toward the imperial palace.

They crossed the River of Pearls, which led from Old Fez into New Fez, into the lustrous-white city of Marinid construction. It was within the fortified new city that the imperial palace was located, its main thoroughfares lined with graceful palms. That this dazzling Moorish structure of mosaic arches, tiled halls, and flowing fountains was a royal seat was obvious.

While Alberto and Hermosa were being led to the palace, the other Jews in the caravan were directed by the royal soldiers to an area outside the city walls.

Alberto asked Hakim for an explanation.

Hakim said, "The Moslems do not want any more Jews in the city. They fear that the Jews will drive up the prices of food and housing. There are already five thousand Jewish families in the *mellah*. They feel that is more than enough. All other Jews, especially the new ones from Spain, must live outside the city walls. The King has listened to these requests of his Moslem subjects."

Alberto was unhappy to hear this. The King of Fez would not let the Jews of Spain enter his capital city? If so, why had so many Jews bothered to come here? As he dwelled on these questions, Hermosa asked, "What is a *mellah*, Captain Hassan?" Hakim replied, "The *mellah* is the Jewish quarter. *Mellah* means salt in Arabic, and the Jewish quarter in Fez is on salty ground. The *mellah* has been in existence only about 50 years. One of the Marinid kings forced the Jews to move out of Old Fez and to settle in New Fez in an area next to the imperial palace."

"Why?" asked Alberto flatly.

"Protection," answered Hakim. "Protection for the Jews. The King wanted the Jews close to him in case there were any outbursts of Moslem fanaticism, as there have been in the past. In fact the Jewish community was almost totally destroyed 30 years ago during such an outbreak. So you see, there is good reason for having the *mellah*. However, that is not the only reason."

"What other reason is there?" asked Alberto. What he was hearing was causing more concern than satisfaction.

Hakim smiled, "You may not believe this, but the Jews were regarded by the Marinid kings as members of the Zenata tribe, deserving special protection."

Alberto's concern turned to amusement. "Jews . . . members of the

Zenata tribe? Did you hear that, Abrahen?"

Zenete smiled widely on hearing this. "Zenata . . . Zenete . . . what is the difference? If Galante is a Zenata, I for sure must be one too. Is that not right, brother?"

Alberto chuckled in agreement. "Absolutely correct, brother Zenata."

Hakim did not want to feel left out. "The Wattasids are an offshoot of the Zenatas. That makes me one, too, I suppose."

"Of course, Brother Hakim," chimed Abrahen.

Everyone laughed. Zenatas all, they arrived at the imperial palace in good humor. Alberto Galante was presented by Abrahen Zenete to the dignified Emir of Granada as one worthy of service in the royal army, seconded heartily by Captain Hassan. The word of Zenete and the recommendation of Hassan were more than sufficient. The Emir, impressed by the glowing reports of Alberto Galante, offered to speak personally with the King of Fez on the newcomer's behalf. It was agreed that a warrior of such exceptional talent deserved an appointment in the military service of the King.

"Nothing less than a captain," insisted Zenete.

"Nothing less," the Emir assured him as they parted.

It was further agreed that Alberto and Hermosa would be allowed to settle in the *mellah*, pending the King's approval. A document to this effect, bearing the imprint of a palace official, was handed to them. It was not often that such exceptions were made.

It was soon time for Alberto and Hermosa to take leave of his comrade-in-arms. Alberto embraced Zenete. They laughingly promised to have a limited Zenata tribal reunion as soon as possible.

Hakim led Alberto and Hermosa to the *mellah*. It looked very much like Old Fez. Along its main street were artisan shops — goldsmiths, tailors, money-changers, glass workers, combmakers, tanners, weavers, leather workers, textile workers, and the like. Many of its dark-complexioned citizens wore straw sandals, others went barefoot; only a few still went about with leather shoes. As they walked further into the quarter, Alberto and Hermosa attracted the friendly attention of its mild-mannered residents. People smiled at them as they walked by. Others came to greet them warmly in an Arabic they did not understand. Unable to communicate in their native tongue, the Jews of the *mellah* gestured with graceful hand movements and smiled with bright-eyed friendly faces.

People were so friendly in the *mellah*. Alberto and Hermosa could feel the good-hearted warmth of the local Jews as well as their courtesy and kindness. The temper of life in the *mellah*, the loving geniality of the people, all brought Alberto and Hermosa to tears.

This was what they had been searching for. It mattered little to them that the *mellah* was small or that it might be lacking in comforts. Jewishness, this was what Alberto and Hermosa had been searching for. It was what they wanted most to make their own, a Jewish life without pretense and without fetters. And now they had found it in the confines of the *mellah* of Fez.

"It is wonderful," said Alberto, his voice choking, a sentiment echoed by Hermosa.

"Good," said Hakim as he walked on. "Very good."

Soon they arrived at a two-story building. The tenant of the building, a lanky pleasant-mannered Jew in a bright-colored tunic, opened the door and welcomed Captain Hassan in Arabic. While Alberto could not understand what they were saying, he suspected they were talking about Hermosa and himself. The excited Jewish tenant, while speaking with Captain Hassan, would look every now and then at Alberto. The tenant's bright eyes shone with approval, and his head nodded eagerly at the captain's request.

Hakim turned towards Alberto. "My good friend, Isaac Wakhnine, has agreed to have you as his guests. You will stay with him until you have a house of your own. He is able to show you the *mellah* far better than I can."

The Jewish tenant bowed graciously, hands outstretched. Alberto bowed in turn, acknowledging the man's warm hospitality.

"*Shalom*! Welcome to my house," said Isaac in a poorly pronounced Castilian.

"My wife and I are most grateful, Señor Wakhnine, for allowing us to stay with you."

"The pleasure, it is mine. Come, come, my children. Make yourself at home. And your names, please?"

"Alberto Galante . . . and this is my wife, Hermosa."

Hermosa bowed when her name was mentioned. Wakhnine smiled widely, bowed again, and turned towards the captain. "Hakim, we'll see you soon. I'll take good care of them."

Hakim thanked Wakhnine for his help. The captain exchanged an appreciative farewell with Alberto and, satisfied that all was being taken care of properly, Hakim excused himself and left.

Alberto and Hermosa entered the dwelling. Its interior was cool, its immaculate blue-white mosaic floor covered by soft rectangular rugs. In the entry way were pieces of furniture with intricately carved insets and brilliantly polished brass urns. Through one of the many white archways, Alberto could see a small courtyard with a water fountain at its center. Two servants rushed outside to their pack mule and began to unload it. This was clearly a home of affluence in the *mellah*; Hakim had brought them to a place where they would be comfortable.

"You go wash, then we eat," said Wakhnine. Before Hermosa had a chance to respond, a servant whisked her away to her room. Alberto, too, was led to his sleeping quarters. Using the large bowls of water at his disposal, he washed off the dust of the road. A short while later, Alberto emerged from his room, his skin cool and cleansed. As he went to meet Hermosa, he saw her coming to the dinner table in a brightly colored tunic. She looked entrancing in the garment, her lovely brown hair flowing as if she were an Oriental princess. She took her place on one of the cushions around a low table, tucking her feet under her, as if she had done it a thousand times before, smiling sweetly to all about her, her tender eyes soft and glowing, her gentle smile drawing her blissful face into one of dreamy contentment. The princess was happy. And so was the gallant knight at her side.

* * * * *

It was during a trip to the southwest of Morocco that Abrahen Zenete heard of a spice merchant from Sevilla who lived in the *mellah* of the city of Marrakesh. He passed on the information to his fighting companion, Captain Alberto Galante.

Alberto felt compelled to follow every lead that might lead him to his parents. Although Hermosa's parents were lost to the Inquisition, his own might still be living. Reluctantly he took leave of Hermosa and their three-year old son Davico. The child had been a blessing for them; his birth eased the grief in Hermosa's heart over the loss of her parents. The child's playfulness and winning smile were a source of joy to both of them.

There were other pleasures as well. With the aid of a private tutor, Alberto had learned enough Hebrew to participate in the synagogue services. At home, he recited the benedictions over the Sabbath bread and wine. Hermosa was still active with the local synagogue's charity organization, although somewhat less than before because caring for

Davico took up most of her time.

Zenete's information about Marrakesh had been sparse. The city of Marrakesh was situated at the foot of the Atlas mountains. Although some native Moroccan Jews lived there, the community had become famous lately as a center for New Christians who wished to return to the Jewish fold. The ruling chieftain in Marrakesh was occupied in fighting off the violent attacks of bands of wild Berbers from the Atlas mountains and requested immediate assistance from the Sultan of Fez. For this purpose, the mighty Abrahen Zenete was dispatched to quell the disturbances and bring law and order to this city — which he did.

Alberto decided to ride alone, as his horse crossed the hills and sands of the Mogreb faster than any other. With his beard, turban, and red sash, Alberto looked like any other royal officer. Only his sword was different: he did not use the traditional crescent-shaped scimitar, but a straight sword of hard Toledo steel. Stopping at the Ouzoud waterfalls to refresh himself, he continued on his weeklong trek, using the trails that paralleled the snow-capped Atlas mountains.

Finally, he saw the rouge-colored city of Marrakesh in the distance, its ramparts enclosing multiple minarets pointing skyward. Passing through a forest of palm trees, he joined the bustling camel traffic heading toward the city gates. At the local marketplace, he sought directions to the local *mellah*.

When he arrived at the merchant's adobe home in Marrakesh, he dismounted cautiously from his horse. He sighed, adjusted his turban, and tightened his sash. Finally, he struck the iron bar on the door to announce his presence to those within.

A head peeked through a side window. Wild happiness welled up in his heart as he recognized his sister Ana, ten years older but beautiful as ever. He wanted to shout out her name, but his voice was so choked with emotion that he could not speak. Flushed with excitement, he waited for her to open the door.

He heard voices inside speaking the language of Castile. It was his sister Ana talking, "Do not open the doors, Papa. I do not know who he is. I have never seen him before at the store. How dare he come to our home with a sword? Speak to him from the window, if you must."

Then he heard a calmer voice, that of his father Vicente Galante. "Many of my customers carry swords, my daughter. Carrying a sword does not make a person dangerous."

Now a third voice, that of his worried mother. "Are you sure, Vicente? What business does a customer of yours have at our house?"

Ana was insistent. "He may not be a customer. Who knows who he is?"

Alberto shouted out. "Señor Galante!"

Inside the whispered voices became more excited. The rising voice of Vicente Galante could be heard saying, "Did you hear that? He spoke my name. We may not know him, but he apparently knows me. And Señor he called me ... Señor ... in Castilian. I am opening the door."

"*Cuidado, Papa. Tiene una espada,*" said Ana again. "Be careful, Papa. He has a sword."

Vicente Galante opened the door and bowed cautiously in front of the stranger. His eyes lingered nervously on the visitor's sword, then dwelled on the beard and turban. Those eyes, where had he seen them before? Somehow the figure looked strangely familiar.

"*Salam Aleikum!*" Vicente greeted his unexpected guest.

"*Aleikum Salam!*", came the response from the man at the door. Vicente thought to himself: those eyes, where had he seen those eyes?

"Welcome, dear sir, to our humble abode. You will, kind sir, forgive my ignorance. You know who I am, but I do not have the pleasure and the privilege of knowing who you are. May I ask how it is that you know me?"

The uniformed figure did not reply. Rather, the armed Moor unexpectedly lowered his head and removed his turban. Having done this, he raised his head upwards once again for inspection. "Do you not know me?," asked the guest with a jesting smile, his outstretched arms ready to receive his father.

This time, Vicente recognized the eyes.

"Alberto!" he screamed jubilantly. He leaped at his son, whom he had not seen for a decade, holding him so tightly it seemed he would never let go. Alberto's mother and sister shouted with joy, ran to the door, and showered him with kisses saved for many a year.

The reunion continued unabated all evening, as Alberto and his family came to know each other once again. The spontaneous hugs and kisses continued amid the recalling of memorable experiences sustained during the years of separation. The united family of the Galantes, now grown wider with the addition of Hermosa and Davico, looked forward to the good times that only a future of freedom could offer.

Tomorrow beckoned brightly for Alberto; the cavalier of Málaga, then of Segovia, knew that his star was rising fast on the Moroccan horizon. Having established his reputation as a great fighter and swordsman, he could look forward to a bright future in the royal Moroccan militia, as Abrahen Zenete repeatedly told him. But deep inside, he knew that living only by the sword was not what he wanted.

With his family together again, he felt a part of himself fulfilled, while yet another part of him ached for satisfaction. Perhaps now, knowing that the quest for his missing family had ended in success, he could begin to sink deeper roots in his newly adopted Moroccan homeland, devote himself to his family and to Torah learning, transform himself into a scholar, cultivate his mind and not just his muscle. Was it possible to become a soldier and a scholar, or were the two lives mutually incompatible? Grappling with the challenge of fusing these two disparate types of existence, Alberto Galante could not suppress the peculiar feeling that this adventure would not be his last.

AUTHOR'S NOTE

This depiction of Converso life is intended to complement my earlier work, **The Alhambra Decree**, which dealt with the 1492 Spanish expulsion of the Jews. Although the principal Converso characters are fictional, the main historical events in which they participate are not.

Ferdinand and Isabella's siege of the Moorish fortress at Málaga is well described by Andres Bernáldez in his *Historia de los Reyes Católicos* and by Washington Irving in his *Chronicles of the Conquest of Granada*. The taking of the fortress was a major turning point in the nine-year campaign to conquer the kingdom of Granada. The Moors were led at Málaga by El Zegri and by the Moorish captain, Abrahen Zenete, who distinguished himself on the battlefield. Concerning one of Zenete's attacks on the Christian encampment, Bernáldez writes: ". . . And Zenete on horseback came across a group of Christian children, where he could have killed seven or eight of them. Instead, he flipped his lance around and hit them harmlessly on the back of their heads with its handle, saying, "Get on, young ones, and get back to your mothers!" The other Moorish warriors, seeing the children flee, began to argue with Zenete because he had not killed them, and he replied: "I did not kill them because I did not see beards." And this was regarded as an act of great virtue, worthy of a Spanish nobleman, even though committed by a Moor . . ."

The greatest of the Spanish cavaliers was Don Rodrigo Ponce De León, the Marquis of Cádiz. A model of Spanish chivalry, he gained fame for leading the successive assaults on the Moorish fortresses, often placing himself and his men in great danger. That the Marquis was historically a great friend of the Jews is evinced by his sheltering of eight thousand Conversos who fled to his estate from Sevilla upon the establishment of the Inquisition in that city.

The Dominican-inspired massacres and forced conversions of 1391 resulted in widespread Judaizing by the forcibly baptized Conversos and their descendants. To combat this heretical 'Mosaic depravity,' the Inquisition was established in 1480 by Ferdinand and Isabella; in this decision, the sovereigns were influenced by the sermons of the Dominican priest Alonso de Hojeda. It is of interest that Hojeda was one of the first victims of the plague that ravaged Sevilla in 1483.

The first *Auto-de-Fe* took place in Sevilla on February 6, 1481. Its first victims included Diego de Susan, the prominent Converso merchant, who along with other Judaizers conspired to resist the introduction of the Holy Tribunal into Sevilla. However, the Converso conspiracy was disclosed by Diego's beautiful daughter to her Christian lover. The conspirators were caught, condemned, and burned at the stake. Diego's daughter, *La Susanna* as she was called, was spared and was placed in a monastery from which she soon escaped; she adopted a notorious life of ill repute, shifting from one lover to the other, and ultimately died in poverty.

For further reading on the Spanish Inquisition, the reader is referred to the works by Cecil Roth and Henry Kamen. The definitive work on this subject is H.C. Lea's *A History of the Inquisition in Spain*; the dungeon torture scene in this novel is modeled after the incredibly detailed account left behind by the Inquisitors in Toledo in the year 1567, an account which is reproduced by Lea and others. On Christian accusations of alleged ritual murder and host desecration, such as in the infamous Niño de la Guardia trial, much can be gained by a reading of Joshua Trachtenberg's *The Devil and The Jews* and of the relevant chapters in Yitzhak Baer's *A History of the Jews in Christian Spain*.

On Converso life, I made use of C. Roth's *A History of the Marranos*, B. Netanyahu's *The Marranos of Spain*, and the articles by Haim Beinart in R. Barnett's *The Sephardic Heritage*. For a more detailed list on related topics, the reader is referred to the bibliography provided in *The Alhambra Decree*.

Juan Arias Dávila, the Segovia Bishop of Jewish descent, was noted for having executed several Conversos for Judaizing activities. Nonetheless, the Inquisition later leveled charges against him of protecting his kinsfolk, and Dávila was sent to Rome for trial. It remains speculative, however, as to whether he was actively involved in Judaizing activities.

Dr. Pinto's discussion of Spanish chivalry reflects the influence of Maurice Samuel's *The Gentleman and the Jew*. The description of activities of the Holy Brotherhood is based upon Martin Lunenfeld's *The Council of the Santa Hermandad*. For those interested in medieval Moroccan Jewish life, I highly recommend Jane Gerber's *Jewish Society in Fez: 1450-1700*.

Historically, it is known that as Don Isaac Abravanel and his family were about to leave Spain, an attempt was made to abduct Abravanel's grandson, but the plot was somehow foiled.

ACKNOWLEDGEMENTS

In the preparation of this manuscript, I would like to acknowledge the valuable editorial assistance provided by Dr. Phyllis Albert-Mitzman of Harvard University.

I would like to express my appreciation of the efforts of Dr. José A. Nessim, a modern-day Sephardic cavalier, and to Mr. Jebb Levy, a caring Sephardi, who together have rallied Sephardim worldwide to the cause of Spanish Jewish culture.

Finally, I cannot thank my wife enough for her deep devotion and loving support during this literary undertaking.